THE SYMMET[...]

T0037412

ALEX MYERS is a writer, teacher, and speaker.

Born in Maine, Alex was raised as a girl and left to attend boarding school. At school, Alex came out as transgender, returning his senior year as a man, and was the first transgender student in his academy's history.

Alex earned his bachelor's at Harvard University, studying Near Eastern Languages and Civilizations. He was the first openly transgender student at Harvard and worked to change the University's nondiscrimination clause to include gender identity.

Since earning a master's degree in religion at Brown, Alex has pursued a career in teaching, as a transgender advocate, and as an active journalist contributing to the *Guardian*, *Slate*, *THEM* and other publications. He currently lives in New Hampshire with his wife and two cats.

Also by Alex Myers

The Story of Silence

ALEX MYERS

The SYMMETRY *of* STARS

HARPER
Voyager

Harper*Voyager*
An imprint of HarperCollins*Publishers* Ltd
1 London Bridge Street
London SE1 9GF

www.harpercollins.co.uk

HarperCollins*Publishers*
1st Floor, Watermarque Building, Ringsend Road
Dublin 4, Ireland

First published by HarperCollins*Publishers* 2021

This paperback edition 2022
1

ISBN: 978-0-00-835277-6

Typeset in Sabon LT Std by Palimpsest Book Production Ltd, Falkirk, Stirlingshire

Printed and Bound in the UK using 100% Renewable Electricity
at CPI Group (UK) Ltd

MIX
Paper from
responsible sources
FSC
www.fsc.org   FSC™ C007454

This book is produced from independently certified FSC™ paper
to ensure responsible forest management.

For more information visit: www.harpercollins.co.uk/green

To Ilona, Again and Always.

The stars were creaking in the farthest sphere, shifting and arcing and drawing a dazzle of sparks across the rich dark of Celestial Space, tracing out the shape of a New Age. It would dawn soon.

And in that darkness, two Immortal beings slumbered. Humans are always reaching for words to explain powers they cannot comprehend: angels, archons, demigods, demons, muses. None of those words fit the beings that slumbered as the stars groaned. These two, bound together like magnetic poles, like sides of the same coin. Two beings invested with opposing forces: Nature and Nurture, forever linked to one another. Forever at war. What they are is powerful, complex, eternal. The one stands for Nature – the belief that everything is innate, settled, stamped in human flesh from the start. The other, Nurture – the belief that all is potential, coiled within a fascinating yet frail body, that the true human self is coaxed out through love, training, and care.

There is no tidy name for these beings, but names are important. Let them be called Godlings.

1

PROLOGUE

It must have been the creaking that woke us up. Woke *me* up. I'm not sure that the ... Other one ... , Nature, ever even sleeps. And I *know* they wouldn't have woken me up if I had somehow managed to sleep through all this grinding and groaning anyway. No, they would have let the New Age dawn and set themself as its ruler, allowing me to slumber through those crucial, crepuscular hours when all matters were determined – only to wake in the impossible glare of a morning ... a morning that was entirely theirs.

But luckily I stirred before the stars had fully settled into their course, before the New Age had been fully delivered. I woke and in doing so spoiled that Other one's ... my ... my (though it pains me to put it so plainly) *twin*'s plans. Here, in the space beyond, neither of us need be burdened by anything so mundane as a body. We exist in our truer forms, a shapeless shift of colour, like the sheen of oil on water. My Other, Nature, stood gazing out at the stars, and just as sparks raced through the depths, so, too, did orange and red and yellow glare and flare across their form. I took this to mean they were excited.

'Greetings, Other,' I said. It was nice to see them give a little jump. But their form had smoothed over, the reds and oranges muting to blue and grey, by the time they turned and offered a reply.

'Greetings, Nurture. Welcome to this New Age.'

Nurture is not my name. Nurture is simply what I am, what shapes me and how, in turn, I shape the world around me. The sound of myself – Nurture – emerged in my Other's voice with a rasping, rotten taste. We really do not get along well.

I stood and stretched and went to my Other's side, the two of us peering over the Deeps, which writhed and roiled, out into the expanse of the farthest sphere. 'It has not yet arrived.' The stars were still settling – bolts of fire now and then flaming out, sparks fizzling, and the creaking grated on as well. Even for us, it was an awesome sight.

'What sort of age will it be?' Nature murmured, a question that had no proper answer, that spoke of potential and danger.

It was difficult to stand so close to them. We are meant to be together and yet meant to be opposed. It's not such a paradox. The world is full of such pairings. Whatever divinity or demonity created this universe must have loved polarity, dichotomy, duality. They loved, I'd say, twins. Some would say my Other was my missing half, that we completed each other. Others would say that we negated each other, cancelled one another out. I felt them strongly, repulsingly – every atom within me twisting away from them. But I also heard them, an echo of myself. Myself turned inside out, front to back. I fought to keep my form steady, a roil of calm green and blue.

'A New Age,' I equivocated. 'Ripe to be ruled.' (I did not need to say 'by me'. My intentions were loud enough to be heard, or felt.)

'It is my turn,' they said. 'In the last age we were both awake for, the rule was yours.' They stared over the Deeps, their form drawn in and concentrated, thick enough to look like smoke.

'Ah, yes,' I said, sarcasm dripping from my every word. 'It was ordained to be my age. But you horned in and interfered . . .'

'Just once.'

'A dozen times! You couldn't keep your wretched . . .'

'You were mangling things. I sought only to help . . .' They pivoted, turning their attention from the Deeps to me. A shiver ran through me, a vein of dark purple. 'Let us share this age, Nurture,' they said. 'We are . . . siblings . . . after all.'

'Share?'

'Yes. I will take the, er, left half of the world and you take the right half, and away we shall go.'

I hunched together, gathering my substance, anticipating a long argument (arguments with Nature are always long. One might even say, eternal). 'Firstly, my *beloved* Other, the world does not have halves. It cannot be split like a melon. Second, even if we *could* divide it cleanly in half, you would still intrude. We know this about ourselves. We cannot share.'

'We can do anything we want,' they muttered. 'At least *I* can.'

'We are in a state of bonded opposition, you idiot. We exist only because we are opposed to each other.'

'I know,' they sulked.

I ignored their pouting, grey shape. 'We are two sides of the same coin. You can't crawl over onto my side, not without wrecking the coin.' I paused. This metaphor (like most metaphors) was not exactly right. 'Forget the coin. We are like . . .'

'You can forgo the comparison. I know what we are. We are twins.' Their voice curled unpleasantly around the word. 'And like any siblings, we fight to differentiate ourselves. I am only myself because I am not like you.'

'Exactly. So you cannot do anything *you* want. What you

do will always be, in some way, linked to and shaped by your need to oppose me.' That is how creation works – the power to create something from nothing . . . yes, it comes from playing opposites against each other.

They were still sulking, glooming over the edge, staring into the endless field of stars. 'What would you even *do* with this age, if you were to rule?' they said at last.

I relaxed a touch, let my substance spread out, washed through with green-gold. 'Let Nurture reign,' I replied.

'Well, obviously,' they snarked.

My threads of green-gold snapped back, flared orange. 'If I were to rule . . . without *your* interference . . .'

'I am Nature. I do not *interfere*. I simply am,' they insisted. 'It is you who nudges in and messes things up. Nurture. Coddling and cooing and shaping and meddling.'

'Nature,' I scoffed, and I couldn't damp down the flickers of red that coursed through me. 'You ought to rename yourself Neglect. I don't meddle, and I resent that implication. I simply open humans' minds to their full potential, allow them to see within themselves and others that they have the capacity to change and grow and develop. That's Nurture. You idiot.'

'Oh, good grief. Be quiet.'

'Who are you to tell me . . .'

We both fell silent as the stars gave a particularly loud groan. Who were we to be making such a scene before *them*?

My Other hunched closer, their words little more than a hiss. 'You're ridiculous. Humans don't care about capacity and potential. They care about hunger and thirst and power and . . .'

I cut them off. 'And what would your rule look like?'

They gave a shrug, if a formless thing can be said to give a shrug. (I said it, so there. They gave a shrug.) 'People are born. Some are strong and healthy and wise and they succeed. Others perish or suffer.'

'That's no kind of world.'

'On the contrary, Sibling. I'd say it's Nature. Human nature, at least.'

They had a point. Humans could be rather brutal. And simple-minded. In fact, if I had to be honest (which I don't) I would admit that if you left a group of human children entirely alone to raise themselves, the results would be much what my Other had outlined. Which is why Nurture is so important. 'We will never settle this. We can't rule together – we would just . . . cancel each other out. And we've proven that you can't be trusted to take turns and leave my age well enough alone.'

They bristled at this, a glisten of orange flares. 'I don't trust that you'd give me a turn, after having taken yours. Very well. We can't share and we can't take turns. So let's fight for it. Winner takes all.'

If I had eyes, I would have rolled them (in general, I prefer being unincorporated, but this is one (significant) drawback). 'We cannot fight each other. Or rather, neither one of us can win in any decisive way. That's what it means to be in bonded opposition. Remember what I was saying about the coin, the sides thereof?'

'I know,' they whispered and I could feel – like a deep, cold shiver – their resentment and hate. If they could get rid of me, they would. Even if it meant getting rid of themself. They shook their form, like a dog in from the rain.

'Let us . . . pick humans to be our proxies,' I suggested.

They sparkled a bit, gazed back out over the edge. 'Yes. Find two humans, one for each of us, and let them bash each other bloody.'

If I had eyes, I would have rolled them. 'You are so predictably banal. We are superior to mortals, so shall we make it a bit more subtle? A little more substantial?'

'Oh?' Scepticism coated their voice. If my Other were to rule over this planet, they'd be sitting up on some throne, probably made out of charred human bones, munching greasy snacks while the world descended into utter depravity. And they'd declare that a complete success. 'What do you have in mind, Nurture? That we gather two humans, have them hold hands and murmur supportive phrases to one another until one dies of boredom?'

I almost laughed. 'Let me think,' I said.

I shuffled towards the edge of the Firmament, to look down on earth. Clouds scudded below, grey and murky, and I was reminded of such things as wind, moisture, air. I turned and again stared at the stars; they groaned only intermittently now. The gears no longer shrieked. The age was slowly settling in. It was too early to perceive the scope of the stars' realigned orbits. They would take their time to establish the new routes, the patterns that would stamp this age. They would rustle and shift through the dawning and then settle down. I turned my gaze back to earth, sat on the edge. From here, I could see the ripples of the ocean, the humped green and grey of mountains. If I squinted, I could bring into focus a ship cutting across the waves or the slate tiles of a towering roof. *Humans.* They are endearing. In their way. Mostly because they are, just a little, like us. A shadow to our True Forms, a reflection in a warped glass. We see humans and know both what we are and what we are not.

'Let us each choose a set of twins,' I proposed, slowly, the seed of an idea taking root within me. 'They will be a sort of mirror to us.'

'Charming,' my Other smirked. 'And will we use them as puppets? To test our skills against each other?'

'Let us each raise our twins according to our . . . essences, our directives.'

They snorted. 'Our Natures, you mean?'

'As you will,' I said, decorously (though my thoughts were not decorous). 'Let us preordain a time when the two sets of twins will meet and then . . .'

'Then they will bash each other?' my Other said hopefully.

'What would be the point of them bashing each other at some future interval rather than having two idiots bash each other right now?'

'Well, I suppose that we'd have the pleasure of anticipating . . .'

'That was a rhetorical question. No . . . we need to have a contest that truly pits our essences against each other. Your twins will be ruled and raised all Nature. My twins will be fully nurtured.'

My Other leaned back, stretching their form out along the Firmament, staring up at the stars, at the velvety Deeps. 'I see,' they said. 'The twins should mature at about the time the age settles in. And when they are mature, what then? They meet and . . .' I prepared to interject before they could say *bash each other*, but to my surprise they continued in another vein. 'The twins will compete in the three areas of human ability – strong body, strong mind, strong spirit,' they said.

I nodded. 'That is good. But there are many possible contests that might test such abilities.'

My Other waved a tendril at me, a flare of amused yellow. 'You fuss over the details.'

'That's a nurturer's way,' I glowed.

'Very well. I can see that you won't be appeased. Shall we cast lots?' They gathered their substance and began to search around, groping at the surface of the Firmament and finally coming up with a hefty chunk of rock. This gave me pause, and I prepared to dodge; it would not be out of the question for my Other to grow tired of this conversation and try to resolve matters by bashing my head in (metaphorically; I have no head). But, no, they simply turned the rock one way, then the other, and then gently tapped it. The rock obligingly split into dozens of thin leaves; they spread the stone leaves towards me. 'For each area – body, mind, spirit – let us each inscribe three of these lots. Then we will cast, one area at a time, to set the . . . nature . . . of each contest'. For each of the three areas, and then cast to determine.'

'Agreed.'

'A test to determine strength of body,' they said.

I formed a tendril and pressed it against the rock, paused. What would be timeless, fair, worthy contests that measured strength and fortitude . . . *weight-lifting*, I inscribed on one leaf. *Sprinting*, I wrote on another. A bit of doubt crept in. What if my twins weren't able in body? What if, despite my nurture, they couldn't run fast? Well, this was only one avenue of competition. They might fail here and win in the others . . . I inscribed *wrestling* on the third. It seemed like a classic. Then I dropped my three stones into my Other's outstretched tendril. They shook their form vigorously, the stones rattling, and tossed all six into the air. I reached out and plucked one, letting the others clatter to the Firmament. We leaned close to read the inscription: *trial by combat; using whatever the arms of the era are*. I groaned. That would be what my Other wanted. Bashing, by another name. I stooped down to collect the other chips. Goodbye, foot race. Goodbye, weight-lifting. Goodbye, pure and noble contests. I turned over the other two stones that Nature had inscribed. Both read, *trial by combat; using whatever the arms of the era are*. 'You put in three of the same,' I spluttered.

'That's not against the rules,' they retorted.

'I can see we will need to settle the full rules. Carefully.'

'Let us finish deciding the contests.'

10

'A contest of the mind,' I said, seizing my leaves of stone. My Other inscribed theirs with confidence, if not haste, but I hesitated, mulling. If my twins were feeble in body, beyond my capacity to nurture them to success, then their minds must be their crowning glory. (Truly, little is beyond my ability to nurture to success, but when dealing with my Other, it is best to be cautious . . . they never are.) *Mathematics*, I inscribed, my letters growing cramped as I added, *computing without aid algebraic equations of fifteen digits*. Ah, that was a good one. *Navigation*, I wrote, *using tools only of their own construction and the earth's features*. Pleasing. I pondered, staring into the Deeps. Strong mind. Deep mind. I didn't want some mechanistic memorization, rote-learned . . . no, something with texture, richness. *Extemporaneous poetic composition with metric and rhyming structures, according to aesthetics of the era.*

This time, my Other dropped their leaves into my outstretched tendril. I shook and tossed and they plucked one from the air, turning it over so that I could see that it read: *Story-telling. Of original invention.*

'Story-telling?' My voice rippled with disbelief. 'You actually believe this to be a worthy measure of mental strength?' It wasn't that I disliked story-telling; I was surprised my Other believed it to be of any worth. But then, I wasn't sure what they valued in humans, beyond bashing brains.

They tossed the stone aside. 'It is but one of the three. I couldn't think of anything else. Human minds are so feeble . . . On to strength of spirit.'

Again, I took a moment to ponder. To listen to the stars creaking. It seemed my Other did as well, for their diaphanous form rippled and wavered and coursed through with threads of silver and red. There were the classics, of course, like withstanding torture. In truth, many of those trials seemed so . . .

unpleasant. *Withstand complete darkness for a week*, I wrote.
Fast for four days. Charm a savage beast. I was disappointed
in my lack of originality, disappointed in the trepidation (not
fear!) I felt in thinking of what my Other might be inscribing
at this moment . . . I *could* nurture strong spirit, yes, I could.

I gave the stones to my Other, watched them fling the shards
high. I reached out and seized one, closing my form tightly
around it, feeling the sharp edges bite.

'Well?' my Other insisted.

I turned the shard over and read: 'Dance with beauty and
abandon.' I blinked, gazed up at my Other. '*You* wrote that?'

They didn't meet my gaze, but instead turned over the other
shards – the ones not chosen. I read the discarded lots – mine
and theirs: *Predict the future. Levitate objects to a height of
at least ten feet without touching them.* I shook my head.
These stones were a fair summary of how my Other and I
are opposites, how we understand human capacity so differ-
ently. (And I am right and they are wrong.) Only this one
stone, the one in my hand, gave me pause. *Dance with beauty
and abandon.* It is almost something I would write. Almost.
But I did not say this to my Other. Instead, I scoffed (such is
our mode with each other). 'Telekinesis? Soothsaying? Humans
can't do such things.'

'My twins will be able to,' they replied. 'Shall we carry on?
Finish sealing the wager? Or do you wish to save us all time
and agony and concede now?'

I glared. Surely this was all bravura on their part. 'Let us
state the rules. Firmly and clearly. Then select our twins. These
are the three areas of competition: contest by arms of the age,
story-telling, and dancing with beauty and abandon.'

'Agreed.'

'We will agree on a fair and impartial judge on the day of
the contest.'

'Agreed.'

'We will not interfere with each other's twins in any way. Nor will we use any magic or supernatural enhancement on our twins.'

'Agreed,' they said, then added, 'and the loser of the competition will be exiled for the duration of the age into the Darkness beyond the Deeps, to be retrieved by the victor when the age is done.'

I gasped. Exile? And I'd trust my Other to release me? They had such a smug look about them, such an insufferable glow. I knew they expected me to back down. 'Agreed. And to be clear, when you say "age" you mean the span of four human generations or a time not exceeding a century.'

Their form curled with a pleased green-yellow. 'How legalistic of you, Nurture. Concerned about the length of your exile?'

'Concerned about how often Nature seems to cheat,' I replied. 'Let us set the time of the competition.' We turned and stared up at the stars.

'It must occur before the age has fully settled, so that I . . . the victor . . . might claim the rule.' We watched a meteor streak through the Deeps, a brief trail of fire. 'Mars and Venus.' My Other pointed.

'Yes,' I said, staring. The one, a blot of red. The other, a glow of sea-green. 'A good pair. Well opposed. When they move into . . . when they align with Gemini.' I pointed to those blue-bright stars, waiting in the Deeps.

'Indeed,' my Other agreed. 'We will need to shift their orbits, then seal our agreement. It pleases me. A profound symmetry. A doubling of twins.' My Other's voice took on a greasy, contented tone. 'Well, now. The nature of the competition is settled, and we've chosen our time keeper, as it were. So, on to the selection of . . . souls.'

They used that word to tease me. In the almost-endless

stretches of space between one age and the next (or at least in those stretches when I am not asleep – sleep is of such value to Immortal beings) my Other and I have had more than enough time to discuss the metaphysical, physical, existential, hermeneutical . . . essence of the universe. I believe in souls. I believe that humans have them. I believe that gives humans free will. Which in turn gives them passion and desire and the ability to change and grow. That souls are what make humans nurturable. My Other believes that humans are granted only an animating force, a spark, they might say. Nothing more.

'Yes,' I replied, all tart courtesy. 'On to the souls.'

In this interstitial period, as the stars continued to shift and settle, the souls that would come into being in this age were all nestled together, awaiting their time on the stage. I find it strange that whatever being fashioned these souls left them here, on the edge of the Deep, to find their own way into the world . . . or to be toyed with by me and my Other. But, then, I think of the two of us, and wonder, sometimes, where we came from (we each have different versions of that story) and why it is that we seem forgotten as well. No matter. These were thoughts for the timeless stretches between ages. Now was the moment for action.

My Other was sifting through the souls. 'This is the only moment that matters,' they said. 'If I choose correctly, my work is done. My twins will grow according to their Natures: strong, robust, clever, insightful . . .'

'Just choose,' I snapped, suddenly, surprisingly, on edge.

My Other's colours swirled with delight. They knew they had got under my skin. As it were. They held aloft two souls, little spheres, transparent but with solid bits inside, like the cat's-eye marbles kids play with in certain eras. I extended a tendril and after a moment of reluctance my Other let me hold the souls they had selected. They were like metal – heavy, cool to the touch. I could even taste the tang of iron as I grasped them tight. I passed them back to my Other, who looked unbearably smug (smugness is a horrible lilac shade).

'You shouldn't need to dally much with your choice,' they said, sounding intolerably like a schoolmarm. (Bashing each other now seemed like a very good idea.) 'Just pluck any old two out of there and nurture them up, right?'

I didn't even bother to glare. Just plunged a tendril into the nest of souls and felt around. My Other was right. I *shouldn't* need to feel around too much. Even to try and sense souls that felt nurturable would be to imply that their Nature mattered . . . oh, I was going to tie myself in knots if I thought too much about this. I let the souls run across my form, cool brushes with potential life, and plucked up two. They were not as heavy as my Other's souls. They were warmer as well. I offered them to my Other and they rolled them around before returning them. 'Like putty,' they said. 'Disgusting.'

'Shall we?' I turned and faced the stars, checking on the location of Mars and Venus, calculating the arc, how they would move as the age settled in. I reached out, with infinite tenderness and care, and placed my two souls in the velvety Deeps. My Other flicked their – one, then the other – shooting them off, as a human might flick away an ant crawling on their arm, and into the depths. Then we both leaned close and traced the path we'd chosen, towards the twin stars, Gemini. Our gesture left a trail of sparks, glistening against the dark, and at the moment we'd selected, the alignment, the convergence, we pressed down, leaving our imprint.

'It is enough,' I said, inspecting our work. 'Their paths will cross only here, which will be the time of our three contests.' I leaned closer, studying the faint traces of our sparks that still lingered in the dark. 'I wonder if they will feel what we've wrought,' I murmured. 'Some pull upon them . . .'

'It's done,' my Other declared, settling themself down on the ground, sighing. 'Stop fussing. Time for a short nap, maybe? Wake in a year, see how things are going down there?'

'Oh no,' I replied. 'We need to keep an eye on our twins.'

'You do. But my work is done. I made my choice. We set their course. What'll happen will happen.' They gave a cosmic shrug.

'Well. I have to go down and do some nurturing. And I don't trust you one inch to stay up here and not meddle with things.' I gestured to the stars, the souls, the Deeps . . . everything.

'What? Go down?' they squawked. 'Corporate? Can we not watch matters from here?' They wrinkled themselves up, as if the odour of earth already offended them. 'I know you intend to nurture your twins. You'll need to coo to them and sing them little songs, but surely you could send emissaries . . . those big . . .' Words failed them and they stretched out their arms.

'Birds?' I said. 'That does it. We are going down. If you want to rule this age, you ought to at least know the word for the winged creatures that ply their sky. It'll be fun. You can watch as my twins grow and improve and yours wither and fade while you sit idle and believe that only Nature matters.'

'I hate incorporating,' they said with a little shudder. 'So vile. Base.'

'I don't *enjoy* it,' I said, 'But I do admit that Nurture is more easily delivered to humans when one shares their form. It is more than the cooing you keep mentioning. True Nurture is about love and faith and care. True Nurture is about listening, about being attuned . . .'

My Other made a sound as if they might vomit.

I flared red-orange. 'You can only properly retch if you have a body.'

They quit their gagging sounds and said wearily, 'We will

16

have to maintain our polarity with each other if we take on a physical form, whatever we do, or the fabric of things will wither and there'll be no Age to rule at all.' Then their voice brightened. 'Shall we cast lots to decide what we'll be? Toss coins, as it were? Make a little game of it?'

It is wise to be wary of all their suggestions, but I couldn't see the harm in this one. 'Very well,' I agreed.

'One of us names a pair of opposites, the other chooses one of the pair so that we are each assigned a half and maintain our polarity.'

'Oh, I like that. I'll start. Light or Dark?'

'Dark,' they said quickly. 'Fire or Water?'

'Water,' I replied. 'Hot or Cold?'

'Hot, of course. Young or Old?'

'Young, please,' I smiled back. They'd look great with wrinkles. 'Air or Rock?'

'Rock. Male or Female?'

I paused, glared at them in a flare of orange. 'That is not a universal, eternal dichotomy.'

'Oh, please. It is a meaningful polarity on earth. In almost every species . . .'

'There are plenty of exceptions, and you can't boil it down to a binary, which you'd *know* if you bothered to learn *anything* about these creatures that you purport to want to rule.'

'And if you cared about the basic truth and not your fancy, ridiculous *theories*, you'd know that – accurate or not – Male or Female form the basis of identity in most human societies.'

They had me there. I didn't like it, but I couldn't deny it. I could, however, subvert it. Nurture is all about subversion (if it's done right). 'Female,' I said.

They glowed with a smug yellow. 'Fool. I know you're only trying to make things difficult for me. I am not so ignorant that I don't know the human belief in Mother Nature. But go ahead. Choose female. You've just selected the harder path for yourself.'

'Cats or Dogs?' I fired back. That *is* an eternal dichotomy.

'Now you're being ridiculous.' They waved a dismissive hand. 'We ought to have decided enough to maintain our polarity.' They stared at me. 'Female, eh? Watery, cold, light and female. I hereby name you Melissa.'

I bristled. Who were they to claim the right to name *me*? But arguing would do no good. I would simply return the favour. 'And you . . . I call you . . . Atlante.'

'Atlante? What kind of name is that?'

'Yours,' I said.

Together, for this one moment, the two of us stepped to the edge of the Firmament.

And fell.

CHAPTER ONE

There was a rush of air and around me, I sensed the laws of physics, the demands of earth, coalescing. We were passing through the in-between. Not yet plunging until gravity took hold, not yet ageing until time came into play. Time. It opened up, a flower unfurling, the pages of a book ruffling past. I could not hear the stars any longer. I knew they were still creaking and moaning but they were settled enough to have dropped our twins into time and so we dropped, too, and now I did feel the pull of earth and now I gasped and choked as air was forced through my throat. My throat . . . I was encased in flesh now. The dichotomies we'd invoked began to take hold and I could feel their essences trickle into me, through me. They worked upon me, a twisting flow, making me not-me, making me new-me. Oh . . . incorporating is difficult.

Far below verdant forests and patchwork fields stretched and the further we fell, the more I saw. Mud-walled huts. Thatched roofs. Piles of stone . . . ah, there were castles. Ugh. I was hoping for a more modern age. Something this primitive was bound to aid my Other . . . now, my brother, and his brain-bashing tendencies.

I do believe I heard him chuckle with delight before he turned himself, spinning away to wherever in this world his twins awaited. For myself, I aimed towards a patch of thick forest, alighting in the lower boughs of an oak tree, and then shimmied down the trunk. Truth be told, I had forgotten that humans can't fly and so I had thought I would make a gentle final descent. Instead, I arrived on the ground in a most unflattering scatter of bark and acorns. At least there were no witnesses.

I am no expert on human history. Why bother? It is, more or less, as far as I can tell, all the same. It tends to be men, men, men, kill, kill, kill. Change the weapons. Trot in a new background (now desert, now mountains, now forest, now jungle) and switch around the order of vowels and consonants in the men's names, and there you have human history. Though, that said, I do prefer a more modern age. Partially the aesthetic. I know it's an unpopular view to some, but I *like* those towers of shimmering glass and steel. Wattle and daub doesn't do it for me. And that's just appearances; since I'd cast my lot as a female for this wager, I would have rather preferred to land in a more enlightened age . . . alas. I would have to work a little harder to gain the advantage. That's what Nurture is all about.

I sat down on the mossy forest floor, stretching and flexing and trying to remember the names of all these human body parts that were now mine. Fingers: useful but fragile. Kneecaps: strange. The choices I had made to maintain polarity with my . . . brother . . . had come to peculiar fruition. My skin, pale as a fish's belly, but taut and firm with Youth. I could trace the blue-green of veins (that's what they're called, right?) beneath my flesh. They were a pale shadow of the colours that flowed through our forms above. I stroked the hair that had grown from my head, long blond strands. This – blond hair, pale skin – was this a manifestation of Light? The goosebumps that rose on my arms and legs were assuredly a testament to my choice of Cold. (I hadn't thought that one through. I had imagined it would be more . . . temperamental.) Or maybe these were just chance aspects of the flesh and not manifestations of the lots. I couldn't be sure until I found my brother – it was only in each other's presence that we became defined. Bonded opposition is such a torturous pain.

But I was undeniably Female: if I turned my attention to it, I could sense mammary glands, the glisten of eggs waiting within me. Fascinating. I knew on a level beyond even the intellectual that this didn't matter. That who and what I was (am, will be) has nothing to do with any of the details of my flesh. And yet, this is the trick of incorporating. I have rendered myself flesh, and I must, to some extent, play by its rules. And humans love rules of the flesh, particularly rules ascribed to female bodies. It would be a good challenge. It would keep me on my (no-longer metaphorical) toes.

I lay on my back and stared up at the clouds. My heart pumped blood through my veins. Air flowed into my lungs. I knew that in a day or two I would cease to be aware of it, unless I chose to be, but for now it was a distraction. How is it that humans walk about trusting that this conglomeration of flesh will continue to do its myriad minor tasks? That is a testament to faith, and they aren't even aware of it.

Clouds came and went, the sky pinkened, reddened, darkened. I played a bit with my form, feeling my magic (that is what it is, now that I am on earth – above, it is my power, my self) flow through me. I could diminish the feeling of cold; I could make myself almost warm. I could shade my hair a delightful orange-red, but no darker, indicating that these were likely aspects of our polarity. The stars appeared. Down here, they are too many, too small, too far away. They don't chime and creak and whisper to us, to me, as they do above.

Nonetheless, they are there. And if I relaxed and let this flesh that is now mine sink into the moss of the forest, let these two gelatinous eyeballs just look, accepting that they will see only a very limited range of colour, alas, then I can let my other senses range over the earth's meagre stars and find my two souls . . . nearby, as I thought when I fell. Not yet in this world, but coming close. Already, I want to nurture – I want to reach out and comfort them. Offer them reassurance that being born will cause pain and confusion, but life is worth that momentary terror. I want to tell them that I am here, that I already care for them. But I know such efforts are futile until they are in this world, fully descended.

Forests are such delights. Fallow deer. Spring-hungry bears. Truffle-rooting boars. I was not hungry this morning (surprising) so I caught only a tender rabbit and was halfway through stripping its bones bare when I recalled that in this era, humans cook their food and look askance at those who do not. A good chance to test my abilities; I conjured up flame and, to my surprise, easily managed to produce a typical human fire – those merry little orange-yellow flames that devour wood. I could not summon up Fire, that magical combustion that allows for transformation, transportation: that would be my brother's terrain. So, though I could have finished this raw meal (and eaten the bones as well), I roasted the rest of the carcass. The cooking meat did smell good.

I drew in deep lungfuls, not just of the woodsmoke, not just of the forest air (redolent of fungus spore, skittish wolves, one lost child), but of the world that lurked beyond. Churches of stone. Houses of wood and mud. Iron. A faint trace of silver and gold. This told me all I needed to know. I settled back, waiting for the meat to cook through, recalling the details I have learned of human history, and almost fell asleep.

But the crackling of a branch startled me awake and in a moment I was on my feet and the hunter, snares dangling from his belt, who had crept up behind me, lay crumpled on the forest floor. A line of blue-black cut across his body, a thin but lethal laceration. In another age, they might think a high-tension cable had snapped and whipped his flesh. But in this era, it is a clear mark of what they will call magic.

A moment of hesitation, remorse. Was he only curious? A hard-working man, laying his trap lines, trying to catch his daily morsel? How many children have I un-fathered? Or was he hoping to catch me unaware? Have his way with me? I glanced down at my own body and then, despite the corpse at my feet, laughed. I was naked. Bare flesh from top to toe. It would take me a while to adjust to this body, to this world. Humans and their insistence (most of the time) on clothing. I would have to remember to complain of heat and cold, as they do. No wonder the hunter was curious. Aroused. Perhaps had nefarious intentions. This was the downside of free will . . . though I suppose my brother would insist that this was just the Nature of man. A flick of my fingers and the corpse dissolved. I would have expected it to turn to ash, but apparently that was a function of Fire. And as I was now Water, I achieved different results: a little puddle of once-flesh. Nearly as satisfying as ash. It would take me a while to get used to the limits of my power . . . of my self.

Another flick, and I was clothed. I took for reference what the hunter was wearing – cloth of homespun wool. Worn leather boots. Adjusted it for what I thought would suit a woman in this era, adding a roughly knitted shawl and a canvas apron. I thought of the man's approach, the hint of a leer I caught on his face before he fell, and I made myself crouched, stooped, older. I couldn't make myself truly Old – that was my brother's domain – but I managed some grey hair and a couple of wrinkles and lumpened up my body a bit. It was time to take the measure of this world, and it was time to find my twins.

Thatched cottages dotted the edge of the woods, and I emerged slowly from the shadows of the trees. Warier since the hunter. Not that I couldn't handle this entire village (this entire world) but that's not the best way to get acquainted. Nary a person about, though. Too bad. I had hoped to study their attire, their mannerisms. Hear their speech. It is never good to be seen as a foreigner. Above the modest thatched roofs and crowns of trees, a single church spire reached towards the sky. I aimed towards it, the houses coming closer now, the trees fewer. A goat tethered in a patch of grass. Pigs wallowing in mud. Chickens everywhere, clucking at me. But no humans.

At last, a babble of voices. I listened and for a few minutes, I thought that the chickens made more sense. Then the language coalesced for me. Another moment, and I had its grammar. The town, as I supposed they call this collection of houses, was enclosed by walls of heaped earth, reinforced here and there with wood and stone. I supposed they call this effort engineering, though I could sneeze the whole thing down.

I didn't. I hobbled to the opening, where guards eyed me from beneath the iron bowls they wore on their heads, and began their careful study. My clothes were not notable, nor, it seemed, was my face, for the guards waved me along. I hobbled on, enjoying the pretence of feebleness. Imagine being feeble! Shutters were pulled tight, though the day was bright and clear, and I wondered if I had arrived after an attack – no, there was no rubble, no sign of breakage. Or on a fasting day? But ahead I heard shouts and lurid cheering. I hobbled faster.

At last, I turned the corner, passing beneath the carved sign of an inn – the Three Leaves, if I correctly interpreted the crude design – and emerged onto the main square. There, the cheering crowd. There, the press of bodies, an onslaught of odour that nearly overwhelmed me. In the midst of those bodies, a pile of sticks and straw and . . . a woman, tied tightly to a wooden pole. By the time I made sense of everything – my ears adjusting to the babble of voices, sorting grunts and whistles into sensible words (not all of them were sensible); my nose adjusting to the morass of decay and flesh – the flames were already leaping, crackling through the straw and the sticks and climbing up the woman's dress. She shrieked, a sound beyond language but clearer at communication than any word I had heard thus far on earth.

I turned to the nearest person, a man in a hole-pocked woollen smock. 'Why are you burning her?' I demanded. I should have made my voice more gentle. I should have chosen my words with care. I realized all of this when the man jumped, recoiling from me (as if I were the one who smelled like a latrine hole), making a quick motion of his hands across his torso. 'She practised sorcery upon the priest,' he said, his voice high and scampering, like a terrier. Then he regained some of his composure and squinted at me. 'Who're you?'

'No one,' I said. The woman shrieked again and we both turned to look. The flames had taken hold of her dress, enveloped her legs; the smoke made her cough, but the wind came in, flattening the flames and dispersing the smoke, and prolonging the misery. I could see, for an instant, the features of her face, her hair tied up on her head. She did not look so different from me, I supposed. A middle-aged woman, greasy, greying hair. No doubt she hobbled when she walked.

'You talk funny,' the man insisted.

And though I could say the same of him, I merely ducked my head in a little bow of deference, and said, 'Begging your pardon.'

It appeased him, or perhaps I was merely boring, for he turned away, his attention back on the burning woman, who ceased her shrieking and was only moaning and coughing and twitching. I kept my head bowed and backed away, until I was clear of the crowd, though not of the smoke. Is it terrible of me to say that the smoke and its charred scent of flesh smelled better to me than the stench of the crowd? So be it. If I am terrible, humans are ten times worse. It will be better when I rule this age. I will make certain that humans understand empathy and love, even if I have to beat it into them.

By the stoop of the Inn of the Three Leaves I caught my breath. Burning a woman for sorcery. No doubt she had fallen asleep during Mass or crossed her eyes at the priest or some such. This era, like most eras on earth, has no actual magic. The power my brother and I manifest comes from our origins beyond the earth – that's where true magic (as humans call it) originates. The truth is humans will burn anyone any time they feel like it for any reason. In some eras, it isn't a literal burning with fiery flames, but the idea is the same. And humans are twice as quick to burn a woman as a man. Especially a woman with power. All of which meant I had to watch my step.

And step I did. One foot at a time, feeling for my twins. Ah, good, they were still yet to fully arrive in the world. Just their shadows, cast across this time, were discernable to me – so they would be here soon. A step, a step. Away from the inn. Down the mucky streets. With each step, I gradually let my appearance change. Nothing sudden. Humans notice sudden change. But gradual change can creep up on them. Like the tide. An inch at a time until they find themselves underwater. My hair went from greying to yellow. The wrinkles of my face receded into smoothness. My spine straightened, the hunch disappearing, and soon enough I wasn't hobbling.

But no good to be notably pretty, or notable in any way. So I was not. Unnoticed, I descended through the town towards the river, where spindly wharves poked out into the current, and a few tattered boats and barges disgorged cargo. This era – whatever it is, wherever I am – has yet to make use of pulleys, and I paused to watch men heave bales of wool onto a donkey cart, thinking that I needed no magic to bedazzle them . . . I could merely construct a crane and show them how to effortlessly lift their burdens. But . . . no doubt the crane would be considered sorcery and burned (along with me). No, best be off.

I added a few pox scars to my cheeks. A cast to one eye. I crossed the river on a flat-bottomed ferry boat, poled by an old man, aided by his sons and grandsons. The timbers shivered in the current – the old man's pole was largely ineffectual and it was only the sons, hauling at the ropes that connected the boat to either bank, that got me across. Delivered to another muddy bank. One son offered an arm to help me ashore and squeezed my bosom as he lifted me off the boat.

It took much effort not to offer him a few choice words or even a glare. As I climbed up the bank, I shrank my chest some, still feeling the creep of his hands upon me. The mud pulled at my feet as I climbed up to the cart track that wove from the river to the timber-and-stone walls that surrounded what was clearly the local lord's abode. A great pile of rocks, heaped into the latest style of aristocratic power. My twins would be born here? To the lord? Or to some scullery maid? The twins' shadows were lengthening, and so I hastened my steps.

The gate stood open, the yard within boasted modest activity – a farrier working shoes onto a horse, two girls scrubbing root vegetables heaped in a dirty basket. A laundress and her young assistant hanging linens to dry. I peered through the gate and studied the scene, watching and listening and also sensing the world beyond. The servants were well-dressed, in the sense that their clothes were sturdy and uniform – shades of tan and blue – and they were clean (at least by this era's standards, meaning it didn't look as though they'd been wallowing with pigs in the last hour). I adjusted my own clothes to be nicer, removing the moth holes, tightening the weave of my shawl. I dispensed with the apron, added as much brown as I could to my yellow hair, and made it a little more glossy, my cheeks rosy.

I could feel them. My twins. Their tiny souls arcing through the atmosphere, racing as if delighted to arrive, descending right towards the manor. From an upper window, I could hear a woman wail. Nothing like the shrieks of the supposed witch, but still full of pain. An hour in this town and I had heard more women screaming than I had full sentences. Nonetheless, her pain was my summons, and I stepped through the gate.

No one challenged me as I walked across the yard and up to the front door. There, a man in a tunic of tan and blue held out a hand to pause my approach. 'What business have you here?'

I plucked the edges of my skirt and gave him more courtesy than he deserved. (I would never admit it to my brother, but there are times when heads do need to be bashed. However, unlike him, whenever I feel the temptation, I at least try to find a different course of action. To him, Nature is brutal and violent and quick. Nurture is slow and patient . . . and it is not as simple as just love. No, Nurture is subtle. Nurture is about shaping, sculpting, allowing for possibilities and potentials to be realized. Sometimes, most times, that does require love. And sometimes, it requires a good bashing.) 'My good and kind sir,' I said, choosing my words slowly and trying to mimic the accent of this region. 'I had heard that my lady within needed a wet nurse.'

He furrowed his brow and opened his mouth and no doubt would have denied my claim had not the lady herself intruded with a harrowing scream that wound down the stairs to assault us. He winced.

'She will be delivered of twins,' I said, quickly adding, 'so I have surmised. And certainly need my aid.'

'I have heard no such thing,' he said, but the scream had flustered him, and he turned to go within, holding a finger up to me. 'Wait here.'

I waited.

The servant returned with another man, his cheeks flushed, his dark hair streaked with white. He, too, wore a tan and blue tunic, but surmounted with a robe lined with fur and worked on its outside with fancy needlepoint showing leaping stags.

'My lord, Duke Aymon, this is the woman.'

I again dropped low in a curtsy.

'How knew you that my lady was having twins?'

I kept my eyes downcast. 'My good lord, I saw her walking in the garden, some weeks ago and knew from how the babies rode in her belly that it would be twins.'

'Impossible,' he spluttered. 'The physician did not discern such things. And even the midwife who attends her now was shocked when the second babe emerged.'

I dared to raise my eyes and met his, a distant blue, thin as a winter sky. 'I come to offer my services, to help her nurse the children.'

He stared blatantly at my chest. 'I do not see how you could do much good.'

Curses. I had forgotten that detail. I swept into my lowest curtsy yet, one knee touching the dirt, my head ducked. 'I was lately delivered of a child, who emerged already departed, sad to say. It was but a day ago. My milk should descend soon. In a moment.' As I crouched there, I let my bosom increase and swell until it assumed rather prominent proportions. 'There,' I said. 'It has come.' And I stood up.

The duke stared at me even more. 'For a woman recently delivered of a child, and bereaved at that, you seem quite hale.'

'I come from hearty stock.'

'I wish the same could be said of my wife.' The duke stroked his beard and gazed, for a moment, off into the distance. He was a handsome man, with dark whiskers on his cheek and chin that stood in sharp contrast to his pale skin. He sighed. 'The Lady Beatrice ailed after the delivery of our first child, Rinaldo.' He turned to the servant. 'I should not be chattering here. I should fetch the priest to bless the babes.' He tipped his head towards me. 'Bring her within and present her to the midwife and Lady Beatrice. They may judge her suitable or not.'

The servant ushered me within and led me up the stairs, swaggering as he walked and muttering how I ought to be grateful the lord had given me this opportunity and so on. But he was only too glad to leave me at the entrance of the lady's chamber, where moans and mewls and various other moist sounds were emerging unpleasantly. He opened the door and called out – as one might call out into a chasm, expecting only an echo – 'My good lord sent this woman, to see if she might be a suitable wet nurse.' With a shove on the small of my back (most unnecessary) he propelled me within and shut the chamber door.

Sweat prickled my hairline as I dropped into a curtsy. Not from nerves, but from the stuffiness of the room. The hearth blazed and braziers of coals stood near the bed. I longed to throw the shutters of the windows open, but held myself back.

Instead, I stayed in my bowed position and said, 'My lady, good midwife. If I can be of service. I come from a line of very . . . bounteous . . . milk-full . . . capable nurses.' I finished awkwardly. I was not yet accustomed to the times, to the body, to human speech. But no matter. Straightening, I tuned the flow of my energy, my self, my *magic*, exuding a sense of comfort, calm. 'May I?' I said and reached for one of the babies.

'Of course,' said the midwife, already under my spell (it took shockingly little effort). I picked up one, then the other. Lady Beatrice, for her part, raised one hand from the richly embroidered coverlet and then let it fall. I took that as a sign of blessing. The moment I had the babes in my arms, they quieted, ceasing their mewling and squirming. The midwife sighed and turned her attention to Beatrice.

I looked down into two faces, beet-red and scrunched. They felt nothing like putty. They felt solid. They felt almost too heavy, as if something vast and weighty coiled within them, waiting to expand. In truth, it did. My brother would name it falsely: Destiny. I would name it true: Potential. Possibility. Just waiting to be nurtured.

Settling as near to the shutters as I could, I plumped down on a bench and with a deft motion (and some magic) had a babe latched on to each breast and the shutter cracked open a hair's breadth. The breeze came tickling in and the twins tugged at me. I sighed. I was in my elements. Cool air, milky flow, young life, the chance to nurture.

And so I began my service in Duke Aymon's household.

I solemnly swear that I upheld the rules that I agreed to with my brother. The milk that flowed into my twins was not molecularly the same as mother's milk . . . but I worked no magic upon their little persons as they sucked and sucked and sucked. Never have I met such a hungry pair.

And what a pair they were. A boy and a girl. Ricardetto

and Bradamante. Their lady mother lay abed, as drawn and drained as if she were the one having gallons of milk extracted from her body (I suppose, to be fair, she had nourished and generated several pounds of flesh and blood herself) for the better part of their first year. I was left alone with them for all but a few moments of daily visits from various aunts and grandmothers and godmothers and cousins, all who came to dote upon the babies and gossip with the recovering lady mother. The twins were to be washed and dressed and brought in their cleanest, quietest state to the duke once a day, and other than that, their daily engagements were left up to me.

In other circumstances, I would assuredly take a more measured approach to nurturing babies. I would, in fact, wish to let infants be as infantile as they wanted – merely being a loving and doting presence – and, as they develop, explore the world broadly, enquire into their own interests, and be able to pursue those avenues that intrigue them the most. But this was not most circumstances. I was not taking any chances. Not with the opportunity before me to defeat my brother and gain control of this age. (And not with the risk of exile to the Farthest Deeps. I couldn't quite forget that detail.)

And so, as I carried the twins about their chamber, or strolled with them in their baskets about the gardens and grounds, I told them stories. I seized upon any book I could and gobbled up the tales, regurgitating them for the twins. They learned of saints and dragons, sailors and orphans. I made sure to tell stories about prowess of arms and made only minor editorial adjustments, to allow for female warriors. I embellished any tale that included a ball, describing the dances in minute detail; how the men leapt and twirled, how the women swayed and spun. And in the night-time, when the rest of the manor slept, I danced with the twins. I took them one at a time, or sometimes one in each arm, and we waltzed or fox-trotted or simply sashayed around the chamber. It would be a couple of years before I could get swords into their hands, but I would have them dancing before they could walk, and telling stories with their first words.

Soon enough, though, they could walk. And talk. And exert their own wills. Dressed in the simple smocks I put them in most days, the two looked interchangeable. Their hair had grown in thickly, matching the red-brown of their mother's tresses, rather than the raven-dark of their father. But their eyes were Aymon's eyes, ice-blue. And their skin matched his as well, pale as snow and prone to flush red when angry or cold or embarrassed (strawberries and cream, one of their aunts had said, pinching Ricardetto's cheek on a visit. This had only made him blush deeper).

Just looking at them, many – sometimes even their father – couldn't tell them apart. (This pleased me – it matched on a superficial level what I held to be deeply true, that despite minor differences in bits and bobs beneath their tunics, there was no substantial marker in their selves.) However, once you let them move about, their differences emerged quite readily and, to my delight, in marked contrast to each other. (This would be better for the competition: if their talents were overlapping, I'd have a narrower range of competency to rely on.)

In their early years of walking and talking – when their words were still babble and their steps still toddling – I kept to my regime: stories, dancing. Dancing, stories. You would think that any child would find this a delightful routine. I held them on my lap and told them nonsense tales of angels (as if such things exist). I let them braid my hair as I unfolded the legends of the trolls on fog-wreathed mountains. I worked tricky magics so that music played only for our ears, polkas and drum circles and plaintive flute melodies, and we danced and danced.

I admit that I made one mistake in those early years. Stories and dancing were easy. These were, in this era, completely appropriate occupations for infants and toddlers (it was peculiar that I, a wet nurse, could read; the dances I did were bizarre, but these were deemed oddities and (mostly) overlooked). I should have been content to prepare them in two out of the three contests. That would be sufficient to win. But I wanted all three victories – or was I nervous that perhaps their dancing would not be deemed beautiful (how does one judge beauty fairly?) – or perhaps I really, really, really wanted to see my twins bash my brother's twins.

At any rate, this desire led me to bring them, not long after they had toddled their first steps, down to the stables. Putting wooden swords in their hands would be frowned upon (particularly concerning Bradamante) but horses were a non-negotiable part of 'arms of the era'. Not that I saw many (any) knights about the manor, but the stories were replete with knights and their steeds and even the guardsmen rode about on their horses. The height, the speed; it was a necessary advantage.

I found the knob ends of carrots in the kitchen, gave one to each child and, at the stable door, asked the groom to kindly direct me and the twins to the gentlest of horses. I even bobbed a little curtsy. He spoke directly to my bosom and told me that Lady Beatrice kept a pleasant pony, Patches by name, in the stall on the end and any other morning he would happily put on its saddle, but this morning he was busy readying the duke's horses for a hunt, but truly I was welcome any time in his stable. My bosom had nothing to say in return.

Patches the pony was well-named. A brindled sort of beast with a dark mane and tail. 'Up!' Bradamante demanded when we stood by the stall door.

'Give the horse the carrot, dear,' I urged.

Bradamante held her palm flat, the carrot in the centre, and lifted it towards Patches, who whuffled and leaned forward, lips slobbering across her palm until it got purchase on the carrot. One crunch and it disappeared. Bradamante giggled in delight. 'It tickles.'

Made bold by his sister's success, Ricardetto stepped closer and held his carrot aloft, pinching it in his fingers. Patches, also emboldened, stretched its neck forward and crunched down on the carrot. And on Ricardetto's fingers. The boy shrieked. The pony kicked the stall door. I grabbed Ricardetto about the waist, visions of a one-handed swordsman spinning in my head. Patches crunched the carrot and, I imagined, a few finger bones. But then Bradamante seized her brother's hand and scoffed: 'You're not even *bleeding*.'

He wasn't. No visible mark. But the damage was done. 'I hate horses,' Ricardetto declared. And though I needed him to ride, I could not bring myself to force him. I would have to regrow that trust. That was what true Nurture means.

As their steps became more sturdy and their words more defiant (*take us outside, Melissa*), I began to take them, most mornings, to the manor's gardens and orchards and sometimes to the woods just beyond. Close to the walls, the grounds were cultivated in an ornamented fashion, with walking paths and manicured hedges. But as one rambled down from the walls towards the river's banks, the cultivation decreased and the branches grew crookedly and the vines draped luxuriously. We would walk, Bradamante holding my left hand, Ricardetto holding my right. I would name each tree and flower that we passed.

On one particular morning, I readied them in their chamber in identical smocks, tying on soft leather shoes. Bradamante drummed her feet most unhelpfully. 'I want to swim,' she insisted.

'Yes, dear, you've said that,' I replied, withholding the precise quantity: ten times just this morning.

'Well, I want to. And so does Ricardetto.'

She did this often, speaking for her twin. 'Indeed. Do you?' I turned to her brother.

'I shouldn't mind,' he said. His words still had a slight lisp to them, his palate not quite hardened, yet he spoke with the cadence of an adult.

'Well. We shall have swimming lessons at some point in the future,' I said, seizing her foot rather tightly and shoving the shoe on. 'But this morning, we must . . .'

'Learn more stories,' Bradamante droned. 'It's always stories.'

'And dancing,' Ricardetto supplied.

'Time's a-wasting,' I said. How could children resent such delightful lessons? They weren't being forced to memorize times tables or learn endless conjugations of Latin. Stories! Dancing! I refrained from telling them they were ingrates and instead held out my hands. They took hold and off we went.

As we emerged from the manor, I could see the sun glinting off the river's surface, far down the slope, and hear a jackdaw crankily croaking away. We paused in the yard as a groom brought out one of Duke Aymon's fine hunting horses, all glossy chestnut and dark brown mane. Bradamante ran towards it. 'I want to ride,' she cried.

The groom laughed and said, 'Not this horse, you don't.' But he lofted her up and set her in the saddle, keeping one hand firmly gripped on her, the other on the bridle. 'This is a man's horse. But we'll get Patches set for you, soon as your father says the word.' He held out a hand to Ricardetto. 'Young master? Would you care to sit up here?' He lifted Bradamante down.

I gave the boy a slight nudge, but Ricardetto just shook his head. Perhaps he would have stepped forward with a little more urging, but the horse at that moment pawed the ground and bared its blocky yellow teeth. 'Never,' Ricardetto said, and withdrew behind my skirts.

Bradamante had not budged from the horse's side, even as its hooves worked at the ground. She merely lifted her chin, levelling her gaze at the groom. The way she stood you would have thought her smock was a suit of armour, or a flowing gown. 'I will be riding that very horse. Soon.'

The groom gave an indulgent smile. 'As you say, mistress,' and he offered a mocking bow. Bradamante answered with a meagre curtsy, and turned dismissively on her heel. The groom added in a low voice, 'Two ducats I'll never see that happen.'

'It's a wager,' I hissed back and was pleased to see his eyes widen in surprise.

The twins and I left the yard for the garden, Ricardetto holding my hand, and Bradamante running off ahead. The carefully trimmed pathways gave way to brambly bits, and I could hear Bradamante crashing through the undergrowth nearby. How to get Ricardetto over this particular fear . . . I could not fathom . . . and so settled for distraction and pointed to a plant beside the path. 'Look, that's rue. Good for so many ills.' Little Ricardetto, fingers still clammily clamped in mine, squatted down and squinted at the plant. 'Which ills, Melissa?'

Bradamante emerged from a prickle bush, leaves in her hair. 'I don't like that groom. I shall tell Father.'

'Which ills, Melissa?' Ricardetto asked again, now turning the rue leaves over in his hand.

And Bradamante, face flushed, ran back into the brambles. 'Insect bites, minor fevers, and warts,' I told Ricardetto.

'Look how the new leaves curl up,' he said. 'I wonder . . .'

'Come on!' Bradamante thundered. She had climbed into the lower boughs of a scrub oak tree and now jumped down.

'Dearest,' I said. 'How are you going to learn what rue is

good for if you keep running off? Such knowledge might aid you some day. You should attend to what I tell you. You may find it boring, but I have your best interests at—'

'It heals insect bites and fevers and warts. And two days ago you said that it was good for stomach cramps as well. Not to mention that in one of the stories you tell us, there's a witch who uses rue in a potion, which means that it is also good for magic. And I wish you would teach us *magic* rather than stupid things, like stories and dancing.'

Well. That rather brought me up short. Before I could think of a reply, she had darted off again. Ricardetto still squatted by the rue, studying the undersides of the leaves. There, on the path below the manor's walls, I had a moment of profound self-doubt. Had my attempt to nurture failed already? Was I proving my own self wrong? No, that couldn't be. Bradamante was acting out . . . a normal human stage of development. Should I rein her in? Or let her explore? Surely I should let her explore . . . but still nurture . . .

My thoughts were abruptly ended by the sound of a splash, then a scream. I grabbed Ricardetto's arm and pelted down the path, around a curve, through a copse of trees, and to the bank of the river, where Bradamante's tunic lay cast aside in the mud, the girl herself splashing in the water. 'I'm swimming, Melissa, look!' she crowed.

'You're almost drowning!' I snapped. But she wasn't. She was paddling her arms and thrashing her legs and keeping herself mostly afloat.

'Come in, Ricky!' she called to her brother.

He studied her flailing movements, craning his neck. 'How do I do that?' he asked me.

I clenched my teeth and fought the desire to summon a gust of wind to get the girl out of the water. Instead, I knitted together some mild breezes to give us a vapour of privacy and stepped out of my dress and leggings, then helped Ricardetto shrug off his tunic. I waded into the river beside him and made sure his feet were planted firmly on the river bottom, then encouraged him to put his face in the water. 'Breathe out,' I told him. 'Now turn your head to the air. And breathe in.' He obeyed, gasping a breath, then blowing out a string of bubbles. The river water flowed around us, the current strong, but Bradamante still splashed and paddled, just beyond my reach. 'Now,' I continued, 'try a stroke with your arms.' I demonstrated, reaching forward and making a little cup of my fingers, to pull efficiently through the water. He studied my movements, his red-brown hair plastered against his skull. Then he bent forward, put his face in the water and copied my motions. I put my hands beneath him, to support his weight and help him float. 'Kick,' I said, and he did. Stroking with his arms, kicking with his little legs. I held him as he practised and then let him go. For a brief moment, he sank, and I worried he might gulp in some water, but he righted himself and shot off, his kicks frothing the water.

When he reached her side, Bradamante paused in her paddling. 'Race you to the bank,' she said. Ricardetto had barely accepted her challenge when she launched off, thrashing her arms and legs. Ricardetto stretched out, stroking the water as I'd shown him, finding a rhythm with his kicks. Halfway in, he gained the lead, and he reached the bank three body lengths before his sister, scrabbling in the mud to stand upright. 'Well done,' I told him.

'You cheated,' Bradamante said.

'Did not,' he insisted, his cheeks flushing red.

'Did so. You learned a trick. From her!' She pointed a shaking finger at me.

'I taught him a skill, dearest. A skill that I will gladly teach you now, if you'll allow me to.'

But Bradamante waded into the water, her back to me. 'I heard you the first time.' And she began to mimic the stroke that I had taught Ricardetto. It took her the goodly part of an hour, by which time Ricardetto's lips were blue with cold (though he wouldn't come out of the water), but she mastered the stroke and kick on her own and could, to her great satisfaction, even best her brother in a race.

If most days were going to be like this, I feared I would sprout grey hairs despite my embodiment of Youth. But still, even though her stubbornness rankled me, I had to admire Bradamante's fortitude. When they had at last grown weary with swimming, I gathered them to me and summoned balmy breezes (as balmy as I could manage) to warm and dry them, before getting them into their tunics. They clutched my hands as we climbed back up towards the manor. 'Melissa,' Bradamante said, when we were halfway up the slope, 'will you tell us a story, please?'

In the summer of my fifth year of service to Duke Aymon's household, something woke me in the night, and I could not get back to sleep. I checked on my two charges, Bradamante curled in a tight knot – knees almost to chin – and Ricardetto sprawled out – limbs flung wide. Both sound asleep. I moved softly through the manor's halls, past the banked coals in the kitchen's ovens and out of the rear door into the yard. There, assured of the privacy that darkness could offer, I studied the night sky. Cloudless and clear, the stars glared down at me. So tiny, so cold in their demeanour. I found Mars. Venus was nowhere to be seen. And there, half a turn away, Gemini. There were many years to go before all things converged. A sigh escaped me. Many years had already passed . . . and what had I to show for it? Would all the Nurture, all the patience, all the attention, all the instruction, matter? I stared up, hoping, like a fool, for some sign. But of course, the stars paid me no heed.

I should have known my night-time restlessness was an ill omen, the fruit of which was born the following day. Early afternoon and all the sultry summer warmth had settled on the manor like a wet wool blanket. I had convinced (with some magical persuasion) Duke Aymon to buy a book of stories from a passing pedlar and now read these to the twins. The pedlar had been surprised at my interest, for the book was written in Arabic, but that made me doubly eager: something new for my twins. Perhaps it would give them an edge in their future competition.

They sat, despite the day's heat, curled against me. (I did, owing to my half of the polarity, exude a coolness they might have found comfortable.) I leaned against the stone wall of the garden, where lime trees had been espaliered and cast a meagre shade. I turned the page of the book. 'Oooh,' Ricardetto said at the sight of the illumination there. A scene of the royal court, rendered in gem-coloured tones. Lapis blue, ruby red, and all of it edged in gold.

'So pretty,' Bradamante said, her finger gently tracing the gold filigree of the king's turban. 'I would like a golden hat. Or a golden crown.'

Ricardetto leaned even closer. 'How do they make the colours so bright, Melissa? And the drawings so small? Could I learn to draw like that?'

I ruffled his hair with my hand. 'I am sure you could, my darling. If you'd like we can try some drawing later.'

'Ffff,' said Bradamante. 'What would you draw anyway? What use is drawing?'

'Now, now.' I patted Bradamante's arm. 'Let your brother do as he wishes. Not everything one does has to be useful.'

'The priest says it ought to be.'

The priest. Duke Aymon had insisted that the two begin lessons with the priest. This meant dull hours for Ricardetto chanting Latin verses and dull hours for Bradamante having Latin verses chanted at her. As well as, apparently, helpful titbits of advice about utility. 'One never knows what might be useful. That's why it's best to learn a great variety of things.' And I turned back to the story. I hadn't made it through another page when shouts – joyful ones – sounded from the gate. We all craned our necks to see four horsemen ride into the manor's yard. The first, and youngest (at least the only one with a whiskerless face), rode a massive black mount with a wide chest, at least a hand taller than Duke Aymon's favourite hunting horse. This rider had a shield slung across the back of the horse, a shield bearing a leaping stag that matched Duke Aymon's device. The rider swung himself down from his saddle, landing smoothly despite the height, and bantered with the grooms and guards who had gathered to greet him.

'Who is it?' Bradamante asked. She had stood up from the bench, but still leaned against me.

'It must be one of our men,' Ricardetto said, 'for he bears Father's stag.' He too stood, and took a firm grip on a wad of my skirts.

Duke Aymon himself came down from the manor's front door and clasped the young rider in an embrace, both of them pounding each other's backs for a moment. Then Aymon stepped past the young man and examined the horse. (Spending rather more time looking at the horse's flanks, or withers, or whatever, than he had embracing the visitor. Typical.) The twins hovered anxiously beside me as the two men turned in our direction, Aymon placing an arm around the young man's shoulders, and started walking towards us. The nearer they drew, the more I noticed how the young man resembled the old: hair dark as coal (though Aymon's had some silver-grey), a thin nose that separated ice-blue eyes a touch close-set. The young man's cheeks were tanned and roughened by sun and wind, but this did nothing to diminish his beauty. His eyebrows – dark as his hair – arched up in merry surprise as he drew near to the twins. I stood up and brushed my skirts to straighten them. (Bradamante, though in a tunic, did the same. Ricardetto, owing to my motions, had to abandon his handful of my dress.)

'Can these two be . . . Ricardetto and Bradamante?' the young man called.

Bradamante dropped a wavery curtsy, lifted her chin, and said, 'I am Bradamante. And who are you?'

The young man's lips quirked into a half-smile, almost a sneer. 'A bold one, eh? I'm Rinaldo. Your brother.' He pointed at Ricardetto. 'That is, if you are Ricardetto? Speak up.'

'He is,' Bradamante said. And she took a step closer to her twin, as if to protect him.

'Has he a voice of his own?' Rinaldo asked. 'Or do you, like most women, speak enough for two people?' He laughed and jostled his father's arm. 'Is that not true, my lord?'

'Well now,' Duke Aymon said. 'Your lady mother seldom harps on at me, but when she gathers with other women,' he waved his hands, 'I worry they'll talk themselves hoarse.'

'That would be a marvellous outcome for the men of their households,' Rinaldo quipped. He held out a hand, still sheathed in a leather riding glove. 'Well, Ricardetto. I have heard much about you and the word is about the manor that you have never ridden a horse.' He frowned at his father, who gave a little shrug, though his cheeks reddened. 'That will not do. Not when your older brother is known as one of the king's finest warriors, the youngest paladin, and among the best riders.'

Not to mention modest, I thought. But, I am proud to note, I did not speak aloud.

'I can't have you tarnishing my reputation. So, you will ride.'

I felt Ricardetto grasping again at my skirts. I put a gentle hand on his shoulder and nudged him. He only grasped tighter. I couldn't blame him. The massive black horse still stood in the yard, tossing its head and stamping at the ground. 'I'd like to ride him,' Bradamante said. 'Could I?'

Rinaldo ignored her and frowned at his father. 'Does the boy ever talk? Or is he mute?'

'It is merely time for their nap, good sir,' I said, and dropped a curtsy. 'Let me take my charges away so they don't interfere with your joyous return. He can ride another day.' I put my hands on their shoulders and gave them a gentle shove. 'Off you go. To your chamber. I'll be there in a moment.'

'Let's get your mount unsaddled, and I'll ask the huntsman about tomorrow,' Duke Aymon said and turned to walk across the yard.

I stooped to pick up what the twins had left behind. A little stick and rag poppet, a pile of smooth stones one of them had gathered from the river, the book of stories.

'You are their nursemaid? How long have you served my father?' Rinaldo asked.

I had been ignoring his presence, hoping he would go away. After all, how could a dowdy nursemaid compete with a horse for a man's attention? Clutching the gathered items to my chest, I kept my gaze on the ground and replied, 'I have been here since the twins' birth, my lord.'

'So you are responsible for coddling Ricardetto so thoroughly.' He shook his head. 'When I was his age, my only toy was a wooden sword. Not this nonsense.' He waved a hand at the poppet I held. Which may have been Bradamante's. And may have been Ricardetto's. Then he leaned closer.

'What's this?' He snatched the book from my hands, opened it, and hissed. 'What the devil? What manner of . . . this is Saracen . . . are you an infidel?'

I dropped another curtsy, deeper, and stayed low. 'My lord. We were merely looking at the pictures. They are very pretty.'

He let the book fall to the ground. Grunted. I lifted my gaze a bit to find him staring at me. Well. Staring at my chest, as if my bosom was engaging him in the most scintillating conversation. (If I let my breasts do the talking, they would have some choice things to say.)

'My lord,' I said, plucking the book from the ground and pressing it once again to my chest. 'I should see to the twins.'

I washed and dressed and readied the twins that evening for their appearance at the dinner table. I brushed Bradamante's auburn hair until it shone in the evening sunlight, then braided and twisted it up, fixing the twirl in place with golden bands and pins that sparkled to match her highlights. She peered into the silvered glass with evident glee. 'Aren't you pretty,' I cooed.

Her smile disappeared and she looked at me sternly. 'No. I am beautiful.'

'My apologies, Your Highness,' I replied dryly.

'The priest says we ought to be modest,' Ricardetto piped up. 'Actually he says *you* ought to be modest.'

Bradamante stuck her tongue out at him. 'You're just jealous that your hair isn't long enough to braid.'

Ah, that jab seemed to strike a little close to home. Ricardetto's chin wobbled for a moment; then he lifted his head and pulled his shoulders back. 'And you're jealous that tomorrow I will get to ride Rinaldo's horse.'

My jaw nearly dropped. I'd been worrying for months over how I would get this child to trust Patches the pony, and here he was, suddenly willing – eager, even – to ride his brother's warhorse. What the . . . and then I realized. Jealousy. Competition. Perhaps, perhaps, the desire to differentiate himself from his sister. That drive – to distinguish, to be different from. I understood that all too well.

'Children,' I chided. 'Enough squabbling.' If I left their words unattended, I had learned, they would soon enough devolve into hair-pulling and scratching and biting. And though this might well be good preparation for one part of their eventual competition, it often left them notably marred, which upset their parents. 'Ricardetto, we need to get you into the new shirt your mother embroidered for you, so sit still.'

He plumped down on the bench that Bradamante had recently vacated (she was now twirling about the chamber, twitching the skirts of her new dress, and dancing around. It was, I thought, a dance with much abandon but not that much beauty). Ricardetto stared into the mirror. 'Melissa,' he said, though he appeared to be talking to his reflection, 'will you brush my hair, too?'

'Of course,' I said and ran the comb through his locks. They were the same russet as his sister's, though his locks curled around his ears, no further.

'Do you think my brother would be upset if I don't want to ride his horse?'

I chose my words with care. One had to with Ricardetto. Where Bradamante would storm, he would sulk. For days. 'Didn't you just say that you wanted to ride the horse?'

'I didn't mean it.'

I leaned down close to his ear, whispering my words softly. 'I think you will be a fantastic rider. Better even than your older brother. But you don't have to be great tomorrow. Tomorrow, you just have to try.' I drew the comb through Ricardetto's hair once more. 'There now, don't you look handsome?'

'No,' he said. 'Beautiful.' He turned his head to the left, the right. 'And handsome. Can I do that, Melissa?'

'Of course you can. You can do anything you want. And if you want something, you can learn to be good at that thing. Whatever it is.' I pulled the shirt over his head and helped him into the jacket. Both were worked with leaping stags his mother had embroidered. He ran his fingers over the intricate threadwork.

'I *would* like to ride a warhorse. And I *would* like to learn to stitch stags just like these. And also to tell stories and perhaps to draw pictures like those in the book . . .' Bradamante, tipsy with spinning, grabbed his hand and twirled him about.

'Make music, Melissa!' she cried.

And so I did. Music just for their ears. I watched as they whirled and swayed and stomped their little feet. 'You can be anything you wish to be,' I murmured. I was surprised (shocked, even) to feel a prickle of tears in the corners of my eyes. Crying! Over what? This feeling of overwhelming potential. This sensation that matched the very core of my being. These two could be anything they wanted to be (I could not. I was locked into being one half of everything. Locked into opposition with the other half . . .). To my surprise, I realized that I loved these twins, as complicated, complex, and vexing as they could be. I put a hand to my chest, feeling the steady beat of a heart that wasn't really mine.

And yet, I needed these twins to be what *I* wanted them to be. What I needed them to be. Contest first, then they could pursue whatever desires were within them . . . when I ruled the age. I wiped the fledgling tears away. Business first. I mustn't forget myself.

* * *

47

The sun sent long shadows across the yard by the stables the next morning. On any other day, I would lead the twins down the manor's steps and into the gardens or through the gate and into the woods the duke kept for hunting. On any other day, the cook's assistant might be grumpily dragging a pail towards the well, or the groom's assistant might be hauling a cart of manure away from the stables. But this morning Rinaldo, resplendent in a shimmering coat of blue silk, embroidered with silver thread, stood in front of the stables, chatting with the groom as his massive warhorse was saddled and readied.

'Ah, there you are!' he called. His voice had the forced-low quality of a young man's – not quite resonant and booming. 'Come along, Ricardetto.'

In answer, Ricardetto squeezed my hand even tighter. 'Go to him,' I whispered. 'Be brave.' I squeezed his hand and Bradamante's, too. 'Isn't he handsome,' I said, fishing about for something encouraging, something expected.

'I like his coat,' Ricardetto said.

'Well. If you learn to ride a horse, you can have a coat like his,' I replied. A little bribery never hurt anyone, did it? He loosened his grip just a little and I took advantage of the moment to pull my hand free and give him a gentle shove towards Rinaldo.

The older boy, the almost-man, gave his little brother a stern look and then fussed with some buckle on the horse's harness. 'How old was I when I first rode, Alphonse?' Rinaldo asked the groom, his voice pitched loud enough to carry.

'Before you could walk, I'd swear,' the groom answered with a laugh. Like any good servant, he knew where his bread and butter came from.

Ricardetto had drawn near and now Rinaldo clamped a hand on his shoulder. 'If the king's campaigns hadn't kept me far from home, I would have taught you long before. As it is, I worry you've been coddled half to death.' Rinaldo shot a look at me, eyes narrowed.

'Curtsy, Bradamante,' I whispered through gritted teeth, and the two of us bent our knees and plucked our skirts. Then I took her hand firmly in my own. 'Let's leave your brother to ride.'

'I want to ride,' she insisted.

'Another day,' I hissed. 'Let's go to the woods.' I hoped this would placate her. I felt so divided. On the one hand, I was quite grateful, despite Rinaldo's egoism, that he had managed to get Ricardetto on a horse. On the other hand, I didn't want Bradamante to pitch a fit in the manor's yard. She was getting old enough that people were beginning to treat her less as a baby or child, and more as a girl. Moreover, in my guise as a nursemaid, I couldn't very well assert dominance over Rinaldo (though a part of me did long to, as my brother would say, bash his arrogant head in).

'I'd rather ride,' Bradamante said.

'I have a surprise for you,' I said. 'In the woods.'

This close to the manor, the woods were well-tended, with paths cut through and underbrush cleared. Bradamante and I walked hand-in-hand until the paths dwindled and the trees grew thicker; she muttered to herself about brothers and unfairness and occasionally looked up at me and said things such as *I like surprises*, until finally she asked, 'What's the surprise?'

'It wouldn't be a surprise if I told you. But, ah! Here we are.' We had arrived in a clearing, edged on one side by brambly bushes, and with oaks standing sentry on the other. 'Close your eyes,' I said. She did so, and I approached one of the oaks. On a branch just at head height a grey squirrel chittered at me, telling me, in no ambiguous terms, to back off and leave his acorns alone.

The wind, the water, moonlight. These are easy for me to bend to my will. Animals are trickier; they have to be reasoned with. Given that, though, squirrels are easier than humans. 'Haven't you wanted to be bigger, ever?' I asked the squirrel. 'Now's your chance.'

The squirrel gave a little hunch of its shoulders. A tilt of its head, a chirrup that clearly said, *What's in it for me?*

'You do my bidding, enlarged, for a short while, and I will leave you in that size for a further hour so you can get vengeance on, or advantage over, any rival you might have.' I suspected, from my observations, that squirrels always have rivals. This squirrel squinted at me. 'Plus fangs. But only for ten minutes.' I didn't want any villagers savaged. The squirrel nodded.

It was a matter of blood, of bone, a small crackle of electricity. That did it for size. Breeze, a touch of water, created the shape, the sensation of a horse. A grey horse. With a bushy tail. But a horse. 'Open your eyes,' I said. The squirrel-horse stared at me. 'Not you,' I whispered.

'Oooooh!' Bradamante said. She reached up and petted its velvety nose. It nipped at her (with two very long front teeth. I hoped she hadn't studied horse anatomy closely).

'Is it mine?'

'For the moment. Up you go.' I lifted her onto its back. The horse looked as if it was eyeing the nearest tree to climb, but it settled for lowering its neck and gnawing at an acorn. Perhaps my magic had not been as completely transformative as I thought.

Bradamante sat at first in an awkward sort of sideways pose; an imitation of her lady mother in her side-saddle. Except without a saddle, the posture hardly worked so as soon as she had swung one leg across the horse's back, her dress bunched up. 'I want a warhorse. Like the one Ricardetto gets to ride,' she declared as she rocked her body against the horse, as if urging it to go faster (the horse-squirrel, to its credit, hardly budged, but took plodding steps).

I might have been able to get the squirrel-horse to be a bit more warlike, but in truth, I was content to let Bradamante begin at a slower pace. She was always rushing off at full tilt and though that was fine in some pursuits, having a warhorse as one's first ride seemed a bit much (I spared a thought for Ricardetto; surely his brother wouldn't let him be maimed). I nudged the horse-squirrel and it bestirred itself into a trot, galumphing inelegantly around the clearing. Bradamante whooped and swung an imaginary sword. 'I'll cut down my enemy! I'll fight beside my brother!'

I cannot express the happiness I felt at hearing Bradamante say this. 'You shall do so, my dearest. In good time,' I said. I had been waiting for the twins to voice some ambition. For the truth of Nurture is this. I could stuff them full of every piece of knowledge. Train them in language and legend and dancing and war. But if they had not the gumption, the *will* . . . all the knowledge would be for naught. (I wonder if this . . . desire . . . is what my brother calls Nature. But it cannot be. Many humans have intentions. Few achieve them. My twins will achieve *my* intentions because I will train them, nurture them, in that direction. That my twins also want to achieve the same goals only makes it more likely they will succeed.) 'Just for the moment,' I said, 'let this be a secret between us.'

'I like secrets,' she said and smiled at me.

Oh, bliss. She would be fun to work with. I watched her dig her heels into her steed's sides and listened to her issue challenges to imaginary foes. Oh! She *had* been listening to all the stories I had told her. Had been thinking about arms and armies and valiant fights. I breathed a happy sigh (and another prayer – to what? – on Ricardetto's behalf) and then helped her down. She scampered across the clearing and I released the horse-form, letting the squirrel remain giant. It opened its mouth. 'Fangs,' I said and stretched bone. It gave a gruesome grin and hopped off between the oaks.

The sun sent slanting angles across the manor's walls when Bradamante and I entered the yard once more. Ricardetto stood outside the stables, on the edge of a group of servants, watching the gangly dog-boy wrestle with one of the kitchen boys. He was the smallest figure there, a little set apart (his older brother nowhere to be seen) and he shifted his weight foot to foot, peering through the press of bodies as the two boys grappled and grunted. Bradamante tore her hand from mine and went running to her brother. 'What are they fighting about?' she piped. The men around her murmured and grumbled, turning their attention to the twins for a moment.

'Young master. Young mistress.' One of servants gave a bow that was almost mockingly low.

Bradamante opened her mouth, and I feared that she was about to command the wrestling to resume, as if the servants were bears trained to entertain her. I grabbed the twins by their wrists and half-dragged them within. 'We must get you presentable. No doubt there will be a dinner this evening.'

'But . . . Melissa . . .' Bradamante whined. 'I wanted to see . . .'

'We'll never know who won.' Ricardetto pouted.

'How was riding?' I asked Ricardetto. 'Did you like your brother's horse?'

'It was . . .' Ricardetto looked around. We had reached the manor's front door; the clutch of servants was distant now, no one else about. 'Scary,' he finished. 'At first. But I got to gallop.' His face split in a wide grin. 'And that was fun.' As quick as it came, the grin disappeared. 'They said that soon I should leave your side, else I would be wearing skirts my whole life.' He frowned. 'I don't mind skirts. I don't want to leave.'

'You are young yet to go,' I said. 'Don't let it worry you.' I gave his hand a squeeze as we passed through the manor door.

'I should like to go. Off to war,' Bradamante crowed. She tugged my hand. 'Can we learn to wrestle, like those two boys in the yard?'

'I prefer you learn to wrestle rather better than they do,' I replied.

'And swords,' she added, now racing ahead.

'A splendid idea,' I replied. 'For the moment, dearies, let us find your mother and learn how she wishes you attired this evening.'

Their mother was, of course, sewing by the fire, cloistered in a room with her lady friends. I rather hoped that she would quickly dismiss the twins – bestow a kiss on each of their brows and order them a bowl of broth and an early bed (the magic with the squirrel had been oddly draining for me). But no, she announced that Rinaldo and Duke Aymon had gone off to try their falcons and she meant to welcome them back with a hearty repast. She let her sewing rest in her lap as she recounted the menu to the ladies, who cooed with approval. I stood by the chamber door, awaiting orders as to how the twins were to be dressed, nodding along to her words, as was expected (I was growing weary of being an obedient servant).

Ricardetto leaned against her side, nestling his head against her ribs. Lady Beatrice absently gave his hair a stroke as she finished her list. '. . . and a berry tart. I have asked Cook specially for it. It's Rinaldo's favourite.'

'He let me ride Bayard,' Ricardetto told his mother, his voice a little muffled in the folds of her gown.

She gave a little sigh. 'That means soon you'll be riding away from here, just like your brother.' Lady Beatrice turned to Bradamante, who had also escaped my grasp and crouched by the fire, using a straw to poke at something – an unfortunate insect, likely. 'Bradamante,' her mother chided. 'Stand up, now. What did you do today?'

Bradamante stood, shot a quick glance at me and then returned her gaze to the floor. 'Went to the forest, Mother. We looked for mushrooms, but there weren't any good ones. Just poisonous ones. With spots.'

'Oh, my.' Her mother shivered and glanced at me. I gave her a bland smile. I would have to teach Bradamante the basics of lying. Keep it simple. Say no more than you have to. Come to think of it, that's the basics of telling the truth as well. Lady Beatrice beckoned for Bradamante to come closer. 'See this, my dear?' She held out the piece of linen she was working all over with briar roses. 'It will be for Rinaldo to take back with him. A keepsake. Wouldn't you like to come and spend an afternoon sewing with us?'

Bradamante gave a curt nod, frowning at the square of linen. 'Yes, Mother, I would,' she said.

'I would, too,' Ricardetto said.

Beatrice gave his hair one more stroke and then gently pushed him away. 'But you'll be down in the yard with your brother, learning to ride. And soon enough, your sister will be sewing a favour for you to carry off.' She said this gaily, as if she were giving the children each a spoonful of sugar. As for the two of them, they looked as if their mouths had clamped on lemons.

I grabbed them each by the collar and tugged them away. 'Let us leave your lady mother to her sewing and her peace.' I gave them a little shake and the three of us dropped into the neatest curtsies you have ever seen. 'A bow, Ricardetto,'

I said through the side of my mouth, and the little boy tried again, bending over at his waist so that his head all but knocked against his knees. 'Very nice.' I pulled them from the chamber.

Back in our own quarters, the twins chattered at me – 'I don't care to sew all day.' 'Did you really find poisonous mushrooms?' 'Could I try Father's horse?' 'Could I learn to embroider?'

'Later, I will show you how to thread a needle and sew. But for now, we must get you ready for dinner,' I said.

Bradamante had stamped over to the one narrow window of our chamber, huffing as she gazed down. The clatter of hooves and the shouts of men rose up to our stuffy room; perhaps Aymon and Rinaldo had returned from flying their falcons.

'If he can learn to sew, why can't I ride Bayard?' She stood beside her twin, the two of them of equal height, the same proportions. Their faces, too, mirror images, down to the bumps at the top of their noses and the dimples in their right cheeks (though only Ricardetto's showed at the moment, for Bradamante was scowling at me). 'How are we different? Why does he get to do what I want to do?'

I sighed. There were dozens upon dozens of ways I might answer this question. But I simply pulled her against me and squeezed her shoulder. 'I will teach you everything you need to know.' This was true, but it was not an answer to her question.

That night, I served the table at the feast Duke Aymon had ordered to celebrate his firstborn, Rinaldo. The knights who had journeyed with the young man joined us, and I was kept busy, scampering to and from the table, attending to the twins, pouring the men wine. I heard snatches of their stories. Heard them teasing Rinaldo, then teasing Ricardetto. Heard one propose marriage to Bradamante (I didn't refill his cup after that). I hauled the children to bed and told them a story of my own design about twins who learned how to fly. I nearly fell asleep myself in that stuffy chamber, the fire banked for the night, the darkness creeping around us. Nurture is a tiring business, but even so I revelled in getting to see my twins make progress. In watching them slowly develop, responding to how I shaped them. I was slipping into dreams when shouts from below roused me, and I went once more down to the feast.

One man leaned back from the bench against the wall, snoring. Two others sang a saucy song. The girl servants from the kitchen rolled their eyes when they saw me. 'Keep your distance,' one whispered. 'They're as pinchy as crabs over there.'

It seemed the Lady Beatrice had withdrawn for the night and now the men ruled the table alone (it rather reminded me of what the age would be like if my brother gained control).

I dodged the fingers and grabbed the wine jugs, catching bits of the stories the knights were pouring into Aymon's ear. How great his eldest son was. Something about jousts and pitching and a king. I returned the jugs to the table; I had considered watering the wine rather heavily, but what did it matter to me if they woke on the morrow with splitting heads and dry mouths? I didn't add a drop to dilute it.

One managed a pinch to my rear as I gathered their abandoned trenchers. I gave him a tight smile that he was probably too drunk to discern and sent a tendril of thought into the mind of the terrier sleeping at the man's feet. The dog shifted slightly, snuffling, then peed voluminously on the man's boots. He wouldn't notice until later – if he noticed at all – but it was a small compensation. When I ruled this age, such behaviour would not be tolerated. Better – when I ruled this age, it wouldn't occur to men to behave in such a manner.

Through the kitchens I emerged into the night air, carrying an empty leather bucket, taking slow steps across the yard, choosing the most circuitous route towards the well, my head tilted back to gaze up, the moon a wicked sickle in the sky. Mars was nowhere to be seen. Nor Venus. Just the two bold lights of Gemini and a span of space waiting to be crossed. Years and years. Time enough for my twins to learn the art of the sword, though I ought to begin that soon. I swung the bucket from my hand. How would I manage that? A nurse-maid couldn't very well become a swordmaster – at least not in this era. And I could only sneak them off to the woods on occasion. A puzzle, indeed.

The well loomed up in front of me and I hoisted my bucket, tying it to the winch line. Before I could drop it in, an arm came around my waist, a hand squeezing my breast from the side. I pulled away, but the arm held me tight. 'Let me go,' I hissed and managed to turn my head to the side, catching a glimpse of the face of the man who held me. It was Rinaldo, his breath heavy with wine.

'I will have my father let you go. Permanently.' He leaned so close his nose almost touched mine. He looked nothing like the twins. His face was a blade: thin nose, pointed chin, arched eyebrows. 'I have heard what the servants say about you. How you sometimes speak in strange languages.'

'A gift of Pentecost, my lord,' I said, letting the bucket fall into the well, and trying to prise his hand from off my breast. 'Our saviour did teach of the speaking of tongues . . .'

'It's witchery. Don't try your spells on me. I saw the books you read.' He pressed closer and I could see the slight move-ment of his other hand, drawing a dagger from a sheath on his belt, pressing its tip against my belly, as if to drive it into my lungs. 'I think you are sent from our enemies. You seem bent on spoiling my brother. No one knows who you are or where you came from. You have worked some sorcery on my father, no doubt.'

'I have worked no magic on anyone. Let me go.' I tried to figure what else I could say. There was no claim I could make. No appeal to an earthly court. No chance to prove my case. No chance even to have my say. He had said it. And his words were law.

He finally took his hand from my breast and instead seized me by the nape of my neck – skin and hair and a bit of my dress's collar as well. 'I'll have my father turn you out.' As if I were a cat. Well. I had claws (not that I was in a position to use them; that would raise more questions than reading storybooks in Arabic).

In short order, he had dragged me before his (thoroughly intoxicated) father. Rinaldo, in his still-breaking boy's voice, declaimed his charges against me and demanded that his father be rid of me. 'She should be brought to the priest,' he insisted, his voice rising in pitch.

The feasting table had all but emptied of men. One snored on the ground beside the bench, a terrier curled up close. Duke Aymon gripped his head. His woe, I suspected came more from the volume of his son's screed than from the nature of the charges. 'Enough, enough, Rinaldo. I hear you. And I agree. She is a strange woman. But she has been good to the twins.' He swallowed thickly and looked at me in the dancing firelight. 'But you are right. It is time she is gone. The twins must have a proper tutor. Not some wet nurse.'

'Father, I would summon the priest . . .'

Aymon lifted a hand and the boy fell silent. 'Enough. Go to bed. I will handle this.' He waited until Rinaldo had withdrawn and then, knees quaking, stood up from his chair. I considered my options. I might gently ensorcel the duke, make him let me keep my spot. But hadn't I just been thinking that teaching the twins the art of the sword would be difficult to manage as a nursemaid? Perhaps this was my cue – perhaps Rinaldo was, in fact, aiding me. I tucked in my chin, as if resigned to my fate.

The duke took a step towards me, another, put a hand on the table to steady himself, then said, 'I fear you must go.' He fumbled at his belt and withdrew two copper coins, thrusting them out in my general direction. He opened his fingers and they fell to the floor with a cheap clatter. The duke turned and stumbled away, leaving me in the dark.

CHAPTER TWO

Walking into the night, into the woods, letting the silly form of my flesh dissipate, I felt a sense of relief. Ah. That was bliss. I wasn't tired, not in the way humans get tired, but I was weary. Weary, weary. Weary in particular of following the orders of an old mortal man who complained all day of how his bowels were gripped up and yet insisted on feasting on nothing but cheese and meat. I would have liked very much to simply return to my proper abode and take a long nap. But my annoyance at the duke and his nasty son Rinaldo grated at me. Particularly because, I slowly realized, if I didn't win this damn bet with my brother, I would be exiling myself to a rather bleak span in the Farthest Deeps. I could not abandon my twins for long, not if I wanted to win this contest. But I deserved a short break.

Deep in the woods beyond the manor, my clothes long ago shed, my sinews and tendons undone, I disincorporated as much as was possible and yet still remain in this realm. Which meant I floated, just above the crowns of the forest's trees, my form diaphanous at best. Likely, if anyone looked up and saw me, I would be thought a ghost. Fine. People of this era are generally terrified of ghosts so, unlike if they thought I was a woman, they would probably just leave me alone.

I floated for a bit, letting the air waft me along over the manor and gradually, when I felt a little rested, I let my attention focus on my brother. It wouldn't do to leave him unobserved for so long. My twins would be fine for a little while without my tutelage. Maybe they'd appreciate me even more after an absence. But my brother . . . Now . . . where was he? To find him, to figure out what he'd been doing, I needed to give myself up not to the winds that breezed over the forest, but to the deeper winds, the thicker winds, the winds above and below, the winds that propelled time, that propelled necessity. I was quite grateful, in this moment, that I had selected Air and not Rock. Air was ever so much more helpful, pliant. To figure out what he was up to and how his plans with his twins were developing, I would need not just to find him, but to trace him back.

Back five years and a few months. Back to the moment of our fall, our descent. The winds caught me up, turned me around. If I'd had wings, I would have spread them out, flexed my pinions, caught the thermal waves and soared. But I didn't. I was a gauzy haze, little more than a fair-weather cloud, in my current state, and so the winds tattered and battered me, but nonetheless hauled me where and when I wanted to go.

I could see my brother hurtling down, waiting until the last possible second until he had to incorporate, then positively popping into his body. To the people below, it must have looked like a meteor streaking through the sky. And the fool didn't even slow down, just tucked himself into a ball and let his new body plunge into the sea with a sizzle and plume of steamy water. Well. Points for showmanship. I watched as he swam – leisurely as a jellyfish – towards an island of humped sand and straggly vegetation. Pulled himself ashore, shook himself dry like a dog, and promptly fell asleep.

Well. I wasn't going to watch the fool snore. I hovered among the lowest layer of cloud and sent my senses out, reaching for the shadows that his twins would cast. I felt them immediately. A tremor went through my substance (insubstantial as it was). These twins . . . felt like iron. And as I sensed them, I was brought back to that moment on the edge of the Deeps, when my brother, my Other, had selected these souls. How weighty they had felt. The winds that bore me aloft tugged at me and I felt frail – my own twins so soft next to these souls. For a moment, I doubted my ability. Perhaps my brother was right. Perhaps he could choose the winning pair that easily, based on their Nature. It curdled my stomach just to think such a thing. I glanced down again at his sleeping form. Would he notice if I . . . no, I would not meddle with his twins. We had agreed on this point; no interference with the other's twins. I would just go . . . check on them.

So off I went, pushed by the wind, following their heavy shadows as easily as a child might follow a trail of gumdrops. Beneath me, the world changed. Blue waves, white-yellow shoreline. Back out over blue waves. Dropping lower, close enough to see hunched grey islands. Here and there big enough to host a clump of trees. Then a darker shoreline. The breeze around me lessened, and I floated, coming to rest on the battlements of a coastal fortress. The air that licked me here was warm, salty, and fresh. I smelled none of the river-mud scent that permeated the air near Duke Aymon's manor. Gone were the sheep and the brambles and the damp fungal woods. The heat here fought against my inner cold, though the sunlight – so bright it was almost unbearable – welcomed me. Ah, the world of opposites. The world of being locked into polarity. That Light and Cold should belong together might seem odd to some – but just think of the moon, the stars. But I digress.

There had been fighting at this coastal fortress. Recent fighting. The walls were battered, a gap broken through on the western side. The gate hanging splintered from its mighty hinges. Piles of rubble had been heaped up, piles of ash and burnt timbers, too. I felt my brother's twins. Hovering near me, oddly enough. They, too, were not yet fully incorporated. I drifted to give them space. I would not be falsely accused of interfering. (I would only be accurately accused of interfering. And then I would deny it.)

Gradually, the western horizon exhaled the last of the sun's light and darkness gathered. I could hear a sentinel's clanking footsteps somewhere on the battlements nearby. The jangle of a horse's bit and bridle from outside the breeched walls. Within the fortress, nothing stirred beyond the mumblings and moans of sleepers.

I grew stiff. I grew bored. I could sense my brother's twins twitching as well, excited, awaiting their moment. I rose up and wafted along, circling around the fortress's watch tower and filtering in through arrow slits. Nothing but guards here and there, peering out into the night as if their feeble eyes could see anything in the dark. These guards, with their shirts of chain mail and spears whose curved blades were wickedly sharp, made Duke Aymon's defensive force seem paltry – little more than the wooden pieces on a chess board. Again, a tremor of uncertainty thrilled through me: what sort of world were these twins entering? How would it shape them, if my brother did not? The moon rose, poured its light over the waves. The guards stared, transfixed at the beauty of that rippling silver.

And in that shadow, that pause, three men crept beneath the watch tower and into the belly of the fortress. I felt the twins' shadows lengthen, beginning their stretch towards their mortal forms. I caught a passing breeze and floated in through the night shutters of a chamber's window. A man and a woman in bed. The woman's belly large with child. Her hair, darker than the growing night, fanned out around her head. And the man, in nothing but a breechclout, with his arm around her waist, cradling both the woman and her swollen stomach.

And there – the two shadows stretched and pooled and swam inside her. The twins, now incorporated. The woman gave a little twitch and sigh, then settled into deeper sleep, nestling closer to the man.

The click of a metal latch. So slight a sound, but in the darkness of the fortress, enough to make the woman wake up, struggle to sit up in bed, the man shifting beside her, raising a hand to rub at his eyes. And there, in the doorway to their chamber, three men. The woman's face registered surprise and then recognition and then confusion as they darted into her chamber. One rushed to her side and drove the pommel of his sword into the top of her head. I was horrified, I was elated: that blow was hard enough to kill. The twins could be done away with before they had even lived . . . she crumpled to the chamber floor as the other two men grabbed her sleeping companion and, in one swift stroke, severed his head. The blood rushed, a deeper dark than the night. Before the pool cooled and congealed, without even a pause for the gold necklace or the purse of coins that sat in the chest at the foot of the bed, the men had swaddled the pregnant woman in her blankets. Two of them carried her, a sagging bundle, and the third, sword drawn and dripping, scouted the corridors ahead.

They met no guard as they descended the servants' stair. The night air was redolent with sea salt, the decay of wrack. They picked their way across rubble, edging through a gap in the wall. Just beyond, a trunk waited, and they stuffed the woman within. It was a tight fit.

The breeze obliged me, twitching me along as the men staggered across the scree of rocks that tilted precipitously towards the shoreline, the trunk banging and dragging between them. At last, they gained the sandy reaches of a cove, where they paused for a breath. One of them sat on the lid of the trunk, another shoved him off, and they scuffled there, arguing in whispers. Humans.

I can imagine how I might shape this into a story – look how my nurturing of my twins has begun to change me, as well! – I might imagine that the woman in the trunk was betrothed to one of the men who entered her chamber, but she had defied him and married another. No, no. Too prosaic. I would say that these men are her brothers, that the woman was taken against her will by the man they murdered and they are, in their tangled mortal way, redeeming her honour. Hmmm. No. They've shoved her in a trunk, half-alive (at best). Better: some madman soothsayer has come to the fortress and warned that the tower will collapse and the kingdom fall if the woman is allowed to give birth . . . Oh. That sounds *exactly* like something my brother would do. I shall have to ask him, the next chance I get (which will hopefully be when I am escorting him to his exile in the Farthest Deeps).

While I was musing, the men roused themselves to their task and resumed hauling the trunk to the waterline. There, they beckoned to a little fishing boat, which was tied at a wharf. An old man sat beside the tiller, mending a net, while a boy busied himself coiling a neat pile of rope. The wharf trembled as they carried the trunk onto it, and the old man pushed himself to his feet, the boy hanging back – he looked ready to jump over the side of the boat at a moment's notice. Wise.

The moon had passed its zenith. The old man ducked and bobbed his head. He took the few coins he was offered. The men heaved the trunk over the gunwales and onto the deck. The boat wobbled, steadied itself, settled lower in the water as two of the three men also stepped aboard. The boy hopped about, unwinding the rope that held them to the wharf, raising the sail. The sea was a dark cauldron, a belly. The cove a pair of arms that sought to enclose them. But the boat slipped through the gap and out into the open night.

If anything, the ocean is the closest you mortals can get to an understanding of the realm from which I come. You think of the sky as a vast emptiness. You think of the stars as beyond. But the sea, you understand. Full. It has depth. It contains multitudes. You can sail upon it. Swim within it. It will buoy you up. It will pull you down. It moves of its own accord and yet you can steer your way across it. Yet you will never, ever know its full extent.

By dawn, the two armed men slept, slumped against the trunk. The old man leaned against the tiller. The boy stood in the bow, looking out, though he kept darting glances back, over his shoulder, at the trunk. I shared his concern – what was going on in that stifling darkness? I gusted as close as I dared, listening, listening. Yes, three scanty hearts beating within. (I felt relief. Ought I? If they were all dead . . . I would win. But I wanted them to live. Odd, that I cared. No, I didn't care, I merely wanted to win the contest, the glory of the fight and my victory. So I told myself.) In the distance, other fishing boats with ragged sails, with old men at the tiller and boys in the bow, plied the waters, but this boat veered away. The men roused themselves, pissed over the side of the boat, coughed and muttered. Beneath the timbers of the boat, the waters changed from light turquoise to murky green-black as they traded the warm waters of the shoreline sea for the true depths of the ocean.

From the stern, the old man called something, and the men jerked in response. A moment of hesitation. Did one of them offer a prayer? He muttered something. And then they grasped the rope handles of the trunk and lifted it up, a pause on the gunwale of the boat, and they heaved it over. I felt a slight pang of . . . sadness. I had grown attached to the little boat. To the old man and the boy, whose throats, I feared, would be slit wide-red-open once they were within the cove again.

But it was the trunk that concerned me and so it was the trunk that I had to follow, letting the boat obey the insistence of its tiller, turning about, tacking its way back to seemingly safe waters. The trunk fell under the sway of the ocean, the current pulling at it. Land-bound mortals often fear deep waters, I have learned. They think that most things sink. But a surprising variety of things actually float. Not stone of course. Bodies do, but only after a time. This trunk floated surprisingly well. It spun about. Now and then a side or corner of it dipped, setting it to wobble momentarily. But I tell you, even planets in their orbits do that, tilting and shifting as they are pulled by others.

Something was pulling this trunk, and not just the current. The sun rose, white-heat that matched the salt of the sea. The trunk floated past rocky crags of islands, some too pitiful to support even a goat, others boasting a lookout post, with some ragged flags asserting domain. The sun set, and the stars emerged, offering their meagre light. So dark was the night, so deep the ocean. The stars floated, sparkling, on the surface of the waves and so it seemed that the trunk sailed through their midst, as if it charted a course in the night sky. As if it was not drifting at all, was not subject to the whims of currents and breeze and chance, but was driven by the will of the universe, the dictates of the stars it floated within.

Then the sun rose and the illusion was dispelled as a seagull, voicing raucous displeasure at something (possibly me. I am realizing, the longer I sojourn on earth, that animals are attuned to my presence), landed on top of the trunk. It befouled the wood immediately with a white splatter, and looked all the more pleased with itself for the effort. For an hour, or more, it sat there, king (or queen, or ruler) of its barren domain, having no sense of what it presided over, of what lay beneath its little claw-some feet. It was only when the sun rose to its greatest height and the current clashed with the pull of the waves towards shore that the bird gave up its perch. The current, too, gave up its hold on the trunk, relinquishing it to the power of the surf, which pitched it up and down, and sucked it ever closer to the sandy shore.

Not a human footprint marred that sand, though other animals had left imprints above the tide line. Past those, a tangle of vines and shrubbery formed a thick barrier. Here and there, a palm tree curved up, thin and winsome, fronds rattling in the breeze. I alighted in one, nestling among the unripe coconuts, and watched the trunk, feeling the sway of the souls – born and unborn – within as the waves pushed it against the shore, pulled it back out, again and again. At length, a rogue wave shoved it far enough up the beach that the trunk's corner stuck in the sand and then the surf commenced a new task of burying it, each wave bringing sand and seaweed that heaped up against it.

The fronds rustled around me, though I felt no breeze, and I tensed. The rattle of the fronds passed to the vine that wound round the palm's trunk, which squeezed, and then the message – for now I perceived that it was a message, went to the roots, the roots to the shrubbery, the shrubbery to denser foliage that stretched from the beach towards the island's interior. Such a system of communication spoke of sophisticated . . . laziness . . . which spoke, of course, of my brother. He hadn't wanted to incorporate in the first place, and I doubted he wanted to do much in the way of anything. Up above, as down below, he liked to lurk and watch.

In another moment, the rustling of the leaves shifted from their gentle dithering into a harsher pattern as he pushed through the tangled vines, kicking the trunk of the palm where I rested (was he hoping for coconuts to fall? Or did he subconsciously sense my presence in the tree?) and then emerging on the beach. He paused at the margin where the shrubbery gave way to sand, blinking in the inescapable sunshine. I floated a shade lower to get a good look at him.

Oh, my brother. What volume of demonology had he looked at before choosing his current appearance? His hair was black as obsidian, and nearly as shiny. Long, it would have reached to his shoulders had he not pulled it back and bound it behind his head. Despite living in this tropical climate, his skin was as pale as moonlight and his eyes, as he blinked in the sun, gleamed red. Oh, my. Might as well give him horns.

He was tall and lean. Lean to the point of seeming gaunt. And oddly ageless. His face had no trace of beard, his hair not a thread of grey. And yet by the way his cheekbones protruded, the way his long fingers bent, he suggested an air of age . . . of wisdom . . . of authority. He wore a long robe, surprisingly plain for him, of sheer white, its hem and cuffs worked in a black needlepoint pattern of waves. Seeing him, I felt myself again. I am not me without him. One cannot be opposite of nothing, after all. I needed him. I hated him. I would defeat him.

He licked his lips. His tongue as red as his eyes. His lips bearing a faint white-grey sheen, chapped from living in this salty clime. Smiled as he saw the trunk there at the surf-line. With one hand (I noted that his fingernails were entirely black, as if he'd painted them with pitch), he lifted his robe a few inches, an almost dainty gesture, and walked down the sand towards the trunk. Blinking, blinking, as if the sunlight still assaulted his eyes, as if he had spent the last month in a cave. (He may have, given that he had chosen Dark to my Light and yet also lived on a tropical island.)

A blue-and-gold parrot alighted in the palm tree next to me, then immediately took flight again with a tremendous squawk and a great flapping of wings. My brother didn't bother to look up, so fixated was he on his prize. Beside the trunk, he fell to his knees in the sand, and began to work at the latch. I wondered if he knew what he'd find inside. How closely he had read the stars.

He dragged the trunk higher in the sand and lifted the lid. His brows arched, a moment of surprise he could not hide. And I knew then that he had hoped to open that trunk and find his two twins, perhaps already walking and talking, ready to run about the island and grow up into their wild, destined selves.

But, no. He gazed down, instead, onto a bedraggled woman, a barely alive body. His nose twitched. From my perch, I could sense how he controlled himself, his desire to recoil, to slam the lid and push it back into the surf. But even I could sense the presence there within the trunk. The woman's swollen belly. The insistence beating there, twin hearts, placed by the stars, demanding to be born.

My brother rolled up his sleeves and reached into the trunk, grabbing the woman beneath her arms and hoisting her out. Her legs hung limply. Her hair matted in bloody clumps. Her belly was swollen to grotesque proportions. How could she still be alive?

And yet her eyelids fluttered as my brother carried her, an arm under her knees, an arm under her shoulders, and set her in the shade (the very meagre shade) of the palm tree I perched in. Her lips moved too, though she made no sound, and my brother reached within his robes and brought out a gourd. He withdrew the stopper – a piece of wood neatly carved to look like a gourd vine – and put the spout against the woman's lips, tipping the gourd until a clear liquid flowed out. Her lips kept moving, and the liquid spilled down her chin, tracing a channel down her neck, dampening the collar of her robe. The fumes rose up, and I knew my brother was giving her a potent brew, something to revive her, or sustain her, something to keep her going long enough to push the twins within her out. Her eyelids shot open, her eyes rolling back to show just white, and she gave a tremendous moan. Her body heaving, shuddering, as if an electric shock had coursed through her, arching her back. Her fingers clawed fruitlessly at the sand, and she groaned again. Had she the strength, no doubt she would have screamed. My brother tipped more liquid down her throat, put a hand on her belly. I peered down waiting to sense some magic from him, some sorcery that would violate our solemn vow. But the magic he worked was on the woman's body, to ease her pain; he left untouched the twins within.

Another wave of pain took her, shook her body as a cat will shake its prey to break its neck. Again, her back arched, her head turned to the side. My brother kept one hand lightly on her abdomen, though if he brought her any comfort from this gesture, it was impossible to tell. Then the wave passed and she lay limp on the sand. My brother lifted her hand, feeling at her wrist for a pulse, then let her hand drop and reached to her neck. In one quick motion, he stood and grabbed at the belt of his robe, drawing out a dagger. Bone handle darkened from use, silver blade oiled and shiny from sharpening.

With the numb efficiency of a butcher, he tore the woman's robe open, poured the contents of the gourd over her swollen belly, and stabbed the knife in, opening her from sternum to navel as one might cut open a papaya. Blood and other fluids welled up. My brother ignored these, let the knife fall to the sand, and plunged his hands into her midst, up to his wrists in gore. He drew out his left hand; in it rested a curled baby. Then his right hand, cradling another.

For a moment, I almost descended to pick up the knife and cut the cords. I was so caught up in the scene that I forgot these twins might be my undoing. But my brother merely bent his head and severed the cords with his teeth before standing up and striding towards the surf. He walked in up to his knees, and lowered his hands, letting the salt water wash the babies clean. The one in his left hand kicked its legs and let out a howl – of displeasure? Of shock? Of joy at freedom? – before a wave washed over it, cleaning its face and setting it spluttering. The one in his right hand remained still as the water licked at it and my brother lifted it up for closer examination. Had he lost a twin already? That would improve my chances significantly . . . but, no, the little body twitched and shivered, as if it didn't dare disappoint my wretched brother. He gave a satisfied smile and walked out of the ocean.

And there he was, a baby in each hand. Now what, brother? What do you know of children, Mr Nature-Will-Take-Its-Course? Are you going to nurse them? I chortled to myself in my palm tree bower. He set the babies in the sand, at the edge of beach, where the vines curled down, a short distance from my palm tree, from their dead mother. He pressed a black-nailed finger into the forehead of one, then the other. I could see from here, a girl and a boy. He stood up and shook his robe; sand clung to its damp hem. He whistled, a low, sharp call. The leaves of the vine rustled. He whistled again.

Belly-low, a lioness crept out from the shrubbery. One massive forepaw placed tentatively on the sand, her haunches higher than her head, as if she meant to pounce. *Oh, eat those babies*, I thought. But my brother just beckoned her nearer. She crept, crouched, right to his feet. He pointed at the twins, and I could feel him working his magic on the creature. She growled low in her throat but crept nearer the children.

Her tawny fur blended in with the sand as she settled herself beside them, tail twitching once, twice, before curling down along her flank. Her tongue flicked out, and I could hear it rasp redly against the girl twin's head as the lioness licked her, gently extended a paw and drew the child near. First the girl, then the boy, pulling them against her stomach, guiding them to nurse at her side. I shivered at the sight. In the stories I read to my twins, when they were tucked in their warm blankets in their soft beds, any child suckled by a wild beast was destined to become a hero. This was not a good omen for me.

My brother heaped the wood from the trunk into a pile, added driftwood and dried fronds and, as lioness and twins slumbered, lit the pile ablaze. The flames rose, as his flames always do, with a blue-green cast, and when they leapt as high as the top of the palm tree in which I perched, he lifted the mother's corpse and placed it – dare I say, tenderly? – atop the wood, and stood watching as it all burned to ash. He stuck his thumbs into the remains of the fire, darkening his skin, and then pressed an ashy print onto each twin's forehead, right between the eyes. They squirmed but, milk-sated, didn't fully rouse. On they slept, the lioness watching, one eye barely cracked, peering towards my brother, the other shut, feigning sleep. The sun dipped low, melting light across the sea, and the lioness rose and stretched in that magnificent way that cats have, haunches high, head low. A yawn that suggested her jaw might unhinge, then sauntered into the vines with barely a rustle. My brother didn't deign to watch her, but stared instead at the sky, the growing dark.

Which stars would be the first to appear? There. And there. Glowing into existence. Polaris. The one that some humans look to for guidance, as if the stars are trustworthy. I searched and couldn't find Gemini yet – their hour was not yet come. The stars are an eternal mystery. Untouchable. Ever-watching. Unknown. As I searched the heavens for some sign, I felt with surprise how similar I am to these mortals – believing that the stars have a message for me. Believing they might care.

My brother reached out his hand, extended one finger with its blackened nail, and traced a pattern in the sky. He nodded, smiled, and stooped to pick up the twins. With one tucked in the crook of each arm, he pushed through the vines; the shrubbery shrank back from him, allowing a clear path, and he strode towards the island's interior. I wafted along above him and watched as he reached the shore of a small fresh-water lagoon. The stars' light reflected in its depths, making the water glow and shiver. He dipped in one twin, the other, washing the ash from their skin, washing away the salt of the ocean, the blood of their mother. Bathing them in starlight and clear water. He examined them with a critical eye: their fingers, toes, nostrils. He gave close attention to a pattern of five moles each bore on their shoulder blades – their own private constellation. Then he set them down, nestled in the roots of a cypress tree.

No sooner had he done so than the lioness reappeared, a palm rat dangling limp from her mouth. With a glance (resentful? One can never tell with a cat, whether it is love or resentment) at my brother, she curled herself around the twins. The boy began to suckle immediately, but the lioness ignored him, intent on pulling rat flesh from rat bone.

*   *   *

I had hoped, I admit, to watch as my brother ran himself ragged trying to raise his twins. I had hoped to watch him fret as fragile babies needed his care and attention at all hours of the night. I had thought he would find it irresistible to try and train them in some way. But, no. He left them to the lioness and the sole extent of his caretaking was to occasionally look over at them while they slept. He read them no stories, sang them no songs. Instead, he studied scrolls and tomes and scratched insensible symbols on pages of parchment. He spoke only to himself and then in mutters that were nearly incoherent even to me. As soon as one of the twins began to whimper or cry, he would stand and withdraw deeper into the island's interior, leaving them to sob themselves dry, or comfort each other, or (I hoped) be eaten by some bird of prey.

But despite his utter neglect, the twins thrived. They grew. They crawled and pulled the lioness's tail, they stood and toddled like little drunkards. They babbled to each other and put fistfuls of sand in their almost toothless maws. I drifted down close as I dared to study them. My twins had not thrived in this manner. Ricardetto had been a wrinkly little thing and even Bradamante, sturdy as she was, had needed coaxing to take her first steps. These two . . . I probed and prodded (not interfering!) to sense if somehow they had power they oughtn't to, some trace of magic, of the eternal, the sublime (it doesn't occur often, but sometimes strange things do happen to souls). But no. They were mortal through and through. I worried, as I watched them grow and learn – teaching themselves, nurturing each other – that my brother was right. Nature alone could make a human superior. Time, I told myself. Time will be the great equalizer here. My twins will age and learn and improve, given a decade or so. I knew I could win this bet.

I watched these twins on the island, pushing the movement of time faster, accelerating through the years, to get just a sense of how they had grown. Rainy seasons lashed the island, whipping palm fronds around, making the lagoon overflow, sending the surf pounding against the beach. And languid weather abounded. Sun and sun and sun. The twins lived in these elements, their skins tanned a deep brown and then stained white with salt. Their hair, dark as coconut husks, grew long and ragged. They ranged up and down the island, over and across. They fought each other with their hands, beat each other with sticks. Cried in each other's arms, held each other as they slept.

I slowed down one afternoon in the rainy season that caught my attention. They had laid snares to catch a particularly tasty kind of bird (a sort of tropical grouse; I am embarrassed to say that I didn't know its name). They lay on their backs and spoke in their twin language (which I could understand just fine). The girl told a meandering story about a giant being who lived in the clouds and looked vaguely like my brother. The boy asked a dozen questions about the clouds. Where did they come from? What were they made of? Could they tie together a hundred birds and have them fly them up there? (Please, try that, young man . . . I'd like to see the result!) Their banter amused me. Would have pleased me, had they been my twins. She was figuring out story-telling, all on her own! Then the boy grabbed the girl's arm and pointed to the distant clouds, where they went from fluffy to flat, from white to grey. The afternoon rains, soon to arrive. But the girl shook him loose and gestured with her chin towards the snares. The first patters of rain rattled the leaves. The boy shrugged, scooted into a hollow among the tree roots. The girl kept her silent vigil. Oh, how much she reminded me of Bradamante. The pout of her lips. The certainty that she was right. The willingness to put up with some discomfort to prove her point. Only, Bradamante would eventually come running to me for help, while this girl merely hugged her knees to her chest and watched the snares as the rain went from pattering to pummelling. I longed to go and check on my twins. I longed to swoop down and summon breezes to dry the girl. But I was merely an observer – no interference.

The longest they were apart was when they played at hide and seek. And then they might spend half a day out of one another's company. The boy crouched in the back of a seaweed-stinking cave. The girl flattened on the upper bough of a banyan tree. Otherwise, everything they did, they did together.

The lioness had a litter of her own, and they slept all a-jumble with the cubs. The twins had learned to make nets from the vines and snare fat lizards, and they would sometimes bring these to my brother, like offerings for a strange and indifferent god, and my brother would cook the animals and together, they'd eat the flesh.

The twins watched my brother with wary eyes. There was no love there. But no hate either. Curiosity. A little fear. But these twins didn't know much fear. They showed the same mixture of interest and wariness towards the fire, coming close to it and then flinching away. My brother never spoke to them directly. He appeared completely absorbed in his studies (what was he studying?). The twins lingered near him, listening, and sometimes I suspected that my brother tuned his mutterings to their ears, changing from reading a scroll on necromancy (why?) to opening a tome concerning legendary warriors. (This, I suspected, was cheating. He was nurturing them. But I knew he'd deny the charges . . . and, moreover, to bring them, I would have to admit that I was spying.) He read aloud about lands full of snow, about mountains that reached through the clouds, and the strange fur-covered beasts that lived on their slopes. He muttered on about cities, bustling and loud, packed with humans who bartered and cheated and stole. These meanderings must have been confusing to the twins, who knew nothing but this isolated tropical island. I wanted, as I watched, to drop down and shake my brother by his shoulders. Stories should help us make sense of the world. Stories should explain how it is we came to be who we are, where we are. So why speak to them of places they'd never go? Of impossibilities?

Ah, that is the core, the pith, of the difference between me and my brother. I believe all can be taught, if one is caring and supportive. He believes such care is useless. You are or you aren't. That is my brother. You can be, you ought to be. That is me.

Once, and once only, there was a night when my brother spoke to the twins directly – showed them anything like concern. The boy and girl had found a wounded rodent – some creature with pink skin and white fur and a thin, rat-like tail (ugly, but cute in its way, too) and had built a small bower out of vines where they intended to nurse it back to health. But no sooner had they left to fetch it water than a lion cub bounded over and ate it up. They were both wailing and upset. No doubt it was just that the noise disturbed my brother's thinking that made him speak to the twins; he ambled over and said, 'What bothers you so?'

And they, with many tears, explained in their babbling twin language what had happened. The boy held the dead rat-thing's tail (the only bit the lion cub hadn't eaten) in his arms, cradling it, and the sight made me think of Ricardetto. How he – my boy – had once found a fallen robin's nest, the chicks already dead and cold within, and fell to sobbing right there on the garden path. Oh, I had cradled him as he had cradled the dead birds, and I wanted, incorporeal as I was, to hug this boy – my brother's boy – as well.

But my brother simply shrugged. 'That is life. And death. That is how Nature works. The strong eat the weak. The same applies to you. Would you have it be another way?'

Their tears had abated somewhat. They shook their heads. Did they agree with my brother? Or did they know it was useless to disagree? He wasn't wrong. But he also wasn't right. Couldn't something that was weak become strong?

'If you aren't strong, you are weak, and you will die. So you must find strength within *yourselves* if you wish to survive.' And with that he turned and went back to his books and his spells.

My brother couldn't possibly be this simple, this fervent in his creed. Yes, his twins were sturdy. Yes, they had learned already self-reliance. But how could that possibly be enough? How could that compete with the knowledge and skills and benefits I would give my twins through teaching and care and tutelage and Nurture?

Speaking of which . . . it was high time that I return to *my* twins, for I had dawdled at this green island long enough, letting the past catch up to the present and, I feared (for the island was, in its lonely way, rather lovely), perhaps even let the present go by and become the past. Which is to say, I might be behind the times when it came to my twins.

So I spent one last night on the island, watching the sun set and the darkness grow, watching the lion cubs tumble against one another and fall asleep. Watching the twins grow sleepy by my brother's fire and then curl up with the lions. And then, watching my brother leave his fire and come to stand over them (the lioness, wary at his presence, raised her hackles, and gave a low growl). But my brother only spoke, plain, simple, in the language we shared at home. He spoke to the twins, who slept, and his words fell on them like a benediction: *You will grow up and become great. That is your destiny. I have seen it written in the stars. You will become great, and I will become great through you.*

Yes, it was high time that I returned to Ricardetto and Bradamante.

CHAPTER THREE

I caught a night wind, the edge of a Coriolis, that spun me away from the island. I sailed through the darkness, flowing through cotton-drift clouds. The stars above me, the water below. Then water gave way to shoreline, to forest, to mountains, and I dropped lower, to a lesser breeze, and wafted my way to a familiar river, a muddy bank.

Oh, how dispirited the humped thatched cottages looked. How menacing and cold the stone church seemed. In comparison to my brother's sun-filled island – sand and salt and garish flowers – this place hung gloomy and despairing. How could children, even with good Nurture, thrive here? What plant could grow in such rocky, chill soil?

I alighted on the banks of the river, next to where the ferry was pulled up for the night. I tilted back to stare at the stars, but they provided no comfort. Only the depths of the darkness between them soothed me. We were all just swimming through the Deeps. My brother knew no more than I did. He only assumed a greater confidence. I could read the stars – such as they could be read – as well as he, and they said nothing about our twins that we did not know.

They cared nothing about our twins. Such minor beings are beneath their notice, are bits for us to play with, if we should care for such dalliances.

With these thoughts I plumped myself up and prepared to resume a fleshly form, lingering only to take one last drifting flight above the walls of Duke Aymon's manor. The twins slept, in the same chamber where I had last stood by their beds. They looked little older than when I had left them, the same age as my brother's twins now. Ricardetto lay with limbs splayed, his mouth a little open, while Bradamante had curled herself into a ball so tight she might as well still be in the womb. I hovered for a while, but heard nothing except their slow breathing. Their chamber held a few books, wooden toy animals, a sleeping spaniel, a basin and ewer ready for their morning ablutions, silver candlesticks . . . they had so much more than my brother's twins. Was it enough?

I drifted to the woods with the dawn light and considered my options. Perhaps the older son, Rinaldo, was still in the manor. Perhaps he had gone back to serve the king (whoever that was). Perhaps he had died of the flux in my absence. But Duke Aymon and Lady Beatrice wouldn't want a wet nurse. The twins had long since passed the age of needing one. What did the twins need? A tutor, for certain. I could teach them to play the lute, or whatever it was that noble children were expected to learn. They had a priest teaching them prayers and Latin, or at least teaching Ricardetto. Perhaps Duke Aymon would take on a tutor, but that came with the inconvenient requirement of being male. My brother had the advantage of not having to make such choices, the wretch.

In the depths of the forest, I played with incorporation. Making myself into a mighty man, barrel chest . . . oh, my lungs felt strange and that deep voice buzzed oddly. And the whiskers! I couldn't bear them, though this form would be perfect to pose as a weapons master and give the twins some training in arms and fighting. But, no, impossible. I felt like an ogre and could barely get a word out of my mouth. I let the form dissolve. Tried a lesser body. Slight and willowy, with just a trace of a moustache. I could be a poet, a singer. My voice a light tenor. I would present myself as one who had trained for the priesthood but was too romantic for such an occupation. That would make me learned . . .

I practised walking around the woods. How would such a man walk? Prance? I kept tilting up onto my toes. No, that would not do. And how would he talk? My voice kept cracking and creaking. How would I pretend to be a singer if I couldn't hold it steady? And the moustache, as minor and downy as it was, itched at me unbearably. I let the form go.

Curse my brother and his insistence on maintaining our polarity . . . it seemed like a game at the time, a mere toss of the coin. And curse this body, too! In my true form, I have no body, no shape. No guts, no brain, no genes, cells. I am . . . mind? Thought? Spirit? I do have self, though. A definite sense of who I am. And I am not used to constraint. I fumed (I did actually, literally, let off smoke) there in the privacy of the forest, calming enough to realize that I ought to be cursing humans and their wretched tendency to create hierarchies of their own design and then worship them as if they were eternal. I shoved myself (rather roughly) into a female form – voluptuous, curvy, full-breasted. Flowing golden hair to my waist, apple-rose blossoms on my pale cheeks – and I shook my very dainty feminine fist at the world at large. I'd show them what a female could do.

Ah. But I'd need clothes. And some explanatory story to gull Aymon and Beatrice. At a distance, the church bell tolled, dolorous and heavy and demanding. I fiddled a bit with my form – a few more inches of height, so I would overtop Aymon (and Rinaldo). Eyes of summer-sky blue. Cheek and jawbones a little more square, a little more prominent than might be considered 'beautiful' for this time and place (currently, roundness was all the rage, so said Beatrice), that gave my face a chiselled look, providing hollows and shadows and sharp edges. I clothed myself in a white robe, worked up and down the sleeves, around the hem, with golden embroidery, flashes of diamonds and rubies, too. Ah, yes. They'd fall for this in an instant.

Where a small rivulet ran through the woods, I paused to take in my image. Mmmm. Too much. The villagers wouldn't let me through if I looked like this. I'd be swarmed and likely have to zap a few of them, and it would cause too much of a stir if Aymon kept me on after that. Away with the jewel-encrusted diadem that I'd perched on my head. Away with the little silvery lyre I'd tucked under my arm. Away with the spotless white robe. Instead, a simpler gown – embroidered round with pomegranates and golden bells (we'd see who had read their scripture closely!) – of blue, the better to set off my eyes. And a grey shawl to cover those golden locks. That would do. I could pass safely through the village as nothing more than a stranger, which was a dangerous enough venture in this time.

I pulled the shawl about me as I passed through the gate into the manor's yard. It still smelled like horse manure and woodsmoke and unwashed bodies. Dogs barked in the kennel and a man shouted at them. I could see why my brother preferred the isolation of his desert island . . . but how would his twins ever be ready for the real world, growing up there? I pushed this from my mind. I had to be focused on my twins. I had to prepare them for three simple contests; I had to nurture them to achieve this. Because this world, this age, would be mine . . . and I would finally have a chance to . . .

'Hey there!' a rough voice called to me. 'What's your business?'

I turned, slowly, trying for a regal stare. It was Bozo, or Boza, or Bazo . . . the head of the stables.

'You can't just wander about. No beggars. The duke don't need another servant . . .' His eyes ranged up and down my form and he squinted at me, nose wrinkling. To him, I was just another piece of horse flesh, and this annoyed me no end.

So I smiled, tight-lipped, and then bowed my head, as if subservient. 'Beg pardon, sir,' I said and backed away. He watched me retreat and then crossed the yard, yanking open the door to the stables. I waited by the gate and just before he disappeared from the doorway I reached out with a little flick of my finger, sending a jolt of energy through him. He jerked rigid, every limb going stiff, then crumpled to the ground. I always forget how fragile humans are, particularly where their hearts are concerned. Pity.

I stepped once more through the gate and into the yard, crossing this time to the door of the manor. It would not do to maim or kill or even mildly injure all of Duke Aymon's servants. They were merely being products of their time and place.

The servant who opened the door gave me a sceptical look, a look I could say I was getting uncomfortably accustomed to. But I was not in the mood to trifle. The progress of my brother's twins had me on edge, and something in the way the now-felled stableman had gazed at me further rankled. It reminded me of the work I had to do. For Bradamante, who would also suffer from such gazes, even though she was noble-born (they'd be more sneering, but they'd be of the same sort) and for Ricardetto who would soon enough be expected to gaze in such a way. Unless I could get in there and get to work.

So I pushed past the servant, doing him no injury, though he huffed at my boldness. 'Get me Duke Aymon,' I said. 'Now.'

I let the grey shawl fall from my head and shoulders, revealing my lustrous golden locks. I was tall enough to look down on him, and I did. Though he frowned, he did hurry from the room. To fetch the duke and spread this gossip, no doubt.

Duke Aymon came out a few minutes later, limping slightly, I noticed. He wore a scarlet doublet, worked on the chest with the stag that was his device, and when he saw me, he narrowed his eyes. 'What do you want?'

'Are you injured, my lord?' I said.

The question took him aback, or perhaps my voice, melodious and honeyed, yet also sharp, surprised him.

'A fall from my horse. No more.'

I licked my lips and examined him. 'A hairline fracture in one of the bones in your ankle. Keep walking on it and it will never heal. Or never heal well.'

'Who are you?' he pressed again.

'I am here to serve your children. The twins. I wish to instruct them.'

'Nonsense. They have all the teachers they need.'

'Oh, do they?'

Duke Aymon winced and shifted his weight to his good leg. 'The boy will be a page soon enough. There's a priest here to teach them their prayers. The girl will be betrothed in a few years' time. What more do they need? And what could *you* possibly teach them? Be on your way.'

I reached out, extended one finger, careful to make it a languid gesture, no visible threat, and pressed the eye of his needlepoint stag. My senses ranged through the duke, blood and sinew and guts, down to his legs and into his bone. There – bone has water and air; bone is a living thing. Easily broken. Easily healed. The duke's eyes widened and he quit slouching to one side.

'How?'

I expected the next word out of his mouth to be one of gratitude or at least a bit more awe, but his wide eyes quickly narrowed and his lips pursed as he hissed.

'Witch!'

I could not help myself. I rolled my eyes back as far as they would go. (Which is much further than the average human's. They came round the other side.) It took but a moment's concentration for me to summon back the white dress, the diamond and silver diadem, the gold ornaments. I increased the lustrousness of my locks, working carefully with air so that it would seem I glowed, just a little.

'Not a witch,' I said. 'An angel.'

His mouth went comically round. 'An angel?' He bobbed down into a bow, then popped back up. 'Where are your wings?'

I restrained myself from another eye roll. 'Good Duke, I couldn't very well walk in here wearing my true form. How would your servants have responded? Your hounds? As it is, I am dimming my brilliance so as not to burn out your eyes and reduce your fine manor to ash and cinder.' I smiled at him and was pleased to see that he could not hold my gaze. 'But since you have asked so nicely, I will show you my wings.' I formed them up quickly, water and light and air, making them transparent and veined, like the wings of a mayfly or a cicada. They folded tight against my body and then I unfurled them, enjoying the way they caught the sun, riffled it into rainbows.

'Oh,' said the duke, frowning at me. 'I rather thought you'd have feathers.'

'Feathers! You think angels look like chickens?' I stormed at him.

'No, no. It's just . . . the pictures.'

'Pictures!' I let my wings disappear. 'Enough of this nonsense. I am here to teach your children.'

'But why?'

He couldn't just be grateful, could he. 'Why?' I straightened myself to my full height and peered down at him. 'I have been sent by the Almighty to train your children that they might be ready when their moment of greatness calls.' That ought to get me all the permission and access I needed.

Someone tapped at the door, cracked it open a hair's-width. 'My lord? The Lady Beatrice wishes entry.' No doubt someone had spied an attractive woman going in to conference with the duke and let Lady Beatrice know.

'Admit her,' the duke said. I was pleased that he at least paused to cast a glance at me and receive my nod. Perhaps I could train him as well as the twins. He could do with a bit of improvement.

'My lord,' Lady Beatrice said, bustling in. 'Oh, pardon. You have a visitor.' Her eyes widened as she took me in and, almost involuntarily, she sank into a curtsy.

'No need for that,' I said. 'I am here to help your children, the twins. Bradamante and Ricardetto. To teach them.'

Again, Duke Aymon cut his eyes towards me and I gave a tiny inclination of my chin. 'She's an angel. She said that Ricardetto is destined for greatness.'

'I did not say such a thing,' I snapped. 'The twins. Both of them. Need to be taught, to prepare them for the chance at greatness.'

I could see the gears of Aymon's mind turn (though to grant him mental gears might be suggesting too much finely tuned machinery in there). 'The girl too?'

My stare would have wilted a pine tree, but this man was more obstinate. 'Yes. The fact that she is of female form makes no difference.' I gave a faint sneer. 'It is not the distribution of *flesh* that makes a child such-and-so. It is how they are shaped in mind, body, and spirit through the love and care and devotion that is shown them.' I turned to Beatrice and continued, 'As a rose might ramble if it is not trimmed and trained with proper pruning.' I didn't say the other piece, the aspect of Nurture. For anyone – even my brother's twins, at some point after their stay on the remote island – might fall into a bit of education and learn a skill or two. It was about the love and concern and support, the bolstering and belief that accompanied each lesson. One must be taught that one is worthy of knowledge. One must believe that one can learn in order to learn well.

'I see,' said Beatrice and her eyes took on the cloudy distance of thought.

I let them stew for a moment in silent contemplation. Beatrice, I imagined, was picturing a neat little hedgerow while Aymon saw luscious blossoms opening pink and sweet. For myself, to hell with the image of roses. I was picturing my chance to forge these two with the hammer and anvil of my vast capabilities. I indulged in a fantasy in which my twins enchanted an audience with a clever and witty tale, while my brother's twins garbled on in their nonsensical language. And even in the contest of arms and strength, my twins would be better fed and trained there, too. If I had my way.

'My lord,' Beatrice sighed when she emerged from whatever her reverie showed her. 'We are so fortunate to have an angel in our household.'

I bristled a bit that I was now included in the household, as one might count up servants or horses or pairs of boots. 'My angelic nature must remain a secret,' I said. 'I will conceal my appearance. Tell no one.' I immediately reduced my glow and changed my dress back to simple, dull wool. I kept my height.

'What should we call you, my . . . er . . . lady?' the duke asked.

'You may call me Melissa,' I said.

The duke frowned at this. 'We had a nursemaid by that name . . .'

'Did you?' I said, quirking an eyebrow. 'I hope you treated her well.'

Duke Aymon swallowed, his Adam's apple dipping up and down. 'I hope so, too, my lady.'

'I am no lady,' I replied.

'They say,' Beatrice began, her voice timid but growing stronger as she spoke, 'they say that angels are neither male nor female.'

'This is true,' I replied.

'It makes it easier for you to remain chaste,' Beatrice said primly.

'Not easy, good lady,' I corrected, 'but the only possibility. Let us not speak further of my nature. I cannot reveal to you any of the secrets of the universe. I have been sent to teach the twins, and more than this I cannot say.'

The two of them clutched each other and cowered, and I could sense a tinge of fright, but a deeper sense of excitement, greed even. Oh, humans. So utterly predictable.

And thus I began my second tenure in Duke Aymon's manor, under the guise of an angel. Those apart from the duke and duchess did not know what I was and it was put out that I was a pious and learned woman, an abbess whose convent, located far to the east, had been sacked by some invading heathen force . . . and here I was. Duke Aymon told some version of this tale to the steward, who rapidly embellished the whole thing, and I generally got the sense that the sacking of my convent was supposed to be a metaphor for what had happened to my person, and those in the duke's household were scandalized, or pitied me, but mostly left me to my own devices. Which suited me fine.

The important part was that Duke Aymon and Lady

Beatrice recognized me as a powerful figure. No more pussy-footing around for me. No more ducking and bobbing and curtsying and yes-sirring for me. And no more acquiescing to the twins' every whim. This time, I would be in charge. This time I would rule.

Oh, that sounds a little . . . authoritarian, doesn't it? I didn't mean to squelch their interests. No, no. I just meant . . . having seen my brothers' twins, growing up so wild and savage and utterly ignored, it made complete sense that my twins ought to be the opposite (polarity, opposites are where power comes from, after all) and so Bradamante and Ricardetto needed to be refined and cultured and attended to in every way. *That's* what I meant when I said I will rule them.

That very evening, while the sun was sinking low, its reflection spreading like a broken egg yolk across the river's water, I summoned the twins to me (I had accepted the duke's offer of a private chamber such as befitted an angel, in my opinion). When the servant's timid knock sounded, I answered, 'Enter!'

Bradamante stepped in first. She wore a dress of peacock blue, a brilliant colour that set off the russet tones of her hair. Two careful steps inside and then she dropped into an impeccable curtsy.

Ricardetto, on the other hand, poked his head into the chamber and stared at me. His eyes went wide. Then he dashed across the room to where I stood and threw his arms about my waist, squeezing me. 'Melissa!' he cried. 'You came back!' I tousled his hair as I looked down at him.

'How on earth did you know it was me?' I said.

He squeezed tighter. 'It's a way you have of looking at us . . .' He let me go and peered up at my face, then over to Bradamante. 'You look at us . . . you see us . . .'

Bradamante had drawn near as well and sniffled a bit. 'And you smell the same,' she said, a touch haughtily.

'Oh, do I?' I laughed. 'And what, pray tell, do I smell like?'
They both drew in deep breaths through their noses.

'Rock,' said Bradamante.

'Rock after a rainstorm.'

For a moment, I felt a surprising warmth spread through
me, and I almost bundled the twins close. But . . . wait. This
was a new moment. Things were going to be different. I was
an angel now. I put a hand on each of their shoulders. Holding
them at arm's length. Staring down at them (commandingly,
I hoped). 'Listen,' I said. 'I have indeed returned to you. And
before, I wore a humble disguise. Now I come you to in
something closer to my true form.' I allowed my hair to glow
slightly, my skin to become luminous, my whole being to swell
and glimmer. Ricardetto's blue eyes went wide as full moons
and Bradamante leaned away from me. 'Have no fear,' I said
(though, truthfully, I hoped they would have a little). 'I will
show you why I am here.'

I took my hands from their shoulders and stepped into the
one slant of sunset light that still entered the chamber. Given
free rein of my preferences, we would have been in a forest,
under the stars, a vast flaming bonfire licking at the dark. But
Fire, and Dark, are my brother's domain. So I made do with
this sliver of light. I summoned Air and set it spinning. Gentle
at first, no more than the twirling of a child's top. It caught
the light up in it, refracting and angling the orange-gold rays.

Ricardetto laughed with delight and whispered, 'beautiful',
while Bradamante dared to stick her hand closer, as if she might
catch an edge of light. I whipped the whirlwind faster. 'Ow,'
she said, withdrawing her hand and sticking her finger in her
mouth. Good. Learn that my power is not to be trifled with.

Higher, faster, I spun the whirlwind. I drew it wider and
the twins stepped back. 'We must go within,' I said, raising
my voice over the swirl of air. 'We must enter the storm.' (A

little melodramatic, I admit. But my sojourn on earth has taught me that melodrama is sometimes the only way to get through to humans.) I kept my hands raised as if my mere fingers could keep this funnel of air spinning, and urged them on. 'Go! Go within! I will follow!' Ricardetto reached for Bradamante's hand and the two of them darted through the wall of air. Good. Brave children. Trusting, too.

A twist of my wrist and the air expanded out, creating a screen between us and the rest of the world. To my twins, it must have seemed that I entered the storm and calmed it. Very well. They stared at me open-mouthed. 'I have been sent,' I told them, 'by a most high power. The very future of the world rests upon your shoulders.'

Bradamante stood up straight, as if to show that her shoulders were, indeed, capable of this burden. Ricardetto merely kept staring.

'In the future, when some years have passed, you will face a formidable set of foes in a series of cleverly constructed contests. I alone can prepare you for this day.' I lifted my hands again and twirled them elegantly (it's all a show – magic is never done with the hands, though often I can't help moving them. Nervous tic). I created little figures of air and water. 'You will be tested in body, mind, and spirit.' I set the figures flowing. Some leapt and ran. Some rode horses or wielded spears. Some twirled and danced. I swept my hand in an arc and the figures scattered, replaced by little shadows that also moved about: climbing, creeping, slashing, swirling. 'But there are two others out there. Your foes. They are training, too. If you listen to me, if you do as I say, you will be ready when the time comes. You will defeat them and bring greatness and glory to the world. Will you do it?'

'Yes,' both the twins breathed.

I sent the shadow figures away. With a flick of the finger,

I summoned the funnel of air, wrapped it around us tightly so that our ears filled with roaring and it seemed as if at any moment the storm would lift us from our feet and then, when the spinning and the pressure had built to its height, I let the whirlwind fizzle to nothing, so that we were back in the chamber in their father's manor, as if nothing had happened. 'You have passed through the storm. You are mine. I will guide you to greatness.'

Ricardetto swept low in a bow. 'Thank you,' he said.

Bradamante licked her lips. 'Can I please have a sword?'

I got her a sword. And a shield. And a set of armour. And a horse, a speckled grey gelding (it somewhat reminded me of the squirrel-horse) that she named Wolf-Fang. (I thought about giving it fangs, but I wanted my twins to be successful, not notorious.) Ricardetto got the same, though his horse was charcoal grey-black and he named him Storm.

There, in the practice yard, I ruled them. They battered heavy leather sacks full of sand with their fists until the seams burst. They rode their horses forward, backwards, blindfolded (the twins, not the horses). They learned the spear, the mace, the axe, and – most of all – the sword.

After mornings toiling at arms, we retired to the gardens and learned stories. I had books purchased and, once, a minstrel wandered by and we spent a week studying with him. Ricardetto, in particular, was taken with this young fellow and wanted to learn the lute. Very well. He got a lute. I found the minstrel's tales fine, but predictable. Beginning, middle, end. Rising action. All that sort of thing. But true story-telling turns one's sense of the world inside out. It doesn't just confirm what we know – it transforms. So I found other samples, like the old woman who lived on the far edge of the woods and was known for her herbal remedies.

Once I ventured to the nearest port and brought back a sailor, just so they could hear tales of the sea, feel the roll of waves in his voice. Bradamante showed a keen memory and could recite any tale she had heard but once; Ricardetto, though, had a flair for invention. A favourite game was for me to toss out three seemingly random words: mud, seagull, haystack! And off he would go, creating some fable or epic or adventure around these bits. Bradamante and I would listen with delight: she might sit behind me and braid my hair, now and then chiming in to add a line or suggest a redirection. 'No, no! Have the seagull drop a shell beside the princess! And there's a pearl inside!' Or she might grow bored and begin to go through her sword forms, empty-handed and wearing a dress, but still with precise cuts.

Each of them showed a certain preference; Bradamante for fighting, for the physical. Ricardetto for the more patient arts. Which meant that while she was good at arms and he was good at story, they were well matched at dance. Dance came in the evenings, when the fires blazed in the manor's hearths and the servants lit reed lamps. A perfect setting, for the shadows of the flames flickered and wavered, a dance unto themselves. Lady Beatrice and her ladies would often join us, a shifting retinue of aunts, cousins, and odd-assorted women who needed a moment of respite at the manor (this age seemed to abound with displaced and disrespected women; I would do something about that when I ruled). Sometimes I would conjure up musicians out of air and water (borrowing a bit of the smoke from the hearth) and have them play. The twins would do the dances of the era – quadrilles and pavanes and jigs. The ladies laughed at these; after all, such dances were for peasants. They preferred the more stately steps of circlets and rounds. The twins could do those, too. They could do them *beautifully*. But no one, not even my twins, could dance such dances with *abandon*. Ah! That was what I tried to nurture within them. When the fires had burned low, when the ladies had gone to bed, when I let my conjured musicians dissipate, I would urge my twins to dance. 'Hear your own music. Make your own steps. *Dance! Truly dance!*' Bradamante looked at me as if I was a madwoman. Ricardetto tried to humour me. He would spin and leap and throw his arms about. Bradamante would only shake her head and perhaps shuffle through some sword forms in her gown, as if I wouldn't notice what she was doing. I would nurture them; I would teach them; I would make them acquire this skill. (But could one acquire abandon? Or did it simply *occur*?) Many nights, foot-sore and tired, I would chide her, 'Bradamante, you must *learn* not to be stubborn.' And she would merely rub her shoulder or roll her neck (making it pop hideously) and stare at me. Stubbornly.

Time passed. Snow fell in the practice yard and we did sword forms nonetheless. Grain ripened in the fields and we learned the local harvest dances. Winter came around again and again, and in the dry, clear air of an especially cold night, I wandered outside the manor to gaze up at the stars. Oh. I had been incorporated for so long that this . . . flesh . . . was starting to feel like *me*. Ugh. How much longer until I could resume my true form? How much longer did I have to put up with this reduction of my powers? (My brother had half of what was rightfully mine – though I'm sure he felt the same way.) How much longer did I have to suffer the stubborn resentment of these humans, until I could rule them? I squinted up into the sky. Mars burned bright. I began to track its progress towards Gemini, but before my eyes found those two stars, a little pop of greenish-blue caught my attention. There. Venus. What? This wasn't the season . . . this wasn't the time . . . Venus came earlier in the night . . . And then my senses cleared and I realized the magic that my brother and I had worked called the two planets out of their proper orbits; they marked time for us. And Venus's appearance above meant the time was drawing nearer. A year, maybe two. I gave a slight shiver and hurried back inside.

For all this training, for every long day of practice and instruction, I think I can boil down my twins' progress and accomplishments (or lack thereof) to two distinct moments, both coinciding with visitors. Not long after Venus appeared in the night sky, Duke Aymon had a messenger from a cousin who had travelled to the far northern lands for his bride, a princess of that icy realm, and was now returning home and wished to stay at the manor for a day or two. Lady Beatrice lived for such things – a foreign woman would bring new fashions, tales of strange people and places, entertainment for days. And Duke Aymon was pleased as well: he could hunt with his cousin by day and indulge in rich feasting by night. I gave the twins some leisure from their training and let them range about. They had reached a somewhat awkward age, each going through a burst of growth. Gazing at their faces, they looked identical still; Ricardetto had yet to sprout a whisker. His voice, though, had cracked and settled into a husky tenor (thank goodness it had settled; listening to him tell stories with all that cracking and jumping was painful). They both had grown at least six inches in the past year, overtopping their lady mother and nearly even with the duke's height. Along with the growth had come even more exaggerated moods, doubts, worries . . . all manner of human things that I had no patience for. Perhaps that was also why I had given them a pause from training.

In the early morning, they were up with Beatrice, sewing new embroidery into the sleeves of Bradamante's gown. In the late morning, they were down in the kennels, readying the hounds for the chase. Listening to the two of them run and banter and laugh, I realized how pent up I kept them, how rigidly I structured their days. That was Nurture, wasn't it? It was certainly the opposite of the neglect my brother's twins received. My brother's twins. I watched as Ricardetto streaked out of the kennel, terriers snapping at his heels, laughing and holding aloft some piece of meat that they all wanted. He stopped, panting, and the dogs mobbed him, biting at the treat. Ricardetto knelt and let the terriers swarm over him. A moment later and Bradamante emerged with Duke Aymon's enormous boarhound on a lead. She brought him towards Ricardetto – the little dogs scattered – and the hound grabbed what was left of the meat, slobbering and licking Ricardetto. Ah, my twins. They were spoiled. They were silly. For all that they had their growth, they were children still. Soft and comfortable. For them, fierce dogs were kept on leads. For my brother's twins . . . they were probably wrestling bears by now. I watched as Ricardetto shoved the boarhound off, bounded to his feet and began to chase his sister. A little tear might have escaped the corner of my eye, but I caught it quickly. They were growing up. The time was coming near. I feared I had not done enough.

That afternoon the cousin and the northern bride, whose name was Fiordispina, arrived. She looked, indeed, as though she had been carved from ice. Pale skin that seemed to glimmer, like a sapphire, white-blue. And blond hair fine as corn silk. Her eyes were brown, with an unexpected warmth to them, fresh-turned soil of spring. The cousin was utterly smitten. And so were my twins. That evening, at the feast, they took turns telling stories. Bradamante recited the entirety of 'The Ode of St Caldar' and Fiordispina clapped with appreciation at the conclusion (so did I; it was a long story. I had to admire Bradamante's ability to retain every. Single. Word. I wished there were other points to admire). Then Ricardetto plucked his lute and began a story – at first, I thought I knew it; a ship, out at sea, a storm, the crew tossed and tumbled, set adrift . . . But no, I didn't know it. Only, he had woven in elements familiar from so many stories, that it seemed so inviting, an old friend. But, ah! The twists he created: the crew landed on an island and discovered a lost civilization . . . Everyone in the hall leaned forward waiting as he plucked his lute and when he finished (I won't spoil the ending), there was silence. And then the words of the northern bride, Fiordispina. 'Oh, my. That was magnificent.' Rosy colour suffused Ricardetto's pale cheeks, and he bowed his head towards the lady.

I forced the twins to leave off story-telling for a moment and pushed food at them. 'Yes, that was lovely. Both of you. Now eat.'

Ricardetto idly tore a piece of bread into bits, staring at the high table, where his parents and the guests sat. 'I think I'm in love,' he said.

Bradamante dipped her finger in her cup of wine and flicked a drop at him. 'Where'd you hear that story? I don't recall learning it.'

'I made it up,' said Ricardetto. The drop of wine slowly slid down his cheek as he continued to stare up at Fiordispina. 'She's lovely.'

'She's married. To your cousin,' I said. 'Now eat.'

'You never eat,' said Bradamante to me, fiddling with the meat on her plate (or, rather, fiddling with the knife that she should be using to cut said meat). 'So why should we?'

Oh, the spoiled stubbornness of this child (not quite a child any more . . . she should have grown out of this). 'I don't need to eat,' I said. 'Unlike you. But if it will make happy, if it will make you eat, very well.' And I picked up a whole roast guinea fowl, unhinged my jaw, crammed the bird in my mouth, and swallowed. 'There,' I said, when I had my jaw back in place. 'I've eaten. Now you eat.'

Bradamante stared at me. Shook her head. 'I'm not a very good story-teller, am I?'

'Eat.' She glared at me, but cut a sliver of meat and, as if to counterpoint my display, put it in her mouth and chewed daintily. 'You are very good at reciting stories,' I said evenly, suppressing a burp as my innards figured out what to do with all those bones.

'But that's not telling stories. It isn't the same.'

'The fact that you know that . . . that you can perceive the difference: you are a very smart girl.'

'But not a good story-teller.'

'Not yet. But I will nurture this talent within . . .'

She held up her knife. 'I am beginning to think that some things can't be taught, or nurtured, or whatever. That we are born with certain innate talents. That Nature dictates, for instance, that . . .'

'Never!' I slammed a fist into the table, startling Ricardetto, who had been staring at Fiordispina. 'Heresy! Blasphemy! Don't let me hear you say it! It is time to dance!'

Perhaps it was my outburst, perhaps it was wishing to prove herself after an admittedly mediocre performance at story-telling, but Bradamante danced as she never had before. I set myself down with Ricardetto's lute and began to play. Once the others were preoccupied with chatter and dancing, I conjured a few additional sounds. The beat of a drum, the piping of a flute. Invisible strains of music that beckoned to the family, that drew them in such that they laughed and spun and twirled, never noticing the magic that was being worked in their midst. Bradamante took a turn with her cousin and her father, and then she approached Fiordispina and curtsied low. The woman gave a delighted laugh and Bradamante put her arms around the lady's waist. There were gasps, a few guffaws, as Bradamante held the woman tight. I felt the music change. Odd. I was the one conjuring it, after all. But something else pulled at the currents of air . . . what was that? And tendrils of flame, drawn from the hearth (metaphorically. No actual flames were leaping about) wove themselves into the music. My music. Which wasn't mine any more, but Bradamante's. She had shifted it. The tune went faster, louder, at a pace that was almost frantic, my fingers flew over the strings of the lute, keeping pace. Others joined in to the dance, their steps awkward and jerking – but Bradamante and the lady moved with grace. I almost recognized it – something like the Charleston . . . But, no, more than that and before I could pin it down, the song ended, a soft note that faded slowly. Fiordispina's pale face was flushed, making her even more beautiful, and all those in the hall clapped loudly. The music resumed its stately beat – the cousin held hands with his wife and they proceeded through the rote steps of the roundel. Lady Beatrice danced with Duke Aymon. Bradamante danced with Ricardetto. I stood to one side and watched. Order was restored. Boring, plain old order. But I knew now that I had seen a dance with beauty and abandon . . . that I had felt the stirrings of Bradamante's power. And I wondered. Had I nurtured that? Or was it something born within her?

When, at last, the fires burned low in the hearths and couples began to retire to chambers or dark corners, I chivvied my twins towards their beds. Bradamante hummed as she walked up the stone staircase. The same tune that she had danced to with Fiordispina. 'What song is that, dearest?' I asked her, half-hoping she would be able to explain what she had done, teach it, perhaps, to her brother.

But she merely kept humming, a smile on her lips, and interrupted her melody only to say, 'I think I'm in love.'

Ricardetto who, I now noticed, had the same goofy smile on his lips, whispered, 'You too? Isn't she perfect?'

'Yes,' gushed Bradamante.

'No, no,' I interrupted. 'You cannot be in love. Neither one of you. Too young. Too distracting.'

'But—' they both began.

'No!' I said and gathered air in a small thunderclap to punctuate my emotion. 'She will be on her way tomorrow, and you will be back to training. Now, go to bed.' And I watched them crawl under the covers and blow out the lamp and I stood there until their breathing evened out, until I calmed down myself, and only then did I notice that I was humming – imperfectly – Bradamante's melody.

The second visitor came not by chance, but by invitation. It happened like this. Every morning, the twins would go through sword forms, ride their horses and practise with lances – aiming at rings, striking wooden targets. Then they would spar. In the years of training them, I had pitted them against every guardsman in Duke Aymon's service. They bested them all. So they fought each other, and Bradamante always won. One morning, when she had disarmed Ricardetto – his sword thudding to the ground – and then tripped him, so that he landed with a *whuff*, and then pinned him, the point of her sword to his throat, I heard a burst of laughter. The guards and grooms, the dog-boys and ostlers, all had gathered around to watch the match. They often did so and usually I ignored them. But this morning, their laughter grated. 'What,' I demanded, turning on them, 'is so funny, you louts?'

'Begging pardon,' the dog-boy said, tugging at his forelock. 'But it's awful funny to see a girl beat a boy. That's all.'

'Is it? Funny?'

He clearly did not recognize a rhetorical question when he heard one. 'Well, yes, my lady. It is. You see, any other boy might be embarrassed to be beaten, but these twins . . .' He shrugged his shoulders, seemed to remember who he was talking to (he was not the brightest candle in chandelier) and tugged his forelock again. 'Begging your pardon, of course, but they aren't quite . . . normal.'

'Of course they're not "normal",' I hissed at him. 'Normal is for dolts like you. They are superior.'

'Peculiar.'

'In a good way.'

'That boy couldn't fight his way out of his mother's sewing room,' the dog-boy said, to general laughter from the gathered group. I glared at them all. 'Begging your pardon,' he said again. 'But you did ask what was funny.'

'He is an able fighter. Perhaps you haven't noticed, but they defeated all the guards here in sparring. And Bradamante is very, very good.'

The dog-boy looked at her (she was now helping Ricardetto to his feet) and said, 'She's a girl. She's not that good. She might get the better of this lot.' He jerked his thumb over his shoulder at the guardsmen. 'But any real knight would topple her in a moment.'

'Top her, too!' the groom guffawed. Then looked at me and knuckled his forehead. 'Begging your pardon.'

That was it. I'd had enough. Clearly I had been too long among this group of cretins. They had grown familiar with me, enough to take my good humour for granted. I was sore tempted to turn them all into caterpillars. But I needed to keep them as men in order to prove my point. I turned up my glow a little. 'Find me Duke Aymon. Now!' I commanded.

At least they obeyed that, for soon Duke Aymon came down

the manor steps, wiping his morning porridge from his whiskers. 'Yes, good Melissa, you called?'

'Find me a knight. A good one. I wish to prove to your men – to everyone – just how well-trained these twins are.' I turned to Bradamante and Ricardetto, who were just now helping each other unbuckle their armour. Bradamante smiled at my words, but Ricardetto paled a bit. 'Both of them,' I said.

'Ah, well. I see. Hmmm.' Duke Aymon scratched his silver-black beard. 'There's Sir Trito, yes. He was wounded last year in a fierce battle, came home to recuperate, but he is healed now, I believe. He would do well.'

'Fetch him, then.'

And so Sir Trito appeared. Tall – almost as tall as me – and broad-shouldered. He rode into Duke Aymon's yard to cheers from the guards (this rankled me; if I am to rule this motley assortment of fools in the coming age, I would prefer that they cheer me . . . but perhaps that will come with time) astride a white-and-chestnut horse. His tabard, bearing a fox and three sheaves, covered freshly oiled mail and he swept down from his saddle gracefully, as if the chain mail weighed nothing. 'Duke Aymon,' he said, with a little bow. 'Who have you summoned me to fight? I did not know there was a war afoot!'

'Not a war, not a war,' Duke Aymon dithered. 'And not so much a fight, as a . . . training match. You see . . .' He led Sir Trito over to where I stood with the twins.

Bradamante let out a long sigh. 'He is very handsome,' she said to me. 'Look at his eyes.'

I looked. They were deep brown, liquid. Rather like a cow's. Cows can be pleasant, I suppose.

'He is handsome,' Ricardetto agreed. 'I hope my shoulders are that broad some day.'

'Enough mooning,' I snapped. 'Stand up straight.'

Sir Trito had drawn near. 'This is most strange,' he said as he took in the three of us. 'Your daughter? Learning to fight?'

'Ah. Erm. Well. We had a . . . holy hermit? Who had a vision? Yes, a vision. Revealed to him by an, uh, angel.' Here, Duke Aymon looked hopefully at me. I should train *him* in story-telling. 'And the angel said that Bradamante should learn the art of war!' he finished dramatically.

I stepped forward, gave Sir Trito a nod. 'I have trained these twins well. But some *people* have their doubts.' I glared over his shoulder at the gathering crowd of guards and grooms and, yes, the dog-boy. They seemed to be taking bets. 'I wish for them to prove their skill against you.'

Sir Trito's eyebrows (the same brown-blond as his hair) shot up. 'You want me to fight them?'

He did overtop the twins by half a foot, at least, and, given that my charges hadn't quite finished their maturation, they were scraggly – all arms and legs and not much thickness to them. Sir Trito was solid. They were willow saplings and he was an oak. But they were very well-trained willow saplings. 'Yes,' I said.

He threw his head back and laughed. If before I was inclining to agree with Bradamante, that this fellow was handsome, by human standards, now I revised my opinion. He had an ugly laugh. 'I'll take them on both at once and be done in a trice.'

'You will not. You will fight one, then the other, with the same rules and rigour that you would use to challenge a fellow knight.'

Sir Trito licked his lips. His gaze glanced over Bradamante, whose hair was sweaty and damp, but whose blue eyes blazed with intensity. Over Ricardetto, who had puffed up his chest as much as he could and thrown his shoulders back. And settled on me, though he spoke to Duke Aymon. 'And what do I get if I win?'

The duke stammered once more. 'I, that is . . . you could . . . well, what would you like? The next foal my hunter sires?'

'I might have asked for your daughter's hand in marriage, but I'm not certain I could get her out of that armour,' he laughed and Duke Aymon's cheeks flushed deep red. 'But I'll take a night with you.' And he reached for my hand, as if I might let him seize it and kiss it. The audacity.

Duke Aymon squawked like a goose that's been kicked and I yanked my hand out of reach, straightening up so that I stared down at Sir Trito. 'How dare you,' I said. 'What are you suggesting?'

He barely blinked his cow-eyes. 'That any *lady* who spends her time in the practice yard knows her way around swords.'

Oh. Turning him into a toad would be too good. 'Very well,' I said. 'If you defeat both of them, I will show you exactly what I know about swords.'

Duke Aymon sent servants scurrying to fetch refreshments for Sir Trito, and then beckoned me aside. 'Good Melissa, are you certain this is . . . wise?'

I gave him as disdainful a look as I could summon (which, if I do say so myself, is very, very disdainful) but said nothing. In truth, I wasn't certain it was wise. I also wasn't certain that *wisdom* was the proper measure for action here. Rightness? Necessity? All I could say was that I felt a deep . . . something . . . like fear? Doubt? Seeing Mars and Venus together in the sky had shaken something in me, made me think of my brother's twins (and I'd been trying – for years – not to think too much of them). And now, looking at Ricardetto as he laced on his leather jerkin and Bradamante as she swung her arms in circles, limbering up, I worried that I had indeed made them skilled but soft. That I had coddled them . . . over-nurtured them? Was such a thing possible? The doubt shook me to my core. And so I needed to test them

– before the time of their true test. They could fail the contest of arms and still win the other two. But if they failed and were maimed. Or failed and died . . . well, then, I would have to grant my brother victory. How terrible. So, at last, I took pity on Duke Aymon who was standing there, wringing his hands, shifting his weight from foot to foot, and said, 'It is the wisest idea I have ever had.' Sometimes feigning certainty creates certainty.

'Oh, good. I do not doubt you, Melissa, but I am a mere mortal, and so I . . .'

'So you are wrapped in ignorance and lack my ability to perceive, discern, and understand.' I patted him on the shoulder. 'That's why I'm here to take care of you.'

'Who shall I beat first?' called Sir Trito. He had thrown back the cup of wine the servants had fetched.

'Bradamante,' I said. I felt Duke Aymon stiffen beside me.

'She's but a girl,' he whispered.

'She has passed out of girlhood and into something else,' I whispered back, speaking more to myself than to him. 'Look at her. She's taller, yes. And she has an edge about her, no?'

'She has her mother's cheekbones,' Duke Aymon mused.

'That's true. But that's not what I meant at all,' I replied. Humans! And their insistence on the flesh meaning something, everything! 'Don't you feel it from her? A certain ferocity? A thirst?'

Duke Aymon cocked his head, studying his daughter as Ricardetto helped her into a shirt of chain mail, buckled greaves to her shins. 'She has always been stubborn.'

'That is also true. And also not what I meant.' I sighed. 'What was Rinaldo like at her age . . . or a few years younger, before he went to be a squire?'

Duke Aymon's whole visage softened and he relaxed enough to give a little chuckle. 'Oh, it was like having a bantam rooster at the dinner table. Strutting around, taking umbrage at the smallest things.' He laughed aloud now. 'He was always facing off to fight with one of the guards or servants over some perceived slight.'

Charming boy. 'He wanted to prove himself. The same with Bradamante. Only her doubts must run deeper.'

Aymon frowned. 'She's a . . .'

I held up a warning finger. 'Don't say it. Unless that last word was going to be warrior. Or fighter.'

He said nothing.

Bradamante was ready: gauntlets, helm, sword, shield. I called for one of Duke Aymon's guardsmen, Nestor, to come forward. He elbowed through the flock of servants, grooms, ostlers, past the dog-boy, and came to the middle of the practice yard. 'Will you judge this contest? Award points when they are scored?'

Nestor, in a blue tunic with Aymon's stag embroidered on it, looked over at Bradamante, then at Sir Trito. He cocked one eyebrow. 'It'll be a quick job, m'lady.'

'Do it fairly, will you not?'

He bowed. 'You can rely on me.'

Doubtful. I nodded to Sir Trito, then to Bradamante. Oh, I wanted to fuss a bit. To tighten the strap on her shield, to whisper a word of encouragement. To tell her I was proud of her already. But she would only shake me off, as a dog shakes off water. The hardest part of nurturing is knowing when not to.

Nestor straightened the wool cap he wore, stepped to the middle, and raised an arm. I stepped back to stand between Ricardetto and Duke Aymon. 'You've bated your swords?' Nestor asked. Bradamante and Sir Trito held out their blades, to show that the edges had been covered with strips of wood. Less chance of bleeding, of severing, of impaling. But still a good deal of bludgeoning possible. 'The first to reach ten points wins. One point for a blow to the arm or leg. Two points for a blow to the body. Three for a blow to the head. And three for knocking your opponent down. If you can't get up in a five count, you forfeit.' Bradamante nodded. Nestor, clearly enjoying his elevation from guardsman to judge, raised his hands, shouted, 'Begin!' and stepped back.

I could hardly watch; I couldn't tear my eyes away. The two of them circled each other, swords held high, shields out in front, a step, a stamp of the foot, testing, probing. Just as I'd taught her. Then Bradamante darted in with a quick slash, her sword making an audible *tink* against Trito's mail. 'Point!' I heard her call.

Nestor shook his head. 'You have to *hit* him. Not just *touch* him.'

Trito laughed, but I could hear – or sense—that the mirth was forced. He was surprised she'd got past his guard.

A moment later, circling again, Trito feinted high and struck low when Bradamante lifted her shield. *Thunk.* His bated sword slammed into her thigh. She leapt back, favouring one leg. 'Point!' Nestor said, his voice rising with excitement. 'That's a strike, now!'

Bradamante tested her leg, putting some weight on it, shaking it out. She'd taken worse in training, I'd seen to that. She set her stance once more; sword held up, cocked slightly outwards, shield at a slight angle. She stepped to the side, a little back, waited as Trito matched her moves. It was a dance, or nearly so, a tidy arrangement of posture and pose. My teeth ached as I ground them together. *Fight, Bradamante!* Indeed, her sword flicked out once more as she stepped around Trito's shield: *clank.* Her bated blade hit against his ribs and he bent over a little to absorb the blow. 'Point,' she called.

Nestor waved his hand. 'No point. Good mistress, you've got to hit him hard.' And he offered a little bow.

Bradamante, brought up short by this blatant unfairness, had to dodge backwards inelegantly as Trito swung his sword; he landed a blow to her shoulder. 'Point!' Nestor called.

'Unfair,' I grated. Ricardetto squeezed my hand, his fingers damp in mine. Duke Aymon shuffled his weight from foot to foot.

'It must be as Nestor says,' he muttered. 'He has served as a guard for years and knows his fighting well. She is a girl. And girls can't hit hard.'

'She can, Father,' Ricardetto said. 'I've the bruises to prove it.'

Again, Bradamante set her stance. Trito made a classic feint, coming in on her left side, and she angled her shield precisely to shunt it off, counter-stepping to avoid his second blow. She ended up nearly behind him and raised her sword, bringing it down on Trito's helm. *Thu-kunk.* The knight took a staggering step forward, but managed to swing his sword up and set his stance.

'Point!' Bradamante insisted when Nestor stayed quiet.

Again, a little mocking bow. 'That was nearly hard enough, good mistress. But a real man's strike would have brought him to his knees. No point.'

Now I could hear her growl. Could feel something rumbling, as if the ground shook with her. She set her stance once more, her front foot turned slightly in, every angle perfect. Trito stepped forward; she stepped back. He jabbed with his blade, she dodged and circled. The watching servants hissed and booed. 'Fight 'im!' someone called. 'Quit dancing around!' I could sense that the calls landed on her as hard as Trito's blows. Saw how her shoulders tensed and her movements became more rigid.

She stepped left and swung her sword at the very instant that Trito did the same: blade met blade. Sir Trito tried to step back, but Bradamante pressed on, her blade sliding down his until the crossguards met, and the blades clinched, locked together. As Trito focused on breaking the clinch, Bradamante stepped closer, hooked her leg behind his knee and brought him crashing down. His head bounced, once, twice, against the hard-packed ground of the practice yard.

'Ooooooh!' the crowd groaned and roared, as if they'd been felled.

'Three points!' Bradamante declared.

'No points!' Nestor waved his arms, as if to clear the air.

'I brought him down. That's the rules. Three points.'

'Ah, mistress. Three points for bringing him down with a blow. From your sword. This is a swordfight, after all. Not wrestling.'

She spun on her heel and twisted her blade free from where it was still tangled with Trito's, then lifted her sword to strike his fallen body.

'Hold!' the guardsman said. 'You can't strike an opponent when he's down!'

'Then start counting,' she retorted.

Nestor's eyebrows scrunched, whether in surprise at her command or because he was struggling to remember his numbers. 'Er . . . One . . . Two . . . Three . . .' Trito stirred then, sat up, got to his knees.

'That's not fair,' Duke Aymon grumbled. 'He's not up, he's not down. But she can't do a thing.'

I agreed, but didn't say anything, though the duke's sentence could well describe the state of women in many situations, in many historical periods. At last, Sir Trito regained his feet and staggered away from Bradamante.

She let him regain his breath and his footing, though I was

mentally urging her to press her advantage. But the crowd would boo even more if she struck now. I could see her, glaring through the slit of her helm, first at Nestor, then at Trito. She lifted her sword, and the blade trembled slightly; I knew that was not from fear, not from fatigue, but from pure rage. I do believe that Bradamante had just figured out exactly how unfair the world could be. Not a bad lesson to learn. Now, what would she do with it?

The crowd hooted and jeered. Even though they were her servants – perhaps because they were – they called out taunts and mocked her. She set her stance again. Trito, at last, did the same. More circling, more howls from the crowd. 'End it, Sir Knight! Stop going gentle on her!'

Trito advanced, using a classic move, one the texts referred to as 'blade parting silk'. Bradamante beat his sword aside easily, starting the preferred counter-strike, when a particularly loud call came from the dog-boy. 'Teach that girl a lesson!'

Bradamante bellowed, jerking her blade out of the neat counter and swinging it around at Trito's ribs. *Thunk*. It landed. She still pressed forward, not even demanding a point for her hit, shoving the knight with her shield, lifting her blade again. No form I'd ever taught her, battering him low on his thigh, then rounding her sword up and bringing it crashing down on his helm. Trito stumbled, backed away, fell to one knee, pushed himself up. Bradamante swung her sword around; Nestor stepped closer and shouted, 'Don't hit him. He's barely got his feet under him.'

She shoved Nestor away with her shield and finished her blow, hitting Trito over the head again. He crumpled to the ground, sword falling loose from his grip. 'One, two, three, four, five,' she counted, standing over him.

Then she turned, sheathed her sword, tugged off her gauntlets, and removed her helm. Sweat had soaked through her auburn hair and her face was flushed a dark red. She spat, once, the gob landing near Nestor's foot. 'I suppose I should thank you for your blatant unfairness,' she said, in a voice loud enough to carry to the ears of the servants, grooms, and dog-boy. 'As I have been raised and trained to think myself capable – to *know* myself capable – it is a good reminder that some will never see me as such.'

I suspected her speech was lost on her listeners (and Sir Trito, though he was sitting up now, was in no condition to absorb her words) but I was glad she delivered them nonetheless. Was proud of her as she stalked off.

Duke Aymon left my side to help Bradamante with her shield and armour and Ricardetto leaned close. 'Do I have to fight him?'

We stared out at the practice yard, where Sir Trito was being helped to his feet by the guardsman. Servants came with a bucket of water, a stool, a cup of wine. 'It'll be a little while before he's ready,' I said. 'But, yes.'

'And if I don't beat him, while my sister did . . .' He left the sentence, the sentiment, hanging.

'Go help her with her armour,' I said. 'And have something to eat. Keep your strength up.' I needed to puzzle over what he was thinking. What I was doing. It didn't bother me too much that Ricardetto was only a mediocre fighter. Certainly, I would have preferred that he be excellent. But Bradamante was good enough for both of them. That should have been enough. Yet. Yet . . . If the roles had been reversed. If Ricardetto had been an excellent fighter and Bradamante not . . . I would not have stood for it. I would have trained and cajoled and battered and perhaps even magicked the girl until she was as good as the boy. Oh, I hated to admit that, but it was true. What human value had I internalized? When I ruled this world, I would fix this wretched system, undo this

113

idiotic hierarchy . . . but I didn't rule. Not yet. And so I had to admit to myself that I had been played by human nonsense. I wanted my girl, my Bradamante, to be the best and I had fallen into the trap of thinking like these people: to be the best, she must be like a man. Had I squashed something true and beautiful within her by insisting on this?

I hurried to her side; her face was flushed, but she'd wiped away the sweat with a kerchief, which was now scrunched in one hand. 'Wonderful. You were spectacular,' I said.

She glared out at the practice yard, her blue eyes fiery. 'It was entirely unfair. I'll have that guardsman Nestor drawn and quartered . . .'

'Well, dear,' I said, soothingly, beckoning for a servant to bring wine. 'You'll find that most of life under the hegemony of this era is quite unfair. If you complain about it, you only make them enjoy it more.'

'That's unfair, too,' she sulked. I held out a cup of wine. She took it and sipped. 'I had to beat him twice over just to win once.'

'You will find that is often the way the game is played, no matter what the rules are.'

Bradamante shook her head and her hair tumbled loose from the tie that had held it beneath her helm. 'What if I don't want to play, then?'

Oh. Six years ago I might have fought with her. I might have insisted – with much love and care and warmth – that she couldn't quit. That she couldn't choose. That she had to do this. But I knew Bradamante better now, knew myself better too, perhaps, and so I said, 'This is something you ought to want. If you don't . . . then . . .'

She stood up suddenly, knocking over the stool she had been sitting on. 'What I want,' she said, 'is to bash in the brains of every idiot man like those three.' She gestured to where Sir Trito sat on his stool laughing and talking with Nestor and the dog-boy. 'But what I really want is for a man not to be an idiot. I feel . . .' She clenched her fists. 'Why are there no stories about people like me, Melissa?'

'Whatever do you mean?' I asked. I had made a point, really, truly, tried, to find or make up stories about women warriors . . . strong women . . . capable and smart women . . .

'I know you want me to fight. To win these contests that you talk about. But why are there no stories about women who are hard on the outside and soft on the inside and who let the softness win . . . without losing everything?'

And she handed her cup back to me and walked away.

It took all of a jug of wine for Sir Trito to laugh off his defeat, blame the angle of the sun, explain that his old injury was bothering him, and challenge Ricardetto. Poor boy. He had been hanging close by my side since Bradamante had disappeared and now seemed rather startled that Trito would fight him. The crowd had mostly dissipated, a few guardsmen lingering about, and I heard the clink of coins as wagers were set. I helped Ricardetto into his armour, and Duke Aymon leaned in to offer some words of 'advice'.

'Watch his feet, my boy,' he said. 'And try to strike with the edge, not the point.'

When the duke had left us, I tightened Ricardetto's shield straps. 'Don't bother with his feet. It's the sword you should mind . . . and strike with point or edge, or shield, or, frankly, whatever you can hit him with.'

Ricardetto nodded and stepped towards Trito. The same guardsman, Nestor, judged this contest; the two combatants faced each other with swords raised. But other than that, there were few similarities to the bouts. Ricardetto executed his forms precisely. He moved with a stately rhythm. He turned at precise angles to deflect blows. In all, then, he fought exactly as he had been taught . . . exactly as I had encouraged him to. And, as a result, he lost quite readily. Oh, he scored points. A solid hit to Sir Trito's leg, a deft counter-strike that earned points for a blow to the ribs. But Trito's blows landed harder, and Ricardetto was lurching, lowering his shield, favouring one leg, allowing more blows – some glancing, some not – and soon enough, he had lost.

To my surprise, Sir Trito clapped the boy on the back at the conclusion of the match. 'Well fought,' he said. 'You show promise with the sword.' He shot a glance at me. 'When I head back to fight for the king, you should come with me, as a squire, though you'd soon earn your knighthood.'

'Thank you, sir,' Ricardetto said and then limped over to me. I wrested his helm off and began to unbuckle his greaves. 'Why,' he asked, 'would he ever praise my fighting over Bradamante's? I'm terrible.'

'You aren't terrible,' I insisted. 'You're quite good. It is just that Bradamante is . . . excellent.'

Ricardetto sighed. 'I don't really like fighting that much.'

'That may be why you aren't excellent at it.'

He nodded. 'Yes, and that's why Sir Trito is wrong. I won't ever be a knight.'

We both stared over to where Trito was enjoying another cup of wine and laughing with the guardsmen. 'My dear,' I said. 'I do believe that if you went to battle you would soon be a knight.'

Ricardetto gave a little laugh. 'Why? Do they reward mediocrity?'

I lifted the mail shirt over his head, tousling his hair. 'That is exactly what men reward in other men.' I examined the links, some dented where Trito's blows had landed. I thought about my brother's twins on that far-off island. How old they would be now. How strong, how savage. They would not spar for points. They would not bate their swords. They would not demand greatness from the female, then disparage her for it; they would not approve of a man's mediocrity because they feared something better. I sighed and set the mail down; the duke's armourer would fix it tomorrow, bend it back to shape and oil it smooth. Would that I could mould my twins so easily.

The thought had flitted across my mind that I might enjoy a stroll in the gardens with the twins. Perhaps down to the river and let them swim. Let them absorb the lessons of today's fighting. Let Ricardetto turn it into a story – one that allowed him and his sister to be the heroes. I wanted to be far from the wagering crowd of servants, the pig-headed Sir Trito, far from them . . . until I could rule them and show them their true potential.

But my plans for a quiet evening were not to be. No sooner had I crossed the yard towards the manor's door when Lady Beatrice flitted down and took my hands in her own. The years seemed scarcely to have touched her face, and looking at her, I thought I might be catching a glimpse of a future Bradamante – the hair softened from fiery towards bronze, the slight lines that radiated from the corners of her eyes that spoke of smiles and laughter. 'Oh, good Melissa,' Lady Beatrice said. 'You will want to hurry and ready yourself. And perhaps the twins, too. Duke Aymon has called for a fine table to be spread for Sir Trito, and a chamber be readied for the knight. What a day of fighting! He must be exhausted.'

'Indeed,' I said. 'He took quite the beating.'

Lady Beatrice's cheeks flushed and she tugged at my hands, leading me inside, her voice dropping to a conspiratorial whisper. 'Melissa,' she said. 'I do not doubt your wisdom. You come from On High.' (I could hear the capitalization in her speech.) 'But perhaps because I am a mere mortal . . . I am so limited . . . And I don't mean to question you . . .'

'Out with it,' I said, though lightly. Women had such a way of qualifying every comment. 'Though I can guess. You don't like Bradamante fighting.'

'You are so wise. That is it precisely.'

'What do you want for your daughter?'

Lady Beatrice nodded to the servant who opened the door for us. 'Well, the comfort of a good home. A husband to care for her so she need not worry much. Children, of course.'

'What you have,' I summarized. 'If Bradamante wants to fight, what is wrong with her fighting?'

Lady Beatrice dithered as we stood at the foot of the stairs, her fingers twisting around a handkerchief. 'Nothing is *wrong*. It's only that . . . truth be told, she is almost past the age of marriage. Another year or two and . . .' She shook her head and her bronze tresses quaked a little bit.

'If Bradamante wants to marry, she will marry. And though I do not know the precise moment when her destiny will arrive . . .' I paused. That word, 'destiny', tasted like ash in my mouth. I did not believe in such things . . . yet I had created the moment. Co-created. And 'destiny' was a word that humans understood (or thought they did). 'I assure you it is soon. Within a year, two at the outmost.' I squeezed Lady Beatrice's hand. 'Your daughter is beautiful and smart and strong and curious and stubborn. Do you not worry that marriage would confine her? Would squeeze out of her what makes her . . . good? Herself?'

Lady Beatrice smiled. A blank and pleasant look. 'It must be nice,' she said, 'to be an angel and to measure oneself by such ideas as goodness and self-worth and potential. Here, on earth, I do believe it is more important . . . easier? Better? . . . for Bradamante to be a good wife than a stubborn, strong woman.'

And she left me there, at the foot of the stairs. I climbed to the twins' chamber and found Bradamante already in a handsome gown, the green of early-spring wheat. Ricardetto was brushing her hair while Bradamante stared into the speckled looking glass, turning her head one way, then the other. 'Sit still,' Ricardetto gently chided.

'Should I put on the blue gown? It favours my eyes . . . but I think this one brings out the colour in my cheeks? Should I colour them more?' she fretted at her image.

'No more colour, or you'll appear to have fever,' I said, frowning at her. 'What do you care for your appearance? Are you hoping to snare Sir Trito for a husband?' I didn't mean to speak harshly to her, but her mother's words had unsettled me. I wanted more for her. So much more.

Now the colour did rise to her cheeks, red and blotchy. She stood up and pushed aside Ricardetto to face me. 'Never,' she said. 'But I wouldn't mind it if he found me beautiful. Or desirable.' She stared at me, and I saw her chin tremble just a bit. Saw her throat move up and down as if she were swallowing words, or tears. 'You may be cold, Melissa. You seem sometimes to come from another realm. But I need warmth. I don't wish to be thought a monster.' And with that, she spun on her heel and fled the chamber.

Ricardetto turned the brush over in his hands. 'I'm sorry for her rudeness.'

'It was honesty,' I replied. 'Let's get you dressed for this feast.'

'There's no one I'm trying to impress,' he sighed.

'Not Sir Trito?'

'I think he took the measure of me in the practice yard.' Now Ricardetto stared into the looking glass, picked at a spot on his chin. Jutted out his lower lip in displeasure. 'Do you think, Melissa, that there will be a day when . . . I get to set the standards? When it is my will that determines how

I will be judged? Or will I always be falling short of someone else's measure?'

I let his question hang there, in the air between us, and helped him into a clean shirt, a coat worked with delicately embroidered flowers (I think he may have done most of the stitching himself; sewing was an art I left to their mother to teach them, lacking the patience myself). I sent him down the stairs and told him that I would decline the dinner invitation. My presence was likely to cause Sir Trito indigestion. Instead, I stood by the chamber window and thought about standards and measure and dualism and balance. My brother's twins: savage and wild. My own: refined and trained. But were my brother's also free? True to themselves? While mine were caged and restrained? I did not know if this, too, this captivity, was a required by-product of Nurture. And, if so, whether it was worth the cost.

I listened to the sounds of dinner. Murmured talk and laughter that floated up to where I stood. Bradamante was likely charming Sir Trito; Ricardetto, too, telling some enchanting tale. I leaned out of the narrow window and drank in the cool night air; it carried the muddy scent of the river below. There was Venus and there was Mars – closer than they had been the other night . . . or was I imagining things? No, the moment was drawing near. A year, no more. How human I was becoming! Worry would do me no good. I needed to take a lesson from my own book: fate was out there, written dimly. What would happen would happen and it was beyond my control. I could only work with what I had – teach and shape and guide and lead and love, in my way.

From below, the sound of the lute rose up. My head ached. It would do me good to check on my brother's twins. To see how they progressed. Perhaps one or both had died. That would make me feel very much improved. And I needed to change my mood for, at the moment, these feelings of mine were altogether too human. I was losing my perspective.

So, while the music poured out from the floor below me, I worked a modest magic. Summon iron. A wash of water. Swirl air about twice. And done. Two suits of armour. Identical. Metal of blue-black. I set them to stand in the beam of moonlight that fell into the chamber. I left a note saying that there was one for each of the twins, a token of their great success in fighting. That the making of this armour had fatigued me, and that I was retiring to my heavenly abode to rest. That I wished them to continue with their practice and training in my absence.

I stood by the window, feeling the cool night air. The moon gleamed down, so lovely. We haven't one up above, where my brother and I normally reside. I leaned out of the window, admiring how the stark light shone upon the river, the leaves of the trees, casting everything in the barest of terms, painting a road of silver-white across the land. I leaned and leaned further and tumbled out, landing, catlike, on that road, and walked away along the moonlight. It was past time I checked on my brother and his twins.

CHAPTER FOUR

Moonlight, taste of cold metal. A faster way to travel than the whims of the wind. Chillier, too. No matter, as to that, for as soon as I descended from that milk-blue path onto my brother's island, the tranquil humidity blanketed me. Suffocating. The clear night revealed not only the moon but also the stars, allowing me to do a quick calculation. By this position, at an incipient angle, taking into account the planetary tilt . . . I slipped into the moonlight once more, shimmied through, and emerged a dozen odd years earlier, not long after I had left the island before.

There were the twins, curled with the lion cubs. There was my brother, not asleep, but bent over a basin full of water. Still, the water mirrored the night sky, and my brother studied this, his red eyes reflected in the basin, too, as if they – like the stars – gave off a faint light of their own. I knew what he was doing; reading the future. But to what end? I could answer that question myself. Not to a good end. If he were to be true to his word (and why would he?), he would let these twins grow up, let the purpose we had drawn pull them towards my twins, and be done with it. But he was trying to read the future. Which could only mean that he was trying to shape it.

I let time flow a little faster. I watched the boy and the girl wander the island, tame colourful parrots, feeding them sticky fruit from their fingers and teaching them to talk, though the only language they spoke was their own twin-language: a polyglot mash-up of sounds, with now and then a word that they might have heard my brother speak. Good, good. I had a strong feeling that the story-telling contest was a lock for Ricardetto.

They grew taller, stronger, deeper brown. They wrestled each other and raced up and down the island's beaches. They swam out into the ocean and then let the surf float them back to shore. They stared at the sea from the island's highest bluffs and occasionally spotted a distant boat, white canvas billowed in the wind. They felled palm trees and sneaked cloth from my brother's stores and tried to build their own ship.

In short, they were clever and resourceful and healthy and capable. And utter savages. They watched my brother, true, but he was hardly a paragon of civilization. He ignored them utterly and focused on some oddities of magic and conjuring. Muttering over scrolls, summoning flames that seemed to have faces. (What was he doing? It seemed sinister. Bizarre. Knowing my brother, I could only interpret it as a threat to me.) The twins viewed these sights as entertainment – the only kind they knew, and even the lioness, grown old and half-toothless, watched from the shadows; her eyes always on my brother, as if she alone knew danger when she saw it. To the twins, my brother was nothing but mystery, fascination. A sometime source of entertainment and a fount of benign indifference.

And then came a certain day. I could feel it coming, the difference of it – a difference that can only be felt because time has gone past it, through it, and woven the peculiarity into itself. So I slowed down my review and let the day play out at a more human pace. At first, it seemed like any other. Bright sun, dazzling water, hot sand. The twins deciding to play hide and seek. They were perhaps eight? It was impossible to tell. They were children, still, that much was certain. It was the girl's turn to hide and she eschewed the predictable spots of shady branches or the hollows of mangrove roots and instead ran off to a cave she had lately discovered on the windward side of the island. (Though she and her brother were two peas in a pod, she did occasionally leave him – often when he was napping – and found time and space of her own. I enjoyed watching her in these times the most – she would comb her hair with her fingers and sing little chanting songs or imitate the whistles of the birds. Simple pleasures, reflecting a simple mind.) At high tide, the seawater would creep past this cave's mouth and at low tide, the sand within the cave would be dry. It smelled of seaweed and dead crabs and endless damp. She crouched there for a while, listening to the pull and suck of the sea, enjoying the cool dark, the brightness of the day just a pinpoint of light at the distant cave's mouth.

She grew bored, as children will, and crept out of her cave. After so long in the dark, the sun stung her eyes. She plunged into the water and swam out towards a series of low, humped rocks. Here, still blinking at the glare, she pulled herself up. If she hadn't hidden so long in the cave, she would have seen the three-masted schooner drop anchor in the waters off the island. If she hadn't been sun-blind, she would have spotted the dinghy that the schooner lowered. But as it was, she had no warning until an oar squeaked in a lock, and by then the little boat and its half a dozen sailors were almost upon her rocks. No retreat – she could not swim faster than they could row.

As they drew closer she bared her teeth, a gesture halfway between a smile and a threat. The sailors nudged the dinghy up to the rock and one of them called to her. 'How'd you arrive at these shores? Do you live on this isle?'

The girl frowned at him, narrowed her eyes, said nothing in reply.

The sailor's next words came slow and halting, as if he judged her stupid. 'Who else lives here?'

'No one,' she said, surprising me with the clear speech. 'I am all alone.' And in hearing those words, I felt a sense of her power and her danger to me. Here was one suckled by a lioness. A little girl. Uneducated in the ways of the world but able to speak a language that had been foreign to her but a moment before. A girl, not without fear of these men – but who, having never met men before, held the correct amount of fear. She was, in short, a more formidable foe than I had thought.

'Then you must come with us,' another man said. The boat thumped against the little rock she stood upon.

'No,' she said, shaking her head. 'I will not.' By the time she saw the flash of the oar, caught sight of it from the corner of her eye, it was too late. The wooden blade crashed against the side of her head. Her mouth formed a small *oh* of surprise, her knees bent, and she fell face forward, the sea cushioning her landing. The men seized her little limbs and dropped her in the bottom of the boat, which stank of half-rotten rope, fish guts.

They rowed then to the shore of the island, leaving one man by the boat, watching not just the girl, but the trees, the vines (they seemed to watch him back; they did watch him back). The others went searching for fresh water. If they found it, they'd signal the ship, which would send the other boat with empty barrels.

The one sailor waited with a bow and arrows near to hand. For humans, for game, to keep him from being afraid. The girl didn't stir; her dark hair clumped damply to her scalp, sticky with seawater, sticky with blood where the oar had struck her. Her limbs, sun-dark and twig-thin, were angled as if she were running. But she lay still. A breeze ruffled the fronds and leaves, made them whisper, made the hairs on the sailor's neck stand up. A single screech from a circling gull made him jump, bite his tongue.

The other men crashed through the dense vines, one hacking at the foliage with his sword, the others cursing and swearing and swatting at the insects that descended upon them. 'Must be water here if that girl survived.'

'Maybe she only just washed ashore.'

They had made landfall on many such islands knowing that fresh water lurked close to the interior, that it was the reason vegetation grew thick. But this wall of green was impenetrable. They lost sight of the sun overhead. If they hadn't reached out, one man putting a hand on the shoulder of the sailor ahead of him, they would have lost sight of each other. It grew dark as night. Still as night, too. Now and then the screech of an owl would sever the darkness and each man could feel the other tense up, then try to laugh it off.

But, after a time that might have been an hour and might have been a day, the trees ahead thinned, and the leader (who had no shoulder in front of him to cling on to) gave a yelp of joy, increasing their pace. That they emerged back onto the beach they had begun from, empty-handed, mattered none. They stumbled, blinking, then ran to the little dinghy and shoved it off the sand, swinging their legs over the side, already laughing and turning it all into a tale for the rest of the crew. Only one sailor paused, waist high in the surf, to turn back and make a sign with his hands, an old gesture to ward off magic.

* * *

I floated up on the breeze, gaining height enough that I could watch the dinghy's progress back to the boat and also see the boy twin emerge onto the beach. He, too, squinted out at the dinghy, fists clenched at his sides. Had he watched the whole scene – afraid to fight them or aware they would overpower him, or hoping that his sister would disappear? Or had he just arrived and would now berate himself for his tardiness, for his failure to protect? When the dinghy reached the ship's wooden sides, the boy turned and sprinted into the island's thick foliage.

I waited until the ship had winched its anchors up and then I drifted down closer to the island's shore, sensing my brother, finding him on the edge of the island's small lagoon. My brother tended a small fire of green-gold flame. In his palm he held four smooth rocks, stones that looked to have lain on the bed of a river. He held them now over the flames, then plunged his hand into the lagoon's limpid waters, his hand hissing and steaming as the water quenched the heat. Then back to the flame.

Here, the boy found him, and panted out his news. 'They. Took. Her. In. A. Boat.' The boy gulped air. 'Can you get her back?'

My brother frowned at the stones in his hand, then closed his eyes, tilting his head back. The boy shifted his weight from one foot to the other; he was a child, a boy, a being of action and growth and swiftness. My brother was a creature of the Deeps and the stars. He could be swift, but he was also profoundly (irritatingly) patient. At last, my brother opened his eyes. 'She is gone,' he said. With his empty hand, he prodded the coals of his fire, making the flames shoot up.

The boy stood, chest still heaving – from the exertion of his run, but more from the way this failure (for he felt it to be a failure, so deeply I could taste it in the breeze) pressed on him. 'Gone?' he stumbled. 'But you . . . you can . . . you have to . . . send . . . or do . . .' To this creature, my brother must seem a god – able to make fire with a snap of his fingers, to tame a lioness at his whim. This boy, wild and unschooled as he was, must have perceived that it was well within my brother's powers to bring the girl back. (What would Ricardetto have done, had this been his plight? He would have come begging to me. He would have cried and wailed. I would have dried his tears . . . and chased down whatever or whoever had stolen Bradamante away. And torn them to pieces. Would that have been a show of strength? Or weakness? Would Ricardetto be the better for it? Or worse?)

'I could,' my brother said. 'But I won't. The stars have written out the fate of you and your sister, and I chose you because of that fate. I will not meddle. I will tell you only that you do have a fate – you are destined for greatness. Let that be your consolation and let the girl . . . go.'

The boy sputtered, but could not summon words to answer. Of course he could not. It is hard to comprehend, when a god disappoints so deeply. At length, he drew a shuddering breath, holding back his tears and kicked savagely at my brother's hand. The four river stones went flying, scattering across the sandy shore of the lagoon, as the boy fled into the trees.

I let time move faster again, floating along, watching the months scroll by. I feared, no, I hoped that my brother had made a colossal mistake. One that I had set him up for by insisting that we incorporate. He didn't realize that everything teaches. There is no such thing as pure Nature. By not nurturing his twins he was, in his way, nurturing them. Just not well.

The months passed by, became years. I trailed after the girl and watched as the sailors brought her to a port city, sold her as a slave to a merchant, drank away her price in a single night. I watched her toil, grow, be sold and sold again. Watched her sent into the hold of ships to seal pitch over leaky planks. Watched her haul buckets of water from distant wells. Watched her travel behind a herd of goats, gathering their dung to dry for fuel, until she had wandered far from the port where she first alighted. I watched her be given a name by one owner, then another, then another. Watched her be beaten; watched her steal food. Watched her pummel another slave – a boy only a little larger than she was – until he was a twitching bloody heap. Watched her grow more, watched her take care to wear the most shapeless of sack-like robes, the better to mask the maturing shape beneath them. Watched her bare her teeth at any man who looked at her. Watched her become someone else, become herself.

And the boy? He sulked for a time, spending hours on top of the island's bluffs, staring out at the horizon, as if the boat might return because he so wished it. The boy pleaded once more with my brother, receiving a sneer as a reply, and then wept himself empty on the shore. The lioness slunk out from the thicket of vines and licked his tears away. He grew, taller and broader. He fashioned for himself a bow and arrows like the ones the sailors had carried. He spoke rarely and then only to the lions, but they seemed to understand quite well and brought him meat, sometimes, and other times lurked and prowled and menaced my brother, bedevilling him by overturning his cauldrons or snatching away the scrolls he was studying. Once I watched as the boy perched on a tree bough, hidden in the thick leaves, and trained his arrow at my brother's heart. Thus do humans scheme against gods that betray them. He did not let the shaft fly. He knew my brother had no heart.

I studied this boy, holding him against the vision I had of Ricardetto at the same ages. It was like comparing silk to wool. This boy was toughened by salt air, heat and wind. The forces of Nature from which he had no respite. He was not as tall as Ricardetto, but was thicker in the chest, broader in the shoulders. Where Ricardetto's auburn hair waved and curled around his ears, this boy's dark locks hung lank and straight. He moved with grace, it is true – the one part of him that was silky – but it was the grace of a predator, stalking prey. Ricardetto moved with the grace of a gazelle, a deer, one kept in a nobleman's game park . . . safe from all fears . . . until the hunters come. Or so I felt, watching this boy. I worried. Oh, I had coddled my twins. They were soft, delicate as eggs, where this one was tough and hardened. But that wasn't the only measure we'd consider – there were three contests, after all.

I watched the boy, and I watched the sky. Saw, at last, Venus appear in the same night as Mars, felt the pull of those two planets. And on that night, or the morning following immediately after, the boy spotted a ship on the horizon. For once, the sails and the wind sang to his wishes, bringing the boat closer and closer. A smaller craft was dispatched towards the island, and the boy flung himself into the surf, arms and legs churning at the water, strong strokes carrying him to the sailors, who hauled him aboard like some strange fish they had angled for. In his half-twin gibberish, he warned them of the demon-infested island, begged them to take him away. They thought him mad with thirst and hunger, but brought him back to the ship, which picked up a new-born wind and sprinted away from the island's shores.

I watched my brother turn from his study of a hefty tome and look up at the sky, cloudless and blue. Watched him feel the boy sail away. Saw him lurch, as if his heart skipped a beat. As if he had a heart.

Watched the lioness dig a shallow pit in the sand of the shore, as beasts will do when they know their time has come. Watched her paw, big and strong and gentle, scoop out the ashes and bones of a long-forgotten fire, stirring up the only traces of a woman, a mother, whose name no one now knew. Watched the creature curl up and set herself to sleep one last time.

I floated on the breezes and gusts. Enjoyed the tropical air. Lingered long enough to enjoy witnessing my brother's panic. Oh, if I only had a way to preserve that sight. He will deny that he ever felt such a thing, that he has the *capacity* to feel such a thing. But human flesh, though not good for much, is good for making plain the pain and worry and vexation that humans all seem constantly to feel. My brother slept, woke, wandered. Found the lioness, nudged her cold, heavy body with a bare toe. And then, his head shot up, as if he had previously been asleep and wakened now at the sound of a beloved's shriek. He stared out at the ocean, and I knew he didn't see the surf that pounded the island's sands but instead sought out the deeper currents, following them as I followed the gusts of air, and traced the passage of his boy twin. Mouth slightly agape, my brother looked almost hurt. Innocent. As if he had been wronged. His boy gone. Willingly gone. Run away from him. My brother's knees, even, gave a little wobble and he sank down onto the sand, landed with an ungraceful thump. My brother. Wounded. By nothing more than emotion.

A moment. Two. A gull wheeled and squawked overhead. My brother blinked and rose and shook the sand from his robe. He gave one last look at the sea and nodded before returning to his lair. And I settled down on the sand he had just vacated, corporated just enough to enjoy the smell of the salt air, the grit of the sand, the heat of the sun. Why had I chosen cold and wet? Why must I suffer the rain and damp and chill of whatever godforsaken valley my twins were born into? I should have put Duke Aymon in mind to relocate. That was an amusing thought. The nobleman with all his hounds and horses, shipping off to live under a palm tree. The terms of my polarity wouldn't allow it, alas, but I enjoyed that image for a moment before setting to the task of burying the lioness. Though old, her pelt was still thick and soft, rich enough to keep a king warm on a winter night. I did not wish to see it ripped by buzzards. So I buried her deep on the beach and then let the sun's shadows stretch long across the sand. And when they had grown long enough, I slipped within one.

Of all the ways to travel, shadows are the most peculiar. My brother picked Fire when we settled our opposites, and I, Water. But shadow is neither of these things. What is shadow? Light? Or the absence of it? Can something be defined by what it is not? I'll leave that puzzle unsolved and simply say, I stepped into the shadow. And in that realm, it is like turning everything sideways. If moonlight frosts the world in black and white and silver and grey, then shadowlight does the same with dimensions.

Flattened, narrowed to an edge, I moved like a blade through time. This is the way to travel if one knows what one is looking for. No drifting on gusts. And no need to walk a bridge of moonlight, beautiful but so chill. A quick slip and I could be in the very spot I wished. For shadows fall everywhere.

And so I let that thin edge of time brush past my fingers, waited to feel what I searched for, and then emerged, let my shadow be cast in that moment.

A good thing I chose to travel by shadows and not the wind; the city where the girl dwelt felt only the occasional sweeping desert gusts that could pull whiskers from a man's beard, but it abounded in shadows, where I could wait and watch with ease. I slipped through, first, in the shadow cast by a guard tower. An unlovely pile of yellow rock, already crumbling back to sand. From the depths of the shadow, I could see the road the tower watched, rutted tracks through rocky, dry hills. Here and there, outside the city walls, bright spots of colour marked the tents of nomads and shepherds, their flocks spread out – no more than puffs of white to me – along the scrubby ground. I turned to face the city, found myself looking down into narrow streets, houses the same yellow stone as the guard tower. It seemed to have been built hodge-podge; there was a central square, open, with what might be a well at the middle. But streets radiated from this square, zig-zagging without sense. Here a warehouse, with some sort of fruit drying on its flat roof. There a rounded dome that might indicate a house of worship. And packed between, canvas awnings of merchants, or pens for camels and donkeys. Packed in, squalid and squalling. Typically human.

With a sigh, I followed the shadow of the tower down to the ground, relinquishing my bird's-eye view. I kept my form all air – easier to float and move. The shadows were plentiful, a welcome coolness in this place of dry, radiating heat. Shadow of a cart. Shadow of stable. Ah, here we were. Shadow of a girl.

Standing in someone's shadow . . . it is not as good as being within their mind (my brother, likely, has perfected this magic: it involves fire, to be certain) but it does give good access to a semblance of their form. A little dark, perhaps. But I find that angle to be just as truthful as anything cast in the best of light. There she was, rubbing at a sore spot on her ankle, wearing a shapeless dress of what looked like sackcloth: scratchy, coarse, beige. Her hair covered with a scarf of similar material, just a lock of darkest brown curling out over her forehead. Even now, she tucked the hair back, hiding it away. I slipped into the depths of her shadow, nestled down. She gave a little shiver, as if she felt my presence, shook it off, and continued with her tasks. I would get to know her now.

The girl was still just 'the girl': she had never been given a name by anyone who had the right to do so. And so, though she was called many things, she knew herself only as the girl. Yet, for all that she was still the girl, memories of the island – the very sense that it had ever been real – had faded away from her. Only certain lingering senses remained indelible: that there was a boy, who matched her, who was meant to be at her side. That there were forces that could be wielded by a red-eyed man; forces that were far beyond her and which she did not wish to meddle with.

The girl had lived in many places and had many owners. Some saw her as a girl and some saw her as an animal and mostly she preferred not to be seen. There in her shadow, I could sense some of her deepest memories, pooled inside of her – dark, oily spots. I sank into one, found myself what must have been years ago – the girl no more than eight or nine. Her owner, a man with a grey beard that hung to his chest. He owned her and half a dozen other child slaves and hundreds upon hundreds of sheep and goats. The girl lived with the flocks and on this day, the day when the shadow-memory pooled, the girl was helping to steer the flocks into a pen just outside some town's walls. The sheep bleated and baah-ed and the girl coaxed and cajoled. A boy, slightly older, drove in some stragglers with a stick; he smiled at the girl as he passed. 'Good job,' he said, and she smiled back. When she smiled – oh, her face transformed. Her eyes, wide-spaced, seemed to turn up just like her lips did, a shy little look of happiness, as if she barely dared. She reached out and slipped her hand into the boy's and for a few moments, the two of them walked

134

together; I could feel what she felt. The gentle pressure of his fingers. The beat of her heart steadying, feeling less like a bird in a cage. She thought of him, almost, as a brother. He had protected her in the night, more than once, as they had slept with the flock in the field – scaring off predators both human and animal with his loud shouts and flailing stick. They had shared memories close-held. He, of a mother who loved him. She, of a brother who was her other half.

Ahead of them, the town walls rose up, the flocks grew denser. Men appeared, in striped robes and leather sandals, bearing long staffs with which they prodded and poked the sheep, sending them off to various pens. Rams over here. Yearlings this way. And then one man, their owner, with the straggly grey beard, waved his stick at them, as if they were sheep. 'You!' He gestured to the boy. 'Get over there.' He pointed with this stick to where the goats were being penned up. 'And you.' He reached for the girl, grabbing her by the back of her tunic and half-dragging her towards another man, this one beardless. 'Here's the one I'm selling,' her owner said. 'Eh? Two ewes?' The girl felt the men's eyes on her, heard those words – two ewes. Her worth, her value, herself. Then she heard a wordless roar, and turned in her owner's grip to see the boy running towards her, his face contorted, holding back tears, his roar a stream of *No, no, no*. But her owner merely released his grip on the girl's tunic, shoved her towards the beardless man, and – as casually as if he were swatting a gnat – lashed out with his staff, catching the boy on the side of the head. The boy crumpled to the ground, a *whuff* of dust rising up. The girl made one effort to get away, twisting in the arms of this new man, but he was too strong and carried her off. I felt the memory constrict, congeal, the shadow grow deeper and darker. This moment, locked away inside her – never love, it only hurts.

Yes, this was one lesson she had learned. And as I moved out of that shadow and into others, I saw that she had also learned early on, in her life off the island, that she was stronger than people expected her to be and so she learned to hide that strength. Anything useful must be hidden. Secrets were good. Secrets were all she had that were her own.

The house of her current owner smelled good. He was a spice trader. The rare and obscure lived in little vials in his shop (there was a trunk of oak, thick wood, with huge iron hinges and a massive lock – this held vials even more valuable, which couldn't be displayed on a shelf, though she wasn't certain they were spices). The more common were the girl's domain: sacks to be lifted and stacked, turned and tended to, kept in cool darkness, kept free of rodents and pests. Barrels of extracts, preserved in alcohol. Vanilla, her favourite, but others, too, mint and almond and citron, imbuing the air of the storeroom with richness and flavour.

She had been owned by this man for a couple of years and found him a master much like all her others. This man had the advantage of being indifferent. The girl slept with the donkeys, at the stable just outside the warehouse. She was treated similarly to the donkeys in other ways, by her master. A useful beast, capable of bearing burdens, could be beaten if disobedient. And she accepted this, could perceive that it was safer to be seen as a donkey than as a woman.

She had no way to know her age accurately and could only compare herself to other girls. But this was difficult, too. (Breathing in her shadow, I judged her to be thirteen or fourteen years old. A year or two shy of how old Bradamante was when I left her with that suit of armour.) She was taller than many of the other enslaved girls who would otherwise appear to be her age. But they, for all their small stature, were often more worldly than she was: more knowing . . . not smarter

. . . but more . . . womanly. They had ways of walking with their hips, ways of fashioning their hair, that, even as slaves, were designed to make men's heads turn. Her master had two such slaves who ran his household. One did the cooking. The other did the cleaning. They took their turns in the master's bed, too. The girl worked only with the spices, with the donkeys, with the merchants and their slaves, who came and went, bought and sold. She slept in no one's bed and had no bed of her own. The two women who served her master's house teased her, chasing her with pots of kohl and offering to paint her eyes (*you could be pretty!*). They called her stupid for not understanding their jokes about the master's bed.

The girl had none of this wisdom and didn't desire it. Her desire was to be invisible. Sometimes she dreamed of this. Of the long-ago island demon-man appearing to her, to apologize, to grant a single wish, and she would wish to be invisible. Not to disappear, but to move through this world unseen. Or not seen as what she was: a slave girl. Usable. Exchangeable.

She learned to make herself as invisible as possible: walk in the shadows, catlike. Talk as infrequently as possible. Never look directly at people. Do every task exactly as commanded. Watch and observe what others do and try to anticipate their actions. Never openly resist. She was very good at being almost invisible.

And thus she often got to remain in rooms, overhear conversations, that other slaves never would have been privy to. Hence her doubts about what the trunk in her master's shop held. She had been in there, cleaning the glass of the vials, dusting the shelves on which they sat, being nearly invisible, when her master had brought in other men, unlocked the trunk (the key on a gold chain around his neck) and opened a small clay jug. It was corked, the cork sealed over with wax, and he would pare this back with his belt knife or sometimes with the sharpened edge of his pinky nail. Pull the cork out, hold the jug to his companion, urging, *smell, smell*. Whatever it was brought a smile, always. A wary smile. Then two little cups, the jug split between (always a little more in the master's cup than in the guest's) and they would drink. Whatever it was, the brew was intoxicating. A sip, two, and soon a look of utter stupor covered their faces. He could be in there for an hour or more, only to emerge almost insensate, wide-eyed and disoriented.

Usually, the girl used this time to climb the city walls. She was friends with the guards up there, having earned their favour first with little paper twists holding peppercorns or cloves, and later by listening to their stories (she loved to listen and they loved to tell). Sometimes she would simply gaze out of the city, at the ramshackle spill of buildings beyond the wall, at how the horizon stretched away to somewhere else, and sometimes she would gaze in at the city, especially when the knights were training, riding through an obstacle course of barrels to dodge and hoops to spear, or hacking at each other with their swords. Sometimes the guards on the wall would watch with her, especially the younger ones, sharing her awe. But the older guards often chided her, telling her that the knights might look nice, but that sort of fighting was fancy and fake. Real fighting – dirty and scrappy and ugly – that's what the guard did. Never mind those knights.

The guards on the wall were lonely and bored and loved not only to tell stories but also – seeing that she was fascinated by the swordplay below – do little tricks with their belt knives. How to flip one up in the air and catch it by the handle. How best to stab someone to kill them in one blow (*though, little one, you won't ever need to do that,* they'd laugh). How to take away the knife of someone threatening you. And when they tired of showing her knife tricks, they taught her hand

138

wrestling: how to break a grip, how to wrench someone's shoulder loose, how to make a man lose his footing.

This she liked. That she could seize the hand of a man half again her size and, knowing the right point of leverage, the right balance of their bodies, send him to the ground . . . she would laugh and laugh and do it as many times as the guards would allow. *Little Mars* they called her, for her warlike interests. Another name that was not her own.

There had come a day when her master started bringing by a new string of men; men not interested in the spices, but in her. The master would call for her to come to his study and the men would gaze at her and ask the master some questions – how old? (he made up a number), where is she from? (he made up a place), has she known a man? (Never. The only truth he spoke.) The girl tried not to tremble, but she would have to be stupider than a sheep not to realize what was going on.

To beg would do no good. And to run away . . . the master had forbidden her to leave the city gates. She knew that if she did so without food, without money . . . either her master would soon fetch her back or she would be forced into a worse situation than the one she faced here. So she remained in service to the spice merchant, duly doing what he demanded. And this morning, as I watched her, she had been ordered to wait by the entry to the warehouse, and so she did.

At last, a delivery of spice came, carried by sullen mules guarded by sullen guards. The master watched as everything was unloaded and then invited the head of the caravan, a man named Ibrahim, into his study. The girl knew Ibrahim well; he had brought wares for years to her master's storehouse. She watched him enter and went to begin sorting the newly arrived spices into the bins and shelves where they belonged. But, no sooner had she entered the warehouse when she heard the master call her.

'Come, come. Now!'

Doggedly, she turned and went to his study.

'What do you think, Ibrahim?' the master said, grabbing her by her upper arm. 'What would such a girl fetch? You travel far and wide, you visit other cities? How much?'

Ibrahim gave the master a pained look. 'I deal in spices. Spices and occasionally mules.' He shook his head. 'Never in girls. Never in humans.'

The master waved a hand. 'There is good money.'

'The prophet says . . .'

'Bah! How about if you took her as a wife?'

'I have a wife already. And this girl is too young. She is useful to you, no? Why not keep her as she is?' Ibrahim looked at the girl, his eyes radiating as much kindness as he could extend. She dropped her gaze. Kindness was not to be trusted. People were not to be trusted. Slaves, she had learned long ago, came and went. A friend made on one day would be sold on the next. Better not to make friends.

'She is worth more this way. Any fool can put spices on the shelves.' The master stood and crossed to his locked chest, bending over to fit the key that he wore around his neck and unlocking it. He drew out coins of gold and silver, counting them on his desk, sliding them to Ibrahim. And then drew out the small jug the girl knew well, its cork sealed over with wax. He extended his little finger and, with the sharp edge of the fingernail, began to pick at the seal. 'Will you partake with me?'

Ibrahim shook a finger at the master. 'The prophet says . . .'

'The prophet! By his beard. A little is fine. That hadith speaks only against excess.'

Ibrahim sighed and began to scoop the coins into his purse.

'Begone,' the master said to the girl, and she bowed and

140

backed out of the room. It seemed only a moment later that Ibrahim was at her side as she worked in the storeroom.

'I had to unlock the door to let myself out,' the man said. 'He is fallen in a drunken stupor. Quite . . .' Ibrahim sighed. 'We all have our weaknesses. I left the key on his desk, but the room is unlocked. See that he isn't robbed while he's asleep.'

And with that, the trader walked away, off to the pens outside the city where his mules were kept.

See that he isn't robbed . . . the girl would never have another opportunity like this. As soon as Ibrahim had disappeared down the warren of streets, she crept into the master's study. He was, indeed, sprawled out on the table, a puddle of drool already forming beneath his mouth. She took the key, which sat on the table not far from his nose, and opened the trunk, extracted a handful of coins without counting them. Then she stood and exited, locking the door from the outside.

In the storeroom, she gathered jars of spices, wrapping them in old sacking and then tying them in a bundle to sling over her shoulders. She lurked by the city gate for a time until one of the guards from the wall was relieved of duty. As he went sloping off to the barracks, she ran up to him. I had been pooled in the deep shadow of the gate, comfortably cool, watching this scene, but as she ran off, I twisted to follow, spinning the air around me. It was a tight fit, to get myself into the meagre shadow that she cast, but it allowed me not just to hear her voice but also her thoughts.

'Little Mars,' he said, smiling down at her, when she drew near. 'Greetings to you.'

'Will you help me?' she said. At her side, her fingers clenched and unclenched, forming fists. Never trust. Never ask for help. These had been lessons she had learned long ago, at great cost. And now, she had to break that rule. 'Please,' she said, through gritted teeth.

I could tell how she hated those words, how much it cost her to utter them. She spoke the words of a beggar, a supplicant, and yet she held her head high. Despite the fact that she was my brother's, I liked her.

'What have you done now?' The guard shook his head, his voice light with indulgent amusement.

She widened her eyes into utter innocence, not the tear-blinking, pity-me expression that many might adopt, but a fiery sort of defiance. She lifted her chin and stared right into the guard's eyes. Nestled in her shadow, I could feel the righteousness course through her, hot enough to singe. 'Nothing. Truly. But my master wishes to sell me to a foul old man . . .' Her rage and, beneath that, her humiliation bubbled up. Now tears did form, of anger and frustration. She wiped one eye, the other, swallowed hard.

'What would you have me do? By law . . .'

'I know,' she said and her voice was steady. 'I would ask you to give me a fair chance. Would you give me the uniform of a guardsman? And a belt knife?' She held a clay jar full to the brim of cloves, no small treasure.

The man laughed, but stopped abruptly, seeing how grim her face was set. He breathed a sigh. 'Little Mars. If I had a daughter, and that daughter was taken from me, I would want her to have a fair chance.' He turned his head and spat. 'Meet me at the barracks; let us not be seen together.' He also took the cloves from her hand.

A few minutes later, she crouched behind the barracks, conveniently enough in a shaded spot where I could stretch out, and soon the guardsman appeared and offered her a messy pile of clothes. She took it, the weight surprising her. 'May God and his angels watch over you,' he said and turned away. She ran, quick as she could, to a spot near the latrines – a place where few lingered, she knew – and unfolded what he had brought. The tan leggings the guardsmen wore, the dark blue tunic, the blue burnoose, and a black sash to tie around her waist. Hurriedly, she put it all on.

It was a profound transformation to behold. In her attire as a slave, she had worn a simple caftan, a shapeless garment, with her head completely uncovered – a mark, I perceived, of her low status. Now, though, the guard's clothing gave her a new shape: leggings that delineated the shape of her calves, a tunic that came to just above her knee, belted with the sash. And the burnoose that she wound around her neck and head, covering her hair and the lower half of her face. She was both revealed and concealed.

I watched her admire the knife the guard had given her. As long as her forearm, sharpened to a wicked edge, it was almost as good as a sword. She held it, unsheathed in her hand, testing its weight and balance. I would have liked to creep closer and get inside her mind once more. Who was she thinking of? Who did she want to stick in the ribs? But the shade kept me near the wall of the latrine and at this angle of the sun, the girl cast no shadow. She sheathed the knife and hung it from her sash before carefully secreting the coins she had stolen from her master in her boots and the inner fold of her sash, keeping just a few in her palm.

A look left, a look right, and she finally left her spot by the latrines. Shadow to shadow, I followed her – funny, we took nearly the same path along the streets until we arrived at the market. There, she purchased dried fruit, hard bread, a water flask, a flint. She bought cheese and olives, too, and ate these in a cool pool of shade not far from the gate. And then she waited until near sunset, waited for that moment of confusion when the detail of guards changed, when the darkness loomed, when tired men want to push into the city and hungry men want to rush out, just as the gate is supposed to clang shut. In the midst of this crowd, she slipped through, out of the gate, beyond the walls, into her first night of freedom in many years.

The girl took measured steps along the road; she must have known that to run would draw attention. Yet even from the shadows, I could sense her tension, her desire to flee. She trudged on, head down, reaching the first rise of land and then turned her head over her shoulder and spat – a big, phlegmy gob – back at the city walls. If I could have laughed, I would have – a shadow can't even wheeze, though – that defiance! It made me think of Bradamante and her stubborn will. I couldn't decide, as I watched her walk along, whether the two, upon meeting, would be friends or enemies. Then I caught myself in this thought. What foolishness, Melissa. We, I, had set it up so that they were opponents, could be nothing but foes.

The girl made it hardly two days' walk out of that dusty city when the first thief attacked her. He lurked in the shadows of some rocks that lay jumbled on the side of the road and moved as if the shadow would also conceal his sound. It didn't. I, innocent observer, watched from those same shadows. By rights, I should have been rooting for the thief; if this girl was dispatched, then my twins would have an easier go of it. But I couldn't root for him. He was a man of middle years, with grey in his patchy beard. He wore a beige robe, the same colour as the sand, with a hood that cast his face in darkness. He lurked by the rocks until the girl had passed and then stepped out – he stood head and shoulders taller than the girl and swung a club the length of his arm, aiming a blow to take her out at the knees. But she easily dodged – a lightning-quick move – and let his momentum carry him past her. The man stumbled, his heavy club hitting the dirt of the road, and the girl stepped behind him, driving the dagger through his robe and between his ribs. The man went to his knees; the girl pulled the dagger out. Dark blood stained the beige of the robe. A gurgle and the man went face-first into the dust.

I studied the girl's face. Was she bloodthirsty? Was she horrified by what she had done? Her lips were set in an even line, though her chest rose and fell with heavy breathing. Her wide-spaced eyes darted over the rocks where the thief had hidden, and her fingers clenched the dagger. Stillness. Just the soundless seep of blood into sand. Then, a crow crying far above as it circled. She knelt, wiped the blade clean on the dead man's robes and rifled his pockets. All I could see on her face was efficiency – the need to do this, the desire to be far from this place, and perhaps a grim sort of satisfaction: she was glad to know she was capable of such violence, though it didn't bring pleasure. For a moment, she rocked back on her heels, squatted by the corpse. I longed to squeeze myself out of the shadow and settle into a long talk with her, help her form an understanding of this moment, of herself . . . but, no. She was my brother's. His to ignore, his to neglect, his to allow to develop on her own. Horrible.

She pushed herself to her feet and trudged on, pausing on the top of the next rise to look back. Crows were already worrying at the flesh of the thief's face. She shivered, though it was not cold. Down the other side of the hill, another pile of rocks awaited. Would it too house a thief? How many dangers would she encounter on this road? I could see the calculations in her eyes, the simple arithmetic: one girl, alone on the road. Many dangers. She hurried to the rocks, sought out their shadows. The two of us there, almost merged in the darkness. I, a shadow, watching, she, unwrapping her burnoose, taking out the knife. Without pause, she sawed off her hair in rough motions. The dark strands that had once stretched to the middle of her back now hung raggedly around her ears. She took off the robe and shook all the stray hair from it, shook the dust of the road as well. As she ran her hand across her scalp, a small smile curved her lips, and her eyes lost some of their keen focus, as if she were looking at something just beyond the next hill. She was, I imagined. She was looking towards her future and, perhaps for the first time since leaving the island, believing it might be better than the present. And then, the moment passed, and she wrapped the tan robe around her shoulders, tied the black sash around her waist to keep the robe closed, and coiled the burnoose around her face, so that only her eyes peeked out. She cleared her throat and tried her voice. 'I am . . .' Coughed, pitched her voice lower.

'I am . . .' Nodded. That gruffness would do. She did not finish the sentence, but took to the road again.

She rode in the back of a cart for part of a day, grateful for a break in walking during the heat. The road went on and on. Her eyes darted between the near hills and the far hills. Flocks of sheep grazed in the mid-distance. A huddle of buildings marked a dusty farm. I rolled along in the shadow of the cart, longing for the deep green of a forest, for a pool of water. All was brown and grey and yellow and sere. But the girl seemed entertained. Merchants and farmers made the road a lively route, calling out greetings and swapping news as they passed. The girl watched them closely, bird-bright eyes studying the wares they had packed on top of donkeys or stacked in carts. When they reached a walled town, the girl drew her burnoose even tighter, and stayed close to the cart, helping the merchant she'd been travelling with unload bags of grain. Even here, close to the gate and walls, the crowds of the city pressed up against them; vendors selling skewers of meat, flat rounds of bread, skins of watered wine. I could see curiosity and anxiety warring within the girl. How she looked at the crowds, fingers twitching; might she hope to lose herself in their midst? But in the end, she helped the merchant load more sacks onto his cart, and then took her place among them. They rode until sunset, when they made camp in the cart's shadows (conveniently close to me). The girl helped the merchant unhitch the donkeys. For a time, the two of them worked in companionable silence and the merchant, a thin man with very long arms and prominent ears, brought out bread and cheese and olives as the girl made a small fire. Then the merchant said, as he handed over a share of the food, 'Have you heard the story of the phoenix and the carpet?'

I hadn't seen the girl smile in such a way since she'd been with her brother. 'Please,' she said, her voice husky. 'I love stories.'

Three days they travelled together. The merchant told stories each night – some the same as I'd told my twins, others I'd never heard before (I took mental notes, to carry back to Ricardetto and Bradamante). Then, when they were camped on a hillside, within sight of a city's walls, the merchant finally said to the girl, 'Now it's your turn. Tell me a story.'

The fire burned before them, casting flickering light. The girl was silent, and I felt the silence might stretch a while, so I hopped from one shadow to the next, wavering and leaping, an echo of the fire's own movement. It was, in its way, a sort of dance, a kind of freedom within form. And then, just when I thought the merchant might give up and go to sleep, the girl said, 'Once, on an island, far out to sea, there lived a demon . . .' and she began to tell the story of my brother – his magics, his powers, the spells he cast to call down lightning, to tame lions. I quit my dancing and settled in the shadow nearest the girl, watching her mouth move, how she paused now and then, tongue settling against lips, to think of what phrase she wanted. The telling wasn't artful; it lacked cadence and a voice of authority. But the story was deep, expansive, beautiful. And it was only as she concluded – the demon vanishing in a cloud of smoke that he had conjured – that I realized she had told the story of the island, of my brother without once ever mentioning herself or her twin. What a strange girl.

Another day's journey brought the two of them to a city – not a village, not a walled town, but a city proper. It sat at the convergence of trade routes and, in a land marked by dryness, it possessed several reliable and sweet wells. As the merchant and girl approached the city's gate, I floated through various shadows to get a sense of the place. So different from the glens and river valleys my twins had grown up in; so different from the lush tropical island of this girl's youth. The land she had been enslaved in was sere, beige, dusty; this city was no different. Yet, for all that the dome of a mosque marked the skyline rather than the steeple of a church, for all that the women wore veils over their faces and the men had turbans perched on their heads, there was not so much that was different. After all, they were humans, separated from each other by a stretch of salt sea, and a couple of hills. Here, a market square, where many of the same goods could be found in baskets and sacks. The men here curled the ends of their moustaches, but otherwise their beards were similar to Duke Aymon's. They wore sandals, not boots. Prized camels as well as horses. But they cursed donkeys in a similar fashion. And that's where the girl left the merchant, cursing his donkey. She said a farewell and joined the stream of travellers flowing into the city. Her eyes darted up to the dome of the mosque, down to the wide gutter, clogged with waste – waiting for a distant rain to wash it clean. She wrinkled her nose at a dozen smells and made her way to the market square.

There, she bought a handful of nuts and perched on a sunny wall – I pooled in the shadows beneath – cracking the nuts with her teeth and watching the people pass by. Clever girl: observe now, that you might blend in later. The girl had lowered her burnoose to eat the nuts, spitting the shells out into the street. Only a few women went by and these practically scurried, paying the girl no more than a cursory glance. With their heads uncovered and clothed in plain caftans, I took these to be servants or slaves. I noticed, too, that the girl studied the women with extra care. Noted their bare feet, noted the bruises on their cheeks. Noted how quickly they moved compared to the leisurely gait of many of the men. I saw, too, how the girl tensed when the richer men – those who had silken robes and fingers heavy with gold rings – came too close. For the most part, men filled the streets. Men in flowing robes with embroidery. Men in tunics belted around the waist. Men with their hands on the hilts of curved daggers. Men with baskets of bread on their heads. The girl eyed each and every one, and I wondered what went on in her mind. My Bradamante, let alone my Ricardetto, were easy to read – their eyes and faces clear maps of their thoughts. But this girl was guarded, and I feared that my twins would be easy prey to her.

I thought I could make a fair surmise, though perhaps I am just assuming her thoughts to be close to my own. There was no question that this city kept its wealthy women sequestered and its poorer women enslaved, or nearly so, by the weight of their work. It is true that, unlike where my twins lived, I'd seen no women burned alive here. But it certainly was a place where, if one had a choice to make, one would choose to live as a man, or a boy. And so, I thought, the girl's mind was turning over similar ideas. (When I ruled, I would be certain that this was among the first perceptions and hierarchies to change: a woman shouldn't have to be like a man to be judged competent. There were far higher standards to be reached for. If only mortals would allow themselves to be nurtured in such directions.)

At length, finished with her nuts, the girl hopped down and wove her way through the market square. I shared an edge of shadow with a dove and caught bits of her conversation as she approached each stall and shop in turn. 'Need a helper?' 'Can I be of use?' 'I am good with sums.' But each vendor turned her away, and with each rejection I saw the girl's shoulders slump further. At last, she turned her steps towards the city gates, where four guardsmen stood. She approached the man with a sash across his chest – a sign of rank.

'Sir,' she said, bowing low. 'How might I join the guard?'

'And who are you?' the man asked.

'They call me Mars,' she replied, making her voice husky and low.

The captain laughed. 'You are rather small for that name. Where do you hail from?'

She had looked the man in the eyes, but now lowered her gaze. 'My parents died in a storm. A tree crushed our house. We herded sheep in the hills.' She gestured vaguely to the lands beyond the gate.

'And why would I take you to be a guard?'

'I am good with a knife. I am strong and young and brave.'

'And modest.' He laughed again.

'Modesty is knowing one's abilities and being honest about them,' she replied.

'I have no need for a guard. Particularly one so small and young as you. But God preaches kindness, particularly to orphans, so a kindness I will bestow. You may come and train with the guard, Little Mars, each morning as soon as dawn prayer ends. We will see what you can do.' He spoke to her with a hand on the hilt of his sword, the other hand with the thumb tucked into his thick leather belt. He wore a dark blue tunic that reached down to his knees, and leggings beneath that once might have been white but were now grey. He looked much like the guards in the town where she'd laboured for the spice merchant, and I could tell by the look in her eyes that she longed to prove herself to him, as she had to those other guards. But she merely bowed low again and hurried away.

Back among the merchants, she sought out those who were itinerant, begging to sleep under their cart in exchange for help with loading (the merchant she had arrived with had already departed). Or for a bowl of food if she carried water for their donkey. A few took her offers of help and she had a bowl of soup to warm her before curling up to sleep in the hay of a donkey's stall. I perched in the rafters, no shortage of shadows for me, and watched her sleep. Even in slumber, she kept her hand on her knife. Now and then, a noise would wake her, but she never started up, only peeled one eye open. Clever. Or, not just clever, but trained by the world to caution.

The caution paid off. In the middle of the night, a man slipped inside the stable, a bag slung across his back, a pointed stick in his hand. He entered, waited, jabbed at the straw piled near the door. The girl awoke and, quick as a spark from a flint, was up and behind the man, knife at his ribs. I could feel her own heart, pounding so much it almost moved the shadow I hovered in . . . and the man's heart racing even more. He gave a frightened squeak.

'What are you doing?' she said, her voice low. She'd seized his arm, given his wrist a savage twist, the sharpened stick clattering to the floor. I heard a small tremor in her voice, as if she were scared, but forcing herself to calm and quiet.

'What are you doing?' the man said in reply.

'Sleeping.'

'Catching rats.' Their words tumbled over each other. She released his arm and he shook his hand out before reaching down for the stick. I noticed the girl did not sheath her knife. But then, a nearby pile of straw emitted a squeak and the man, forgetting the knife that threatened him, plunged his pointed stick into the straw. The squeaking stopped. The man drew the stick out, swung his bag around, and deposited the carcass within. 'I am the city rat-catcher,' he said. 'Two coppers a tail.'

'Do you need an assistant?' she replied.

He smiled, and in the dim light, she could barely make out yellow teeth beneath his stringy moustache. 'Indeed, I do. Particularly one who moves as quietly as you.'

And so she learned to catch rats. In daylight, the rat-catcher looked eerily like his prey: patchy grey whiskers on gaunt grey cheeks. Ears that sprouted grey hair as well. A mouth that twitched and a nose that tilted just a little up. Close-set eyes beneath bushy grey brows. He could whistle very well. Like the other men of this city, he had two types of robes that he wore. One, for festive occasions, or going to the mosque: it was white as could be, with embroidery on the neckline, the cuffs, and the hem, of vines and clusters of grapes. The other, for everyday, a beige-grey robe with many patches. The girl had just the set of clothes the guard had given her, a bit too big (though she was still growing). She belted the knife around her waist every day, but kept it within the robe, carrying instead a sharp stick just like the rat-catcher. The two of them spent hours together yet spoke very little. One had to be quiet when catching rats, and when he wasn't catching rats, the rat-catcher was still inclined to be taciturn. This suited the girl, who did not want him to know she was a girl. Silence would protect. And if it did not, then her knife would.

There are many ways to kill a rat. Poisoned barley worked well. The catcher fashioned traps, too, laying bait to lure the vermin. At times, a home or warehouse would be so infested that they could kill the creatures with little sharpened sticks that served as spears. Whatever the method, after they had gathered their quarry, the rat-catcher, whistling all the while, would carefully skin each carcass, saving the tail to present to the customer to earn their payment.

So each day went, and each morning, the girl would muster with the guard and follow them in their training. With spears. With bows and arrows. With short swords and maces.

They teased her for being small. They teased her for being young. For the smooth skin of her face. For how little she weighed. She let them tease her – better that they think her a stripling boy than that they suspect she was a girl. She bared her teeth at them in a grimace that was not quite a smile, and challenged them to wrestle. She lost a few times, but threw down several men who weighed twice as much as she did. They teased her a little less. Watching her (I grew particularly fond of a shadow by the stables), I thought of Bradamante, missing my girl. The two of them had a similar sense of innovation. They knew the forms, the style, the rules, and they knew when it was better to break them. And both of them . . . so stubborn. The girl moved through the exercises with her teeth gritted. Exhausted, scared, she pushed all this away and, morning after morning, proved herself to these men.

She differed from Bradamante in many other ways, one of them being that she didn't delight in displaying herself. She kept a burnoose wrapped around her face, pulled up over her chin and nose, even when the wind didn't kick up sand and grit. The others thought she was ashamed of her beardless face;

that was fine. She grew taller. Stronger. The rat-catcher was never short of customers and so they ate well. She was quiet, wanting to hide the unavoidable treble of her voice. Most of the other guards gave her a wide berth, bothered by her strangeness; that was fine, too. I paused at the memory of one evening – there was a lovely sliver of shadow, cast by a just-sprouted marigold, that I could not resist. The rat-catcher had readied a meal and brought a bowl to the girl. She set aside the reeds she had been weaving into a trap and took the bowl. 'My thanks,' she said. They both bowed their heads in prayer (I was not close enough to hear what they asked for, nor whom they prayed to. I suppose such things are private, even to me?).

The rat-catcher brought a spoonful of lentils to his lips, blew away the steam. 'Why do you insist on being a guard?' he asked. His nose twitched, just a little rat-like, making his stringy moustache quiver.

The girl did not meet his eyes and shrugged, her voice low as she answered. 'I don't know. I just want to . . . belong.'

'Rat-catching is a solitary trade,' the rat-catcher replied, swallowing his lentils. He pressed his enquiry. 'You say you want to belong, but . . . I don't intend to be cruel, but . . . they don't like you. Most of them don't. You are good – better than they are and they resent you.'

The girl's mouth twisted in a strange amalgam of emotion: pride, fear, hope, anger. 'I know,' she said huskily. 'But I need . . .' She set her spoon down on the table and looked around the room where they lived. A pile of reeds waiting to be woven into traps. Little bottles and jars that contained the makings of poison. Two straw pallets with blankets neatly folded on each. It was almost cosy. 'I know I sound mad.' She tried to laugh. 'Half-crazy at least. But I need to know how to fight. I have to. It is a . . .' She clenched her fist. 'A need. To feel safe. To feel *right*.' She shook her head. 'I can't explain.'

The rat-catcher spooned up more lentils and nodded as he chewed. 'Perhaps it was written for you, in your stars.'

In the slender shadow of the marigold stalk, I shivered, feeling the truth of his words.

And so I kept watching her, letting the days and months spool by quickly. Season turn to season. I had no way of knowing her exact age – but she began to look about the same size as my twins had been when I left them. And so it was inevitable that I would compare them. Watch her fight and imagine her grappling with Bradamante. Or, the stars save me, crossing swords with Ricardetto. This girl lived on the margin of life; would her sufferings, would my brother's neglect, be an aid to her? Would the care and breeding I had bestowed on my twins be to their ultimate advantage, or would it weaken them . . . make them soft? No . . . I knew my twins, though coddled and cosseted, were strong. When the time of their trial came, they would rise to it . . . I was (almost) sure.

In the spring of that year, she finally earned a position with the city guard. That meant a leather jerkin, leather leggings, a coat of mail. These would be worn only if the city came under attack – which seemed unlikely to the girl. For their usual rounds of walking the city streets, keeping a lookout for thieves and rowdies and trouble-makers, the guard wore no armour. But she delighted in the heavy leather gloves that could be tucked into her red sash, a curved sword to wear at her side, and a deep blue cloak to wear to keep off the ever-present dust. It was easy for her to blend in with a uniform, to feel that no one could see her for who and what she was. A liar. A runaway. A girl. A killer.

I watched her don the uniform, saw how it made her stand taller, prouder. Yet she still kept to herself. The barracks in which she now lived with a dozen other young men were tight quarters, and she had to mind her movements, her words, carefully. One of the men played the oud and sometimes in the evening, they would listen to his songs. Another of the men fancied himself a poet and would often recite his verse; the girl didn't always care for the flowery language, but it kept her alert on the long nights of sentry duty. To her, best of all were the guards who liked to tell stories; one of the older men, Nafeez, so old that he was no longer much use as a guard, would tell tales of djinn and giants and sea monsters while they sharpened their blades or patched their cloaks and leggings. The girl listened in awe; she loved stories for the way they transported her, allowed her to escape the worry of the moment, the heat and the dust and the fatigue. The way they allowed her to imagine that a very different world, one that seemed entirely impossible, might, in fact, be possible.

In the summer of that year, as the sun scorched and the stench of the city thickened, a pavilion was erected just beyond the city walls. Tiered benches for viewing, a broad expanse of canvas stretched over a raised platform to provide shade. Rope was strung to demarcate a span of dirt, and boys were hired to remove every stone, twig, and tussock of grass. 'What's happening there?' the girl asked.

The others scoffed at her ignorance. 'The tourney! The festival! The fair!' they told her and then set teasing aside to regale her with stories of past years' fairs. They talked about wrestling matches and contests with the bow and arrow and how jugglers came and merchants of all kinds and acrobats and also, knights, who would put on shows of jousting and swordplay, and new poems would be recited.

The city guard stepped up their patrols; the captain explained that the fair meant more pickpockets. More fights. More need to be vigilant. The girl, out on the city walls one evening with Nafeez, the oldest of the guards, stared down at the growing sprawl of the fair. She could see merchants, wares spread on blankets before their tents, and women hurrying, laden with jugs of water, and men – nobles or knights – wearing silky jackets and plumed hats, swords dangling from their waists as they rode their massive horses. The crowds parted to let them through. 'Why do we need to worry about the fair, if they have knights to guard down there?' she asked Nafeez, her eyes tracking the progress of one particularly gaudy specimen of noble (a scarlet jacket; a yellow-plumed hat . . . Ricardetto would have loved it).

Nafeez chuckled, hawked a glob of phlegm. 'Don't let their swords fool you. Knights aren't there to keep order. Quite the opposite. They'll start more fights'n anyone. Haughty bastards.' He hawked some more phlegm. 'Course, they are fun to watch, when they have contests at the fair.'

The girl scowled down at them, her hands gripping the gritty stone of the wall. 'But you tell stories about knights, Nafeez. You make them sound so . . . noble.'

'Ah, my boy. Those are stories. Stories are play, fantasy. That's the only place knights are good and noble. In real life? The true fighting is done by us.' And he pounded his fist against his chest.

'Careful there, old timer,' another guard called out. 'Don't hurt yourself.'

Nafeez called out a gentle curse. And the guard laughed in response. The girl, still staring down at the knights, allowed a small smile to lift her lips. (I knew, I thought, what she was feeling . . . a sense of belonging. A sense of being good enough. How precious that must be to one like her.)

That following morning, when she rose from her bunk in the barracks, she could hear music rising up from the tents below and found her gaze straying often towards the pavilion

157

as she wondered what went on down there. 'Will you enter?' said Nafeez, who was cleaning and polishing his boots (I had noticed that the boots and the swords were the prized possessions of these guardsmen – what distinguished them from the men of the city, who wore sandals and curved daggers, though many of the men were richer than the guards would ever be. Status . . . humans make so much of it) as he sat outside the barracks.

'Enter what?' the girl asked.

'The contests?'

The girl tipped her head to the side. 'I hadn't considered it. Will you enter?'

'I am too old. But *you* are young. And good at wrestling. You might claim a prize there. I've seen you throw men twice your weight.' Nafeez nodded. 'Or archery. You do well with a bow.'

She smiled a small smile, ducked her chin at the praise. 'Thank you,' she said, making her voice gruff. 'I might do that.'

They looked out over the city together. She looked up at him, a little tender youth left in her voice, yet. 'Have you known any famous archers? Could you tell me one of their stories?'

'I always have time to tell a story,' he said. 'Do you know of Abu Talhah?'

She shook her head and listened to the tale.

The next morning, trading her guard uniform for a plain tan robe and leggings, she belted on her knife. In the shadows of the barracks, she shook out the long white (now almost beige) scarf that she'd carried with her from the spice merchant's house – the single token of her life as a slave. Then she wound it carefully around her head twice, around her neck twice.

She plucked and pulled at the fabric so that it could come up to her jawline, over her ears, but not get in the way of her sight. Such a balance, to cover the delicate parts of herself – the pieces that might give her away as female – but to still be able to hear and see and breathe. Survival should not be so difficult. She picked out a dozen of her best arrows – ones she had fletched herself – and selected two bow strings, tucking them inside waxed cloth.

She walked down to the tents and wandered through the rows, marvelling at glass beads, at shiny jewellery. Skirted an array of spices. I watched her as she moved slowly along the stalls; her gaze was appraising. What did she want? Bradamante might have been taken by the ribbons one merchant had laid out and certainly by the array of knives and daggers on another table. But this girl looked at everything and seemed to want nothing. That's dangerous. For me. Desire is the key to understanding anyone. She must want something.

The girl worked her way through the vendors and found herself at the edge of the pavilion and began asking about the contests, following where others pointed her until she stood before a plump man who was working the blade of his knife on a whetstone. He eyed the unstrung bow she carried, the quiver of arrows. 'Archery is the first contest.' He tipped his head to the side. 'Then a foot race. Then wrestling.' (The shadows here were sparse and distant; here the edge of a tent, there a donkey tethered to a stake. I couldn't stand being this far from the girl; her curiosity and excitement whetted my own, and so I slipped closer and closer until I flowed along the edge of her shadow, close enough to hear her thoughts as well as her voice.)

'Just archery,' she said in her false, deeper voice, and she pointed down the path to the open space beyond. When she arrived there, she found one other guardsman, a man a few

159

years older than she was, named Abdi, and a clutch of other young men. Most she knew by sight, if not name, from patrolling the city streets. But one boy stood out, a stranger, who wore a light blue caftan patterned with embroidery, an intricate pattern of interlocked swirls, around the edges. His eyes almost matched the colour of the fabric and he stared flatly out at the row of targets. He seemed to be nearly her age, without a whisker on his cheeks, and hair as dark and thick as her own. She sneaked glances at him from the corner of her eyes. The boy had skin lighter than hers, and long, delicate fingers.

The girl stood beside the other guardsman, Abdi. 'Who's that?' she whispered, tilting her head in the direction of the strange boy.

Abdi shrugged and ran his fingers over his chin (it had lately sprouted a few dozen whiskers, of which he seemed unduly proud). 'Who knows? Many travel with a fair. The children of merchants, urchins who do odd jobs . . .'

The girl saw the stranger's shoulders go back, the quick snap of his head in their direction. His nostrils flared and he lifted his chin at them, every inch of his body radiating arrogance and anger. In two steps he had closed the distance and stood so near Abdi that their chests almost touched. The stranger quivered with rage, but the guardsman stood in stoic stillness (a posture they had all learned through days of drill). 'I am no son of a merchant. And no urchin,' the boy said – and he was a boy, his voice still light, with just a trace of hoarseness. 'I am a squire to a noble knight, Khalid, who will joust this afternoon, I'll have you know.'

Abdi made a mocking bow, a hand pressed to his chest (though I could see that he had curled his thumb around his fingers in what was a rude gesture in this region). 'My pardon,' he said, sarcasm thick in his voice. 'May you do well in the archery.'

The squire gave both of them a hard look. 'I hope I get a chance to teach you a lesson. I'd challenge you to wrestle later, but I must attend my knight.' He stalked away.

Abdi spat in his direction. 'Nobility. Knights. They think they are better than we are. But who does the real fighting? And who jousts for play?'

The girl considered this. She thought of what Nafeez had said about stories and real life. She liked stories – enjoyed how they transported her to other places; enjoyed how, in telling her own, she could reshape the world – and didn't want to believe that all of them were untrue, but she also liked the idea of the guard – of herself – being the true protectors, the ones of honesty and virtue. She shrugged as the boys and men around her quieted. The plump man stood before them and recited the rules. 'You must shoot from behind the rope. I will call each shot, and you must release at that time, so there is no discrepancy in wind. Five arrows. Then we tally the score.'

I watched her pull her scarf tight about her neck, making sure it covered the lower half of her face. I could feel how nervous she was. Not about this contest, in particular, but about moving through this world. Fear of being revealed. Fear that she would never belong. Fear that she had no place. This could work to my advantage. Fear gave one a momentary burst of energy, but over time it left one weak. She would worry away her strength. The imagined horror would eat at her. When would she be found out . . . what would they do to her when they did discover the truth?

The girl jogged to claim a target. It was a circle, painted in concentric colours. White, yellow, green, red. Each band indicated a point value – more points the closer to the red centre. On either side of her, the men and boys were pulling back the sleeves of their robes. She did the same, rolling the wool tightly so it wouldn't interfere with her draw. She took a deep breath. Another. She stared at the target and stilled herself. She imagined putting an arrow into that red heart. She felt her fingers release, heard the twang of the string. She took another breath. It helped her to imagine things before they happened. Helped to bring her stillness and certainty. Helped to make her calm and ready.

Around her, the other men rustled as they prepared their gear; she heard one of them laugh, another scuffle the sand at his feet. She took out her strings and fitted one to her bow, testing its pull and tautness. Then came the call from the official. 'Nock! Pull! Release!'

The commands came faster than she liked; she had barely drawn the string to her ear, barely aligned the arrow tip with the red centre, when she had to let it fly. Usually, she preferred to take another breath, say a small prayer. But the shaft was released; it sliced the air and landed with a thunk in the wood. Green. And again the commands came, 'Nock! Pull! Release!' Green once more. By the third arrow she was used to this faster cadence, had aligned her breath with the commands, and her last three shots landed in the red.

Young boys ran forward to each target and counted on their fingers. Then the official called for them to report. 'Six points!' the first boy chirped from where he stood at someone else's target.

If a contestant landed all five arrows in the red, they would earn twenty points. All five in the white, five points. Down the line the scores were reported. Ten, fifteen, three. Abdi scored nineteen. The girl eighteen. The blue-eyed squire sixteen. They each earned a small coin and a ribbon to note their achievement. The girl congratulated Abdi, while the squire inspected the tips of his arrows. 'There ought to be several rounds,' the squire said, smoothing the feathers of an arrow. 'Anyone can get lucky once.'

'Yes,' Abdi said. 'If we kept shooting all day, it might even happen to you.'

The girl gave a small laugh as the squire's cheeks flushed deep red.

'Come on,' Abdi said, tucking away his bow string and gesturing to the girl. 'Let's go spend our winnings.' And he turned on his heel and aimed towards the part of the fair filled with food stalls.

But before he could take a step, the squire had given him a vicious shove, sending Abdi to his knees. The girl helped her fellow guardsman up and then looked at the squire. Her voice dripped with disdain and venom as she said, 'Not only a poor archer and a poor loser. But a coward, to wait to attack until his back is turned.'

'I'll beat you bloody right now,' he said.

The girl clenched her fists, bared her teeth. But knew she couldn't fight him. Couldn't risk causing a scene and the head of the guard finding out. Couldn't risk, even, stripping out of her robe and scarf (which would get in the way in a fistfight) for fear of being discovered as a girl. 'Go away,' she said. 'I have better things to do than fight with the likes of you.'

The squire sneered at her, blue eyes flashing. 'Who's a coward now?' he laughed. 'Just as well. I have a knight to attend to.'

He pushed past them, his shoulder bumping in to hers. Abdi spat at the squire, his phlegm missing the mark, and then resumed brushing dust from the knees of his leggings.

'To think,' he murmured, 'when I was a boy, I wanted to be a squire. Or a knight. A noble . . .' He spat again, though the squire was long gone, and then turned to the girl. 'What did you dream of, when you were a little boy?'

Such a look came over her face. Longing, despair. Her lips quirked in a funny smile, and she twitched the scarf higher to cover whatever that expression would become. 'I used to dream of having a brother,' she said at last.

'You can borrow one of mine,' Abdi said. 'I have five.' And he threw his arm around her shoulder. 'Let's forget him, Little Mars. The world is full of arrogant idiots.' He gave a little laugh. 'They tend to cluster around knights. Rather similar to flies on dung. Let's go spend our winnings.'

The girl thanked him but went her own way. She watched the foot races, wandered through the merchants' stalls, bought a skewer of spicy goat meat and chewed it as she watched the wrestling. I could tell that she wished to join in; she winced and shook her head as the men made clumsy grabs for each other. Eventually, the girl wandered off, picking her teeth with the empty skewer, and found herself on the margin of a thick crowd. Worming her way through, she caught sight of the main pavilion, the stretch of flat ground. Then the blast of a horn, the crowd cheered, and hooves thundered. She barely got sight of a flash of a horse with a rider, before there was a screeching impact of wood and metal and more cries from the crowd.

She dodged and elbowed and moved about, finding at last a gap farther along, close to where the stables were. She stared at the scene before her, entranced, the scarf falling away from her face, so that I could see her mouth gape a little open, could see her crane her neck for a better look. For years now – back in the town where the spice merchant had owned her and here in this city – she had gazed from afar at knights. They had always been distant. And she felt, even now, a seething resentment. These nobles knew nothing of the toil and trouble of *lesser* people. Could not imagine a life like hers. And yet she was also entranced.

The knights wore suits of armour worked with gold, and polished so that they were almost too gleaming to behold. A few had painted their armour, and all had painted their shields, with devices showing flowers, leopards, trees, spears . . . so many designs. But the girl liked the helms the best. Most wore a plain steel helmet, pointed at the top and pointed at the front of the visor. Some had decorated their helmets so they looked like the heads of beasts: fangs dripping blood, red eyes staring, even a few with horns protruding. She leaned against the railings that separated the crowd from the pitch. Where others around her hooted and clapped, she simply stared, her mouth a little agape. I could feel, in the depths of her shadow, a hint of what went on in her head. It wasn't greed, wasn't plain avarice and desire for that status. Far from it. But she did want . . . to be in that armour. To be protected, covered. Ah, yes, that made sense. She wanted to be untouchable. What a struggle, within this girl, twin desires that ran counter to each other: the desire to belong, to have a place and a family, and the desire to be invisible and out of reach.

This girl thought like a prey animal, ever on the lookout for the shadow of a raptor passing overhead. My girl was a predator, wasn't she? No. No, to be honest, she was not. She was a well-trained animal. If I may indulge in a somewhat lengthy metaphor I would say that this girl, my brother's twin, was like a feral cat. Cats are odd. They are simultaneously both predator and prey. They will stalk a mouse and in turn be stalked or chased. They must watch the world through both these lenses. My girl, Bradamante, was more like a wolf-hound. I had her on a good leash; she was trained to obey commands. But she was powerful, she was dominant. She knew no fear of predators. And that made her stronger, did it not?

The girl watched the jousts and chewed on the wood of her skewer, squinting up now and then at the sky. No doubt wondering when she ought to return to take her turn at the guard post. Two more knights rode out, this time with swords drawn instead of lances. She watched closely. She knew little of lances (though they didn't seem that different from the spears and pikes the guard sometimes trained with). But swords she did know. These knights fought with grace, their strikes fluid, shifting rapidly to a back-cut. They also fought with excessive flourishes, spinning the blades across their bodies. It looked pretty, but it wouldn't help in a fight.

From behind her, a hand landed on her shoulder, pulled her roughly around. 'It's you. I thought so,' said the blue-eyed squire from before, the one who had shoved Abdi. 'Are you ready for your beating?'

'I have no quarrel with you,' the girl said, though her hands clenched into fists once again. I could read the frustration of her face. She wanted to fight. She thought she could beat him soundly. But was it safe? Could she risk it? Oh, she hated to back down. Hated to seem weak.

'Coward.'

She lifted her eyebrows. 'Why would I fight you? What would I gain?' She gazed at him steadily, her voice calm (though I thought I could sense a smouldering fire within her . . . one that, given the proper fuel, would burst into flame). I could see now why her fellow guardsmen would find her unsettling. Men understand a quick temper. Men understand a loud mouth. Patience and silence – indications of self-control – are deeply troubling to them. (And to me. Good restraint and self-awareness . . . these indicate a level of mastery I would not expect from someone so savagely raised.) This girl could not easily be baited. She cocked her head to the side, her dark eyes staring right into the squire's blue ones. (Would Bradamante have such restraint? No . . . I knew she would not. And Ricardetto? Well, he'd either have told a story or joke to defuse the whole situation or abjectly apologized by now.)

'You're afraid,' the squire taunted.

'Not at all,' said the girl. 'But I have already beaten you today and see no need to do it again.' She gave a shrug and turned back to the jousting.

The hand landed on her shoulder again, pulled her around, and a fist swung towards her face. She ducked, bending her knees low, and shook off the grip on her shoulder. Then she ran a few steps forward and undid the sash at her waist, letting the quiver, the unstrung bow, and her robe fall to the ground. Better not to damage her equipment; better not to fight in a robe that he might grab onto.

The squire faced her, hands clenched into fists that he held level with his shoulders. She stood ready, arms loose at her sides, knees slightly bent. The squire waited, shuffling his feet. Then he seemed to lose his patience and leapt at her, fists flying. She stepped to the side, waited for the punch to pass by, and gently grabbed his arm, steering him in the direction his force already propelled him, then wrenching his arm at the last moment to send him into a flip. Up and over. He landed with a crash on his back. A moment. A groan. (I caught myself in this moment, cheering for the girl as she sent him flying. Cheering for her, when she ought to be my foe. How human I was becoming in my fickle emotions.)

'What are you doing to my squire?' a loud voice demanded. The girl turned and saw a knight, immense in his plated armour, helm under his arm, staring at her. His eyes were hazel-brown, catching the sunlight and showing glints of green and gold, and his face was flushed, his dark hair sweaty and flattened to his high forehead.

The girl straightened, gave the knight a level gaze. 'I beat him at the archery competition this morning. He challenged me to fight him. I said no, and he attacked me anyway.'

The knight crossed over to the squire, offered a hand. He

was tall and barely bent over, so that the squire had to reach up, strain a bit, to get the proffered assistance. The knight didn't take his eyes off the girl as he yanked (none too gently) the squire to his feet. The boy stood up and dusted himself off. 'It's not true,' the squire said. 'He attacked me from behind. Caught me when I wasn't looking.'

'You're a liar,' said another voice. This belonged to a large man. Even taller than the knight and, though he was dressed in a loose caftan – a creamy yellow colour sewn with a pattern of blue waves at the neckline – he commanded attention with his echoing voice. The girl shifted her gaze from the knight to this new man, took in not just his height, but his bulk, a thick chest and thick waist and massive hands. Took in his presence, which was not just his size and his voice, but the deep darkness of his skin; the girl was brown, a few shades tanner than many on the guard, but this man's skin was darker than any she'd ever seen. He met the girl's gaze briefly, his dark eyes blinking once as they met hers, and then returned his attention to the armoured knight. 'I watched almost the whole thing. That fellow tossed your squire into the dirt only after being attacked from behind, Sir Khalid.'

Sir Khalid, the knight in armour, curled his lip as he replied to the large man. 'Rami, have you nothing better to do than watch two squires squabble?'

The large man shrugged and laughed. 'I won my first match. I earned a little rest.' A small smile lifted his lips. 'You lost your first match, so you have to fight again, unless I am much mistaken?'

'I just unhorsed my second opponent. So we are even in the lists.' He turned away from Rami, and faced the girl again; her eyes darted between Rami and the knight. I could sense her question, her calculation: who to trust? And I suspected I knew her answer: no one. I shifted and swirled about in my little pocket at the edge of her shadow. 'You've bloodied my squire. Torn his shirt. You have to answer for this damage.'

The girl looked up at him. 'On my honour. He began the fight. I have nothing to answer for.'

'Your honour. That's worth nothing.'

The girl started back, as if slapped. 'I will fight you to prove that I am telling the truth. To show to you my honour, which you dismiss unjustly. God will not let a liar win.'

Sir Khalid looked around; a few men, servants and other squires mostly, had gathered to watch the argument. Khalid grinned as he met their gazes, clearly trying to win over the crowd. 'You! Will fight me?' And he laughed. A few of the watching men chuckled along with him.

'And win,' the girl said, bristling.

The large man, Rami, stepped forward. For all of his size, he moved with grace, not lumbering as one might expect. 'Allow me to adjudicate this fight.' He turned to the girl. 'Have you mail? A sword?'

'I have,' she replied.

'Then that is how you both will fight.' Rami faced the girl. 'You fight with your honour and your honesty on the line, boy. Sir Khalid.' Rami faced the other knight, spread his arms wide. 'What will you put on the line in exchange?'

Khalid shrugged, as if the matter were below his concern. 'Whatever this liar wants. Name it, for you shan't win it.'

'Your armour and your horse,' she replied.

Khalid laughed. Rami laughed, too, but quickly quieted down after a glance at the girl's serious face. 'Bold! Very well. In a glass's time. Right here.'

The girl scampered up to the city gate – for once the city was deserted, every inhabitant had already gone down to the fair – gathered her mail and sword, and began to descend to the fair again. I waited for her outside the gate, pooled in cool shadow; at length she emerged, her face wrinkled in worry, her teeth chewing at her lower lip. I felt that concern and, to my surprise, echoed it within myself. I should wish for her downfall! And yet, I wanted her to fight this arrogant knight and win. What was wrong with me?

The girl arrived in the designated spot with her mail and her sword. When she stood on the city ramparts for her turn at watch or walked the streets on patrol, this arms and armour – together with her sturdy boots and leather gloves – made her feel safe, like a real soldier. But now, next to the shiny plate and heavy helms, the thick wood and leather of shields, her weapons seemed puny. Rami, in his yellow caftan, watched as she strapped on the heavy shirt. 'No shield,' he observed. 'Then Khalid will forgo his to make it fair. I would give you mine, but if you aren't used to it, it would be a disadvantage rather than an aid. Better to fight just with the sword. It will be more pure. More exact.' He studied her as she swung her arms, limbering up. 'A member of the city guard?' he mused. She gave a little grunt of agreement. 'Few others use swords of that length. More like a long dagger. Better in close quarters and crowds.' He pointed to the weapon on her belt. 'A city guard. And you so young. I imagine you have a story?'

She grunted again. His voice, which had boomed earlier, now soothed, deep and melodious. But the girl continued on with her stretches. 'Ah,' said Rami, 'I'll not distract you more.'

Khalid emerged in his own mail shirt, greaves on his legs, gloves on his hands.

'Just the mail shirt. Leather gloves. No shield,' Rami ordered.

'What's this nonsense?' Khalid said.

'To make it fair. Or are you concerned that you can't fight without a shield? Without greaves?'

'Nonsense.'

Soon the two were identically outfitted. The girl had the round steel helm, visorless, of the guard, the curved blade she had carried and trained with for these past months. Khalid's squire helped him into his mail shirt, its links tightly woven, well-oiled and shining. The knight ran a whetstone along his blade, honing the edge. The rasp grated at my nerves (though I had no nerves in this shadow form, but still), a reminder that these were not bated blades. Surely that was his intent. The girl tugged her leather gloves tighter and waited as Rami walked to the middle of the clear patch of dirt among the tents and stables of the knights. The large man gestured for them to come near. 'Either of you may yield. Just cry out with that word,' Rami instructed. 'There are no points awarded for style or elegance. If you fall unconscious, I will call an end to the match, and declare you the loser.' The girl nodded, her eyes already on Khalid.

The knight lifted his chin to Rami. 'Get on with it, then.' He looked at those who had gathered, forming a rough circle around the cleared area: squires and grooms and servants. 'Who's betting on this boy, eh?' There were a few laughs. Khalid's grin broadened. 'The only question is whether it is one minute or two for me to win this fight.' The crowd laughed louder. The girl drew her sword, held it ready. Khalid did the same, adding, 'And whether I win by running him through or knocking him senseless. I can't decide . . .'

'Begin,' Rami shouted and then quickly backed away.

The girl heard their calls and jeers, but with a deep breath, she squared her shoulders and faced the man before her. I marked how her eyes traced his movements, watching his feet, gauging the length of his arm, how he bent his knees. Taking the full measure of him. (Just as I'd taught Bradamante to do.) After a few moments of circling, Khalid surged forward, striking towards her head. She jumped to the side; his blow had been so quick, much faster than what she was used to. She shuffled back, reset her blade. He struck again, and she met his blade with her own, the metal shrieking and scratching as they locked together, hilt to hilt. The girl pushed against him, then suddenly withdrew the pressure, twisting away and swinging her blade back, catching him on the shoulder.

But just as her blade landed, she felt a thumping impact to her lower back. Sir Khalid had managed a strike as well, and she stumbled forward. He'd driven the mail into her flesh; she could feel the blood start to flow, but nothing had broken, she thought. She steadied herself and faced him, satisfied to note that his shoulder was also bleeding. Again, he struck and she countered. She feinted and he spun. They each managed to hit each other, but dull strikes, nothing landing solidly. Her breath came heavy and quick now. Khalid seemed to sense her fatigue, and pressed his advantage, approaching her with little probing jabs, making her dance away, making her dodge and dart, and expend her energy.

Someone in the crowd called out, 'Look at him! Dancing all around!'

And another voice, 'Run him through!'

Tired, she stumbled just a bit and Khalid caught her, hard, with a strike to her upper arm. The mail bit into her flesh though her bone held; nothing cracked.

The fingers of that arm had gone numb, and it took all her strength to hold onto the sword. Khalid's eyes glinted, as he seemed to register her weakness. Her training had schooled her to retreat, to reserve her strength, and she shuffled in a slow circle, trying to steady her breathing. The crowd around her clapped in a slow rhythm, now and then hooting, calling for her blood. They hated her and they didn't even know her; she was just a nobody, a guard, a nothing.

Khalid's blade shot out in a low strike. Every ounce of

training – every manner of sword form I had seen in this era – called for the girl to retreat, turn the blade away, and circle to the side. It seemed to me that, for a moment, time slowed – a haze came through the air, as heat will do, making everything waver and shimmer. I didn't just see it; I felt it. A tremor, a shake, as if the earth itself were shrugging. And then the girl, ignoring all inherited wisdom, leapt forward, both feet leaving the ground, jumping over his blade. Mid-air, she shifted her sword from her right hand to her left. Khalid was entirely exposed as she brought the blade down, catching him on the side of his head, at the margin of his helm. The haze that had surrounded the girl disappeared. The shaking stopped. Gone, as suddenly as a dream upon waking.

He fell to the ground, his sword dropping from his hand, and the girl landed, catlike, beside him, sword in her left hand. She raised the blade, but paused as Khalid remained inert. She darted a glance to Rami, who held up a hand. 'Khalid! Rise now or forfeit.' The knight didn't stir. 'I declare you winner,' Rami said, pointing at the girl. But his words were nearly swallowed by the crowd, which, having held its collective breath for a moment, now surged forward to see if the fallen knight yet lived.

'He breathes!' one of them called.

The girl backed away, sheathed her sword, and tried to steady her own breath.

'Get some water! Wake him up!' came the calls from those who helped Khalid.

Then a louder, deeper voice. 'Take his armour! And someone bring his horse!' It was Rami, his words cutting through the babble. 'This young man has earned his prize.' His hand, fingers looped with rings, landed on her shoulder, then went to help her remove first the helm, then the mail shirt. She shrugged off the leather gloves she had worn and quickly wound her scarf around her head and face, using it to dry the sweat that had run down her forehead and neck. 'Well fought,' Rami said. He turned to where some men were bringing Khalid's horse over, a sable stallion that tossed its head with barely contained fury. The girl gave it a glance, scarcely believing that it was now hers. 'And the armour,' Rami said again, wading into the crowd of men.

The girl looked around for her robe, wanting the cover that it offered, no doubt. But before she could find it, something slammed into her back, driving her to the ground. She landed hard, taking the impact of the fall on her already numb right hand. Quick as she could, she rolled away, coming up on one knee, as she'd been trained. But she didn't make it to her feet; someone kicked her, hard, in the ribs, and she crashed to the ground again.

Dimly, she was aware of men shouting around her. She clutched one hand against her ribs and again tried to gain her feet. Off the ground; that was the most important thing. She had seen too many men stomped and kicked to pulp in brawls because they could not stay on their feet. A fist struck her, landing on her shoulder as she managed to get to a knee, then stand. But before she could get a clear sense of who was attacking her, they hit again, catching the side of her head. Her scarf fell away from her face, dangled from her neck. Now her attacker grabbed a wad of her shirt and tugged. She tried to pull herself away, to get free, but all that resulted in was a tearing of fabric, a noise that seemed impossibly loud even in the shouting and yells of the crowd.

'Enough!' Rami's voice bellowed. Whoever had been grabbing at her shirt let loose, the fabric going slack. But other hands held her shoulders, pinning her in place. 'This fellow won. He beat Khalid in a fair fight. The horse and armour are his. And anyone who disputes this will fight me next.'

A hush fell over the crowd. I waited, crouched in the shadows, coiled up. Would they tear her limb from limb? I both wanted that and I didn't want that. I didn't want to like this girl; she was my enemy.

No. *She* was not. My brother was. I liked *her*. And she reminded me so of Bradamante. The two of them might have been twins, in another life. What a strange mirror, what a strange symmetry. So similar, so opposite. What would happen when these two met?

The girl tried to wriggle free of the grip that held her. She wanted to cover up, find her robe and scarf. But a man's voice called out, loudly, right over her head, 'Don't look now, Rami. But your young victor isn't much of a man at all.' The hands that held her shook her shoulders hard. The crowd murmured, voices rose, calling, *It's a girl! Blasphemy! A girl! Kill her!*

The girl took one swift look around at all those men staring at her, seeing her bare head. Her torn shirt. Across from her, other men held Khalid's squire; it had been he who had attacked her and ripped her clothes. Then she turned her gaze to the ground, swallowing hard.

'I am looking,' said Rami. 'And I still see the person who felled Khalid in a fair fight. Girl or not. She won. And I stand by my words. The armour and the horse are hers. So is the honour. And if anyone would dispute this, they fight *me*.' He paused and looked around, giving each watching face a hard stare. 'Now, let her go.'

The hands on her shoulders clutched tighter for a brief moment, then released her with a shove, sending her stumbling towards Rami, who caught her by the arm. The crowd around them murmured and shuffled their feet. 'To my tent,' he said, his voice pitched low, just to her. He pulled her along beside him, cutting a way through the crowd.

* * *

Rami's tent smelled of leather and sandalwood; as the large man pushed her inside, she blinked a few times and then saw the coil of smoke rising from the dish of smouldering herbs. Sandalwood and frankincense. She hadn't smelled anything that good since she had worked for the spice merchant. The pleasant fragrance relaxed her for a moment. But just a moment. Then she snapped back to where she was and what had happened, seizing at her torn shirt and trying to tuck it together, then pressing her hand to her ribs, where one of Khalid's blows had landed. She glanced quickly around the tent; Rami stood by the entrance, tying the flaps shut. Elsewhere, the tent was tightly staked, barely a gap of daylight sneaking under the folds, not enough room for her to wriggle easily out (but, pleasantly, plenty of shadows for me to hide in).

Rami turned towards her, gestured at a pile of pillows on one side of the tent, near the smoking brazier of incense. 'Sit, sit.' He sighed. 'You have caused a stir. But it will die down. Or not. Depending on how things play out.'

'What do you mean, sir?' she said, gingerly lowering herself to the pile of cushions. I could see how she winced a bit, how her eyes jittered around; the effects of the fight starting to show.

'Just Rami.' He cocked his head, considering her. 'And your name?'

'They call me Little Mars.'

He laughed, a sound from deep in his belly. 'Fitting! In my native language that would be Marfisa. Most fitting!'

'I am glad you think so,' she said.

'And now, Marfisa, what do you intend to do?'

Rami fiddled with a large silver ring that encircled his thumb, spinning it over the knuckle, while his dark eyes – round and unassuming – stared at her. 'To be honest,' she said, 'I probably intend to run away. The word of . . . what I am will spread, quick as fire, and . . .'

Rami nodded. 'You have run before, no doubt. And you could keep running. But what if you stopped?'

'Here?' Marfisa cocked her head to the side. Her dark brown hair, shaggy and ear-length, still stuck in sweaty clumps against her forehead. 'They would kill me.'

'Ah!' Rami held up a beringed finger. 'They would try to. The trick is to manage it.'

She frowned. 'What do you mean?'

'I mean, if you let them be what they are right now, an angry mob, then, yes, they will kill you. But if you take the reins . . . if you are a knight, you can demand certain rules. Being a knight comes with a code and set of expectations. They would have to fight you one-on-one. Not attack from behind. Cede you riches if you win.'

'But I am not a knight.' She stretched out one leg, emitting a small groan as she did so. 'And I am not certain I want to be one. Better a member of the city guard. At least there is some degree of honour.'

Rami laughed, low in his belly. 'Perhaps there are one or two guardsmen with honour, I grant you.' He waggled his eyebrows. 'And perhaps one or two knights as well?' Then he pointed to the leg she'd stretched out. 'You're bleeding.' With a groan of his own, he pushed himself up from the cushions and seized a ewer of water and a basin from a table, placing them beside Marfisa. Then he lifted the lid of one trunk, another (the tent was nothing if not well-appointed, one might even say, cluttered), until he found a folded pile of fabric scraps, old and soft. 'Here. Clean that cut.' The girl took the cloths, but hesitated. 'I'll turn my back,' Rami said, and did so.

Marfisa eyed him as if still suspicious, but then shimmied

out of her leggings and began to clean the half-dried blood from her shin.

'You now have a horse. And a full suit of armour. It's too big, but the armourer will know how to adjust or will take it in trade. And you have a sword. And most importantly, you have courage and skill and speed.'

'A knight must be a noble. I'm just a member of the city guard. And not even that, any more.' She trailed off, dabbed at the cut once more, and then pulled her leggings back on.

The sounds of the crowd outside began to ebb. Rami poured from a silver pitcher into a matching silver goblet. 'I'm turning around,' he warned her and then offered the goblet. 'Water, with a little wine.' Marfisa took it and sniffed. Even I could smell the mixture: it was mostly wine, with a little water. She took a tiny sip. Rami poured himself a goblet and settled again on the pillows. The hair on his head was curled tightly and shorn close, and he scratched at his scalp before speaking. 'A knight must be made, that is all. No matter. I can make you a knight. You have more than earned it with your courage today.'

'How can you make me a knight?'

Rami smiled. 'I am a prince. My father, the king of Axum, may God keep him, sent me here to recruit good warriors to protect our kingdom.' He held out a hand. 'Will you join me?'

The girl, Marfisa, grasped his hand, finding his palm rough but warm. 'I will.'

Rami raised his goblet to her. 'Most excellent. And I tell you, truly, one does not have to be a nobleman to be a knight. Let me tell you the story of a simple boy, a shepherd, who became one of the most valiant knights of my father's kingdom . . .'

Marfisa leaned against a pillow and relaxed, a rare smile stealing across her face. I, too, uncoiled a bit in the shadows; there's nothing like a good story.

* * *

It is strange, how time feels. Now tense, now loose. A little knot in the thread, or a place where the yarn has begun to unwind. As soon as Rami began to tell his tale, I could feel all the tension in the girl's body relax. Things would spool out now. There had been a time of danger, of massive shift and change, and it had passed. I almost sighed with relief before recalling that this was my enemy. No. The tool of my enemy, my brother. And not the dull tool I'd been hoping she would be. Many other children – even those suckled by a lioness – would have been ground to hopelessness from years of enslavement. But somehow she had pivoted from neglect and abuse and fear and turned all that suffering into a sort of mental toughness. I feared that next to her Bradamante and Ricardetto would look like two glass goblets: precious, sophisticated, and oh, so easy to break. The moment was coming for me to go back and work them into better shape. But first I had to backtrack and find what had become of her brother. In the darkness of the shadow where I hid, I heaved a sigh. All this pattering about through time was tiring. The only thing worse than hopping about was imagining what it would feel like to be stuck in a single span only, one's chance at life pouring out, a drop at a time. Oh, that would feel like being a human. How horrible.

I traced back to when the boy was pulled aboard the ship, got a sense of his thread, ran it through my fingers, as it were. This was the moment of his departure from the island, and though I didn't want to dally too long, I did want to see what he made of the rest of the world, and what the rest of the world made of him. Would he be hardened, forged and seasoned, as his sister had been? Or would the weight of the world beyond the island crush him? (I could only hope.) I saw him on the ship, climbing the ropes. Joining another ship, then taking to land. He journeyed with some cargo, acting as a donkey handler on one journey, a camel driver on another, then a guard, with a cudgel in his hand. He crossed over a great swathe of desert and spent time in a city, then drove a herd of sheep and goats back across the desert. It was, in short, an incredibly dull life, and I was glad not to have to live it out minute-by-minute. At last, I felt some tension creep into his thread, then the surprise of a hard knot. It passed through my fingers, that moment of happening, and I pulled back to visit more closely.

A town by an oasis. One of those peculiar crossroads places, where travellers and merchants of every stripe come to pause. A sort of desert port. There were traders as dark as Rami and others as pale as Fiordispina. A group of dancers swirled and stomped to the beat of a drum; they wore wide-skirted robes that billowed out when they spun. The drumbeats merged with the pounding hammer of a blacksmith's forge, which was rivalled by the shouting match between three camel drivers (speaking three different languages). Another place where shadows would be my safest harbour. I settled into a long, narrow one cast by the trunk of a date palm, and looked about. Ah. There was the boy. The young man, now. He looked stunningly like Marfisa, only thicker in the chest and broader in the shoulders. But the arch of the eyebrow, even the walk, toes turned slightly out, just like her. He was, perhaps, three inches taller, and while I would call her slight or slender, he was just shy of robust. I had caught him at almost the same age as she had been when she escaped from the spice merchant – that age after the first burst of growth. He was just starting to grow into his new height. A strong young man, who walked as if he knew it, with a bit of a swagger.

'Hey, Ruggiero! Get over here and help!' The cry came from a man with an eye-patch and a scruffy beard.

My young man, clearly going by Ruggiero now, turned

from where he had been talking with another fellow and hurried over to the one-eyed man. 'Yes, sir?'

'Load up. Pack things tight, eh, and make sure every cover is tied secure. No gaps.' The man tugged at some of the ropes around the loose canvas. 'We're carrying gum and resin. Sand gets in there, it's ruined. So no sand gets in, eh?'

'I understand.' Ruggiero began to work at the ropes, humming to himself, some melody I did not recognize.

As he worked, the sun settled low in the sky, and a call went up from the muezzin, but Ruggiero didn't turn from his work. A few of the others unrolled little squares of fabric or carpet and began their prayers. Ruggiero patiently tugged on each piece of rope, pushing at the crates, testing that they wouldn't move.

An older man, wearing a mail shirt and leading a white-and-tan horse, approached. He had a sword belted at his side and a shield tied behind his saddle (along with other odd, lumpy baggage). 'Where do you head with these carts?' the man enquired.

Ruggiero looked around for the boss, but found himself alone. He shrugged. 'First to Qhat, then to Jerusalem.'

'My destination as well,' the man replied. 'Your cargo will need guards, I should say.'

'I am the guard,' Ruggiero replied, laying a hand on the cudgel at his belt.

The man smiled, showing crooked teeth. 'No offence to you, but you'll need more guarding than that.'

Ruggiero shrugged again. 'That's for Druss to decide.'

The one-eyed man reappeared, as if summoned by the sound of his name. 'What's this? A knight errant at an oasis?'

The man with the horse bowed in exaggerated fashion. 'I am, as you perceive, a knight. Sir Badr. At your service.'

Druss rolled his one eye at Ruggiero. 'Why would a knight be at this godforsaken place?'

'Tut! God forsakes no place, but gives every spot, every man . . . even every animal and rock . . . its own magnificent destiny,' Sir Badr said, his voice taking on a decided enthusiasm, if not eloquence.

'I have all the guards I need,' Druss said. 'But if you ride along, we'll feed you. And if there's a fight, you fight for us.'

'Done,' Sir Badr replied.

Ruggiero eyed the knight as Druss stalked off again. If the man was a knight . . . why was he here? And from what heights had he fallen to be reduced to working for a share of the common stewpot?

'Ready carts!' Druss's call came. Ruggiero pulled up the donkeys' stakes and wrangled them into the traces. Sir Badr came to lend a hand, was bitten in said hand by a donkey, and ended up atop his horse, trying to staunch the bleeding, as the caravan headed out from the oasis.

'Do you really believe in destiny?' asked Ruggiero. He walked alongside the cart, one hand on his cudgel, the other with a switch, which he whisked over the donkeys' flanks now and then. (I had secreted myself in a donkey's shadow, lumping along with his plodding steps.) 'As you said to Druss? That everyone has it?'

'I do,' Sir Badr replied, looking wise for a man who has just been bitten by a donkey. 'Everyone. As I said, even stones, even trees. Do you doubt it?'

Ruggiero tipped his head to study the clouds and picked his words with care; in that posture, he looked so like his sister. The wide-spaced eyes, the ragged dark hair that peeked out from underneath the scarf he'd wound around his head and neck. The look of introspection, careful consideration – what to tell, what to hide. 'When I was a child, I was told about it. A . . . sorcerer . . . even told me that I was destined for greatness. But I don't feel it.'

'A sorcerer?' The knight leaned forward. 'Say more.'

'He was a madman. Maybe a demon. I call him a sorcerer because I do not know what else to call him. He spoke sometimes of fate. And destiny.' Ruggiero shrugged. 'Yet here I am, driving a donkey through the desert. Was I destined to do this?'

The knight seemed to consider this question for a while. 'Sometimes, we have to search out our destiny,' he said at last. 'That is, in part, why I am on this journey. I must. The destination would not come to me.'

'I suppose that makes sense,' Ruggiero said, though he sounded unconvinced.

Sir Badr sighed. 'I am no wise man, no philosopher who can expound on such at length. I can tell you only what I feel. We are each pulled by our destiny. When we are born, or perhaps even before that, the stars align above and imprint themselves upon us. A certain fate is written in our soul. I believe it is a question. And the destiny that pulls us is the answer. We seek it out, each day of our lives. This question burns within us, desiring to be answered, and so we go forth and try to find the reply.'

Ruggiero listened to this errant nonsense with his mouth hanging open, gawping like a fish. 'Yes,' he breathed at last. 'I do feel a pull. It's as if . . . there's a moment out there waiting for me. A moment that will . . . test me, where I will prove myself.'

In the shadow of the donkey, I gave a little squawk. How could he know? Did he know? Or was he just a mortal, feeling mortal things and, in a bumbling mortal way, getting close to the truth?

'And what do you think that you will have to prove?' the knight asked.

Ruggiero again tipped his head to consider this question

but I noticed that his gaze didn't stay on the clouds this time, but rather scanned the hills and tumbled rocks that sat near the edge of the road ahead. Like his sister, he was a good guard. Then he looked once more at Sir Badr. 'I had a sister. She was stolen from me. Sometimes I think . . . I think my purpose is to find her. But how is that possible? When we are so long parted and the world is so vast?'

Sir Badr nodded sagely. 'To God, all things are possible.' He held up a finger. 'It may be that God is testing you, as He has tested many saints and heroes.'

Ruggiero gave a little smile. 'I am no saint. And no hero.' But I could sense, as his eyes continued their study of the rocks and brush, that he thought that maybe . . . maybe . . . he could become a hero. 'What sort of tests might a man undergo?' he asked.

'For some, it is a test of spirit. Resisting temptation – say, of food, or drink, or of flesh.' The knight paused, nodded at his own wisdom. 'For others, it would be a test of strength – mind and body. Endurance. Capacity.' His words sped up as his excitement grew. 'And of course, there's the quest, the most noble calling of all. A show of faith, to renounce one's home and go to search for some holy and sacred object. Is that what you are called to do, my boy?'

Ruggiero ran a hand across his brow, tucking away a lock of dark hair (a gesture so like his sister's it made me smile). 'I have left my home, I suppose. If the island where I was raised could be called home. And I am searching for my sister, in a way. And sometimes, yes, I feel like I am meant to fight. But sometimes, I feel a call – a need, even – to dance.' He flashed a sharp look at the knight, rolling his shoulders back, as if bracing himself for laughter.

'Dancing? Strange. But quests and destinies take all forms. And did not King David dance before the Holy Ark of the Lord?'

Ruggiero shrugged. 'I'm not certain.'

'He did! Let me tell you the story,' the knight said eagerly.

'I like stories,' Ruggiero replied, his eyes ranging over the hills, searching for danger.

And on they rode, through the desert, up into the hills, and down again. After the story of King David, Sir Badr recounted the tale of his life. It turned out that he had sworn to undertake a pilgrimage. He explained to Ruggiero that he had sinned gravely and killed another knight. It was a long and twisting story, involving a beautiful woman, hand-to-hand combat, lust, blood, swords, and oaths. Ruggiero revelled in every detail. I fell asleep halfway through the telling. But I got the sense of it and a shortened version is all that's needed: Sir Badr felt a great deal of guilt and woe over what he had done and took on a pilgrimage as penance. He had lately visited the cave of St Anthony, and had within his coat of mail a piece of the saint's hair shirt. Now he was on the way to Jerusalem, where he hoped to pray on the hill of Golgotha and find a piece of the true cross.

Ruggiero sighed and shook his head as the knight's tale wound to an end. 'It must be nice,' he said, 'to have such a definite purpose. To know where you are going and what you must do. I feel like a wanderer, just drifting about, waiting for a moment of truth to arrive. But what am I supposed to do in the meantime?'

'Let us figure that out, my boy. Wandering is not such a bad thing, either. Let me tell you the story of a famous wanderer . . .'

At length, they arrived in Qhat and refilled their water skins. Now began the long trek, through the rugged and scrubby desert towards Jerusalem. Druss rode up and down the caravan, adjuring the men to be alert. He sneered at Sir Badr's horse –

'Donkeys're bad enough,' he opined. 'Three times as much water as a camel needs. But horses . . .' He snorted.

'You'll be glad of my steed when the raiders come,' Sir Badr replied stoutly.

And come they did, not three days out of Qhat. The caravan had entered a narrow pass between two crumbly yellow-grey slopes. Druss and the camels out in front, the donkey carts behind. Ruggiero had scrambled up one hill, trying to gain some vantage, and stood, panting, halfway up the slope. From here, he could see down into the pass, and across to the other slope . . . and there, hidden behind a jumble of rocks, were half a dozen men – they would have melded with the shadow, had not one of them drawn his blade prematurely; the flash of light drew Ruggiero's attention. 'Hey!' he shouted. 'Look out!' And he began to run, headlong, down the slope. Pebbles tumbled beneath his feet, rolling away, loosening the ground. It was the rumble that alerted the caravan more than his words, and Ruggiero arrived in a veritable avalanche, just as the raiders leapt out from behind their rock.

It was mayhem. I stayed to the margins, making myself small enough to fit in a pebble's shadow. One of the raiders was hidden up the slope and loosed arrows that picked out man and beast alike. The others rushed in, swinging axes and swords. The caravan guards had mostly cudgels and short blades. Sir Badr waded into the thick of it, and his horse did as much damage as he did, lashing out with its hooves. Ruggiero lay about with his club, bashing at one man, dodging a clumsy strike with a sword. The camels shrieked and tried to break free; the donkeys shied in their traces and attempted to bite anything that came close (but this was typical behaviour for them on any given day). Ruggiero managed to disarm the man he was fighting and the two were soon grappling, then rolling on the ground. This was no tidy contest on the pitch, no match scored with points, like my twins had fought. Now Ruggiero had his hands on the man's throat, now Ruggiero found himself pinned beneath his foe. His face grew red, almost purple, and he thrashed with his limbs, a desperate motion. And then, suddenly, the man he was grappling with slumped down on him, heavy. Dead weight. Sir Badr was leaning over, tugging his sword lose from the man's torso. 'Thought he had you, eh? That's the lot of them.' Sword loose, he leaned down and offered Ruggiero a hand. The boy barely stirred; the red was receding from his face, but his breath came in ragged gasps and his dark eyes were unfocused, staring at the nothingness of near death. Sir Badr seemed unconcerned and grabbed Ruggiero's shoulder, dragging him up as he explained, 'They did some damage, and the archer got away.'

Some damage . . . I spread out to a larger shadow (someone's corpse) and looked about: two camels dead, or as good as. Three members of the caravan as well. Druss had taken an arrow to the shoulder; a camel driver had been bashed over the head and still lay unconscious. But the raiders were fallen – five of them. Sir Badr had skewered three with his blade. Two other guards had teamed up and beaten another. And Ruggiero had smashed the skull of the other. He hadn't realized he had done so until Sir Badr pointed it out. Stiff, bruised, Ruggiero picked up his cudgel. It was caked with blood and dust, and he stared at the corpse he had made. He licked his lips, looking as if he might be ill. From where he sat on the edge of a cart, wincing as a camel driver tended his wounds, Druss called out, 'I owe you, Ruggiero, for killing him. And I'll have to pay the old knight, too.' These words brought a little of the swagger back to the boy's step, though I noticed he looked away from the corpse. Druss continued with his shouting. 'Strip the packs. Load the carts. We'll leave the bodies for the buzzards.'

Sir Badr was studying Ruggiero as the young man stuck his cudgel back in his belt and knelt, checking the raider's body for coins, for anything of value. 'Good,' the knight said at last.

'What's good?' said Ruggiero.

'This is your first kill?'

Ruggiero nodded. His Adam's apple bobbed up and down as he swallowed and tried to speak. He quit his searching and stood up. Sir Badr pounded him on the back in a friendly way.

'It's good that you are rather nauseous. Not bloodthirsty. And yet, you carry on, practically. You are not some blade of grass, some mere lily, to be blown over by the wind. But you are also not a miscreant, who fights and kills for the pleasure of it.'

Ruggiero straightened. 'If I had not struck him and killed him, he would have killed me.'

'Indeed. It was righteous. You have a sense of honour and nobility, even though you are sworn to no code.' Sir Badr nodded solemnly. 'You are one of the few who might not only seek the answer that destiny provides, but find it, gain it, and understand it. I see that within you.'

It was as if Ruggiero was a well-oiled lamp, and Sir Badr had touched a spark to his wick, so suddenly did the boy flare with light. 'Truly?' he breathed.

'I swear it,' the knight answered. 'Remember what we spoke of, quests and destinies. I feel your purpose. A day of reckoning will come to you. And I believe I am called, too. To help prepare you. For now you fight with a crude cudgel and your bare hands. But I will train you to fight with a sword and shield and lance and armour. For glory! For God!'

'Yes,' Ruggiero said and then his voice grew husky and low. 'And perhaps for my sister, too.'

Within my shadow, I felt a tremor, as if the ground shook. It reminded me of . . . the same feeling I'd had when Marfisa was fighting Khalid. There was none of the haziness . . . but that same shaking. I'd swear the earth was moving. It could not be chance, this similar sensation. And it seemed that Ruggiero felt it too. I saw his head snap up, saw him struggle to draw a shuddering breath, as if something shook within him, as well.

What was it? Some magic my brother had worked? I sampled the air around my shadow. Caught a hint of that static charge, taste of lightning about to strike. Oh, Melissa, you fool! The moment was drawing near . . . this was a strange symmetry at work. Both of these twins had found themselves a mentor. The fool knight was correct – they were off on a quest, destiny was awaiting them. And I, I!, had helped to create it.

There was no time to waste. Sir Badr was reciting a prayer as Ruggiero knelt before him. I had to be off. I had my own twins to train. And time was running short.

CHAPTER FIVE

The sky that night, as dark as my shadow form. Oh, the spaces between the stars. I drifted, waiting, in the nothingness between earth and sky. Where do *I* belong? Sometimes . . . sometimes I feel that I have no home. Not the Deeps. Not the Firmament. Not earth (though, I admit, I am finding it pleasant to sojourn there). It is as if I am doomed to be a wanderer, or doomed, at least, to feel unsettled. An exile? But that implies that once, somewhere, I had a home.

Enough! I shook such thoughts off me, like a spaniel rids itself of water after swimming, and stared up at the sky. There . . . Gemini: twin stars burning bright. Lesser suns prickled around them, but I saw only the twins. Focused on them – were they brighter than before? Was I imagining things? And there . . . just now appearing in the night sky (any astronomer looking up would be beside themselves with confusion; any astrologer, with delight), the green-hued Venus. The planet ought to swing higher than the twins, but this night, its arc was lower, bringing it into a straight line with that pair of stars. Closer, closer, and then, a *pop* of red so sudden I thought I could hear it, as Mars was pulled into this sequence, too, the workings of the magic my brother and I had wrought. Yes, right there. The confluence wasn't complete. I squinted and worked the calculation in my head, of angles and orbits and . . . oh. Less than a year. Three seasons. That was nothing. I had to focus. No time to dilly-dally and spy (though I longed to check up on my brother). Focus. Now I knew what I was up against, and I had only a short time to figure out how to improve my twins sufficiently.

I floated back and dissipated among the shadows, still staring up. These stars, though minor compared to what waited above, were pretty, I admit. I really did want to win this contest. The thought of being exiled – the thought of the utter, bleak emptiness of the Farthest Deeps – made me shudder. I couldn't bear it. I had to win.

Three seasons, and the first was autumn.

No time to lose. The woods near Duke Aymon's manor had begun to shed their leaves as I squeezed out of the shadows. A moment to stretch, and then I shrugged myself into some flesh. It felt momentarily *good* to incorporate, I admit. It gets tiresome to be unbounded. It is sometimes nice to have limits, to know where one begins and where one ends. I took in the scent of leaf mould, of woodsmoke, of fishy river mud. Odd, it smelled like home.

In a moment, I had settled the flesh of Melissa, the heaven-sent angel, pale and blond and cool, about me and set out through the forest towards the manor. I paused only once, to study the angle of Mars and Venus from down here and make certain I wasn't mistaken. I wasn't. Three seasons. No more. And what would I find when I reached the manor? A girl, as sharp and honed as her blade, quick and clever like a fox in winter? A boy who believed he could do anything and was strong and smart enough to achieve it? Because that was what we . . . I . . . was up against. I hurried my steps along.

The guard at the manor's gate recognized me and bowed me within, murmuring, 'Good Melissa', as I swept past. I glowed just a little bit – nothing to appear *too* supernatural (though I realized that by now even the dog-boy must have a sense that I wasn't a typical woman) but just something to assert that I meant business. My brother's twins did tend to put me in such a mood. That boy! He had such *faith*, such *hope*. Given his dismal upbringing, I hadn't thought that possible. And the girl . . . don't get me started on the girl. The best I can say is that she showed no sign of being able to dance.

Another guard opened the manor's door and I heard the slippered steps of servants rushing about. Good. They were still a bit intimidated. Inside, cool shadows broken only by a torch in a sconce on the wall – it cast flickering light across the stone. A servant appeared and led me to the manor's main hall. Here, more light. A merry blaze in the giant hearth at one end, a few torches higher up along the wall. Dinner had been eaten, it seemed, and while a few kitchen girls carried out the remains of the meal, a few others carried in new platters, a jug of wine, settling them near the hearth, where the servant led me.

'Melissa!' Bradamante cried as she rose from her chair.

I started just a little; I knew her by her voice, but until she spoke, I had thought her to be her lady mother. But now Beatrice rose and came forward to clasp my hands. 'Oh, how chilled you are, good Melissa. Come close to the fire.' The flames brought out the subtle highlights of their hair: red and gold and brown. And, in Beatrice's, I now saw, strands of grey and white.

'I knew you'd come back,' Ricardetto called. 'You always do.'

Good old dependable Melissa. I smiled at him as he bowed to me over his lute. He wore a delightful little felt cap topped with a grouse feather that wobbled and bobbed with his every move. His bow complete, he resumed his melody.

'And where is your husband, Lady Beatrice?' I asked. 'I hope he is well.'

'He went to the north. It is the wheat harvest there, and the farmers are apt to miscount the sheaves unless someone keeps an eye on them.'

A servant brought a goblet, a platter with choice morsels of meat, slices of apple, briny olives. I took only the goblet, held it in my hands, feeling the beaten metal between my palms as I studied Bradamante. 'Let me look at you, my dear.' (I did love Ricardetto. But Bradamante is my favourite. Is it wrong to have favourites? I will definitely have favourites when I rule this world.)

She gave a shy smile and turned slightly away from me. Her dress was plain wool – after all, they were merely sitting by the fireside at home – but fancifully embroidered. A whole garden scene worked its way up her sleeves and across her bodice. She seemed . . . fuller, broader, rounder. Stronger. And more settled.

'Well, how do I look to you?'

'You seem content,' I said at last. Casting about for some other praise, I added, 'And your needlework is most impressive.' I pointed to where an embroidered rabbit nibbled a strawberry on her sleeve.

'I have been. Most content. Sewing.'

'Indeed,' I said. We settled into chairs by the fire. I felt the tension in her words. 'Sewing.'

Her blue eyes caught the reflection of the flames. She lifted her chin to gaze at me. 'Yes. Sewing. I have ceased to fight.'

A good thing I hadn't taken a swallow of wine, for I would

have spat it out. As it was, I spluttered, fought for control. 'Ceased fighting.' Ricardetto's lute playing grew louder. But there was no melody that could soothe me now.

'Yes.' She shot a glance to her mother, her mirror image, sitting on my other side. Her pale cheeks were flushed a bit by the fire's warmth, but she held her chin high like her daughter.

'Explain, my dear, if you would.'

She took an olive from my platter and chewed it. 'In the months you've been gone, I have had time to think about my contest with Sir Trito. Yes, I have thought about it.' She stared into the firelight, her jaw set, her chin high. There was the stubborn girl I knew. 'And I have come to the conclusion that a woman cannot fight and win.'

'What?' I squawked. I cleared my throat, smoothed my skirts. 'Do explain.'

'You saw it, Melissa, I know you did. That guardsman, Nestor, wouldn't judge any of my strikes fairly. A woman cannot win that way – there is no fair judgement. And then, after the fact, Sir Trito went swaggering about claiming that I had only knocked him down through luck. That he had kept his blows light because I was a girl.'

'You know that is not true,' I said, placing my hand on top of hers. Her fingers were so much warmer than mine; I could feel the pulse of blood beneath the flesh.

'I do,' she said and squeezed my fingers. 'But no man would believe it.'

'I believe it,' Ricardetto said, pausing in his song.

'Thank you, dear brother.' Bradamante smiled at him, and I took a moment to marvel at how, though they were both clearly more mature, they still looked almost identical. The slant of the nose, the line of the jaw. The point their hair came to in the middle of their foreheads. Yes, Ricardetto had a few whiskers on his chin (just a few!) and Bradamante's cheeks were a touch fuller. But otherwise: mirror images. She turned back to me. 'Moreover,' she continued, 'I have endured snide remarks and lewd comments ever since that fight. And did you hear what my very own servants yelled at me as I fought? Yes, you did. You were there. I have thought about it and I have come to the conclusion that a woman cannot fight a man and win.'

'Not unless she kills him,' I said delicately.

'Not even then,' Bradamante replied. 'Admittedly, she does win over *that* man, but it isn't a victory that will bring her any lasting comfort. There will be another man and another and in the meantime, she will be picked apart – by men and women alike – for her *unseemly* ways. No, a woman cannot win.'

I took my hand from hers and gently cracked each and every knuckle of my fingers (enjoying how Lady Beatrice winced). 'Very well,' I said, keeping my voice level. 'And what have you been doing in my absence, Ricardetto?'

'We had word from Rinaldo,' Lady Beatrice said, speaking for her son. It was a miracle the boy could talk at all, so often did he let others make his case. 'And Rinaldo asked for Ricardetto to come and be his squire. The word is that the king gathers an army to . . .'

I held up a hand to stop her words. 'Don't burden me with the details of kings and armies and such. Fleeting fancies. I have more important concerns.' I looked at Ricardetto. 'And do you intend to go, to be a squire?'

He gave a laugh, the grouse feather of his cap flopping to the side. 'Of course! I couldn't very well run away, could I?'

No . . . no, he could not. Marfisa could run away – had run away. Ruggiero had run away and now, seemingly, was running towards something. But my twins. No . . . they had been well-trained.

Ricardetto seemed to perceive my displeasure and said, 'You should be pleased with me, Melissa. I have kept up my training with sword and lance in order to be ready to serve my brother. And who could keep me in fighting shape . . . except my sister? So I have cajoled and insisted that she train with me.'

I turned back to Bradamante. 'So you have been fighting?'

'I have been training my brother. I am permanently retired from contests, wars, sparring, and any other form of public humiliation.'

A smile spread across my face. That was my fiery girl. There was hope yet. 'Your lute playing is excellent, Ricardetto. Did you invent that melody you were playing just now?'

'I did,' he said, basking in my approval. 'Sometimes, it seems that the notes are just waiting for me in the air, hovering there.'

The fire popped, sending out sparks, and a servant hurried near to prod the half-burned log and settle fresh wood on top. A rosy glow, a pleasant warmth. Too comfortable. 'Right,' I said and clapped my hands together, making Beatrice jump. 'We leave tomorrow morning, first light.'

'What . . .' 'Where . . .' 'But . . .' All three of them began to speak at once. I held up a hand. Silence.

'I told you before that I was preparing you for a moment of greatness.' I paused, let the quiet grow. The stillness but for the fire's crackle. Ricardetto gripped the neck of his lute tightly; Bradamante stared at me thirstily. 'That moment approaches. It will ask of you all your wit, all your strength, all your cleverness, all your skill. Trust me. I want what is best for you.' Lady Beatrice gave a little hiccup, put her fingers to her lips. I could see the firelight glint off the brimming tears in her eyes. 'We cannot wait for the moment to come. We must be brave and go off to meet it.' I held out my hand, palm up. Bradamante rose from her chair and put her palm against my own. Then Ricardetto stepped near and seized both of our hands. 'Together,' I said. 'We will set out.'

And so we did. The next morning.

We crossed the river on the ferry and rode up from the valley to the broad track that led through the hills. Ricardetto wore his grouse-feather cap and a cloak of dark brown wool atop Storm, his lute carefully wrapped and stowed behind him. Bradamante wore the same moss-green dress and rode side-saddle on Wolf-Fang, who seemed less than keen with this arrangement. But like anyone who had spent any time with Bradamante, the horse seemed to have figured out there was little point in arguing. Or maybe I was just projecting my thoughts onto the beast.

For myself, I rode a handsome brown gelding; if it had a name, I had forgotten it and had dubbed it, with some irony, Destiny. I wore a split skirt with leather leggings underneath and held in one hand the lead rope to the packhorse that trudged behind us, encumbered with the suits of armour for my twins. Bradamante had haughtily declared that I needn't bring *her* armour on this trip, but I had anyway. And we were off. Above the river valley, the air grew drier and the scents of autumn filled the air. Peasants worked in fields, bundling sheaves of grain, and if you didn't look too closely, you could imagine that they were content.

Ricardetto and Bradamante played a little game, passing a story back and forth, each one trying to leave the other with an impossible situation to untangle. 'And then the gnome threw the treasure over the cliff. Your turn to say what happens next,' was one of Bradamante's offerings to her brother.

It wasn't but two days of riding before we met up with Rinaldo, who was quite surprised to see us. Their brother rode at the forefront of a dozen or so men, a mixture of soft-seeming nobles and war-hardened fighters – including, to my dismay, Sir Trito – with a couple of servants or squires towards the rear, leading packhorses stacked with arms and armour. Rinaldo, wearing a handsome blue coat worked with his father's leaping stag in gold, hailed Ricardetto, trotting forward on his big warhorse and pounding the younger man on the shoulder in what seemed to be a playful manner (though Ricardetto winced with each impact). 'What's this, what's this?' Rinaldo called. 'I see my squire, but who are these ladies in attendance?'

Ricardetto blushed. 'Brother, surely you know your sister, Bradamante?'

Rinaldo gave a little bow. 'I could mistake her for no other, for she looks just like you, and just like our fair mother.' He nudged his mount closer to Bradamante; Wolf-Fang shied back, but Bradamante spoke some words and the horse quieted. Rinaldo seized her hand and kissed it. 'What, pray tell, are you doing on the road? I hope I am not about to have *two* squires on my hands.' He spoke this last loudly, and the assorted men who rode with him laughed sycophantically.

Rinaldo looked even more like his father than last time; he'd grown in his whiskers and trimmed his black hair. His handsome face bore a fresh scar on one cheek, just to the side of his nose, but though it marred the symmetry of his face, it gave him a roguish look that, I admit, served him well. He reined his horse in and said to Ricardetto, 'And who is this other lady accompanying you?'

Oh, forget that I paid his looks a compliment. I cannot abide being spoken about rather than spoken to. When I rule this age . . . but I am getting ahead of myself. Ricardetto gave his brother a broad smile. 'This is the Lady Melissa. She was abbess of a convent. The convent of St Philomena.

High in the hills above Sancy. An isolated convent, it was, and so, as abbess, she trained all the nuns in the finest arts of warfare.'

I widened my eyes, shooting Bradamante a look, but she just shrugged, lips pursed, as if to say, *let him tell the story, it'll be fine.*

Indeed, Ricardetto was continuing. 'And the barbarians came sweeping down from the snowy hills to the north and would have razed the convent and the village below, had not the abbess and her nuns been ready to fight.' He paused and swept his grouse-feather hat from his head. 'Sadly, all the nuns perished from their wounds. Only the abbess survived. Our good mother heard the tale and insisted on giving the abbess refuge. And she has been with us ever since, helping to train me in the sword.'

I fixed what I hoped was a winning smile on my lips and looked demurely at Rinaldo.

'That is as strange a story as I have ever heard. But, very well, I can see now why you bring her along and why she rides astride the horse rather than properly.' And here he gestured to Bradamante (who was, I might note, having trouble keeping Wolf-Fang from skittering away from the warhorses due to her ridiculous perch in side-saddle). 'But why is Bradamante here and not safe at home?'

It seemed that Bradamante didn't wish to leave her fate to her brother's story-telling ability. 'Why else, dear Rinaldo, except to find a suitable suitor? I will be married to no one except the bravest, strongest, fiercest warrior.'

The men who rode with Rinaldo guffawed again, but Bradamante merely swept a level gaze across them. 'I've yet to find the right match, thus I must search further afield.'

'This is all highly irregular,' Rinaldo said. 'And that hat is ridiculous.' He pointed to the grouse feather.

'I like it . . .' Ricardetto began.

'You're my squire now, and that's the end of it.' Rinaldo snatched it from his head. 'We haven't time to dither and dally. Since you've intercepted us, we must return whence we came and make good time. Sister, I am glad to see you, but I fear you'll slow us down.'

'I'll do my best to keep up,' Bradamante said and I could hear brittle restraint, tamped-down resentment in her voice. (Good, good. Get angry. Dislike this treatment. Chafe at it. Want to fight. Want to win.)

And then in a tramping of hooves and a few shouts of frustration, we were off at a trot with Rinaldo and his men. Through hills terraced with grape vines, where young boys and girls ran sticks and brooms, keeping the birds from the nearly ripened fruit. Across another river, this time on a bridge little more stable than the ferry had been. Rinaldo dropped back to ride with me for a time. 'That is a tale of woe Ricardetto told about you.'

'He is a good story-teller,' I replied.

'I see the packhorse has two sets of armour. I have heard odd stories from Sir Trito.'

'One for me and one for Ricardetto. Though I have sworn not to fight unless my life, or the life of your siblings, is at stake. For me, fighting is a holy endeavour.'

He nodded solemnly. 'I am sure you have trained my brother to the best of your ability.'

I smiled in response and he rode away. A moment later, Bradamante had manoeuvred Wolf-Fang next to me and spoke in a low voice. 'I know he is my brother. And my elder. And a paladin. But he is also . . .' Now she whispered. 'Insufferable and egotistical.'

'Ah. This is often the case when one is raised to believe one is, by Nature, and Nature alone, the very best.'

We were lagging behind the troop of men and Rinaldo turned in his saddle to urge us on with a wave. Bradamante patted Wolf-Fang's flank. 'I don't like to be thought incompetent.'

'Mmmmm,' I said. 'Nor do I.'

'And I hate it when people think I'm helpless.'

'It is irritating.'

'I want to bash their brains in.'

'Why don't you, dear?'

And she heaved such a sigh. 'Melissa. I don't know what to do.'

'Let me think. We'll figure something out.'

And so we rode and rode and rode. Rinaldo certainly had a destination in mind: this war that the king was preparing to wage against such-and-so. But he also appeared to be in no great hurry to arrive. Our course zigged and zagged, aiming now north-west towards the manor of some count, now north-east towards the hunting lodge of a certain duke. As we rode, the knights who accompanied Rinaldo took care to slow their mounts and ride beside Bradamante. I played the part of the warrior abbess (has such a thing ever existed? It ought to) and stayed close enough to eavesdrop. The knights usually wanted to tell Bradamante things: where they were headed, for instance. Or the particular positive qualities of the horse she rode. Or, more dullingly, about their latest feats on the tilting pitch.

I was so proud of Bradamante. She tilted her head, just like a little bird in a tree, and listened carefully. Gasping and nodding and laughing exactly as one ought, to draw the speaker out more. She raised a kerchief to hide her face if the knight shared a detail that was gruesome or (mildly) scandalous. I could see how they appreciated her attention, how they warmed to her. Of course, being Bradamante, she wouldn't restrain herself to this role, but was likely – after listening for a good, long while – to add in some perspective of her own. That Wolf-Fang was, as a matter of fact, not bred from the northern stock of horses, but had come to her father from a breeder of Arabians, and you could see that in the line of his withers. Or she might suggest that the next time the knight found himself on the jousting pitch that he . . .

Well, you can imagine how those conversations went. Off the man would ride and out would jut Bradamante's lip, and she would pout beside me for an hour or more. And then sigh and scowl at the backs of the men ahead of us, and glare at her brother, who rode beside the other squires and was forever gesticulating wildly as he told a tale, wreathed in the young men's gales of laughter. And then say to me, 'Is it impossible . . . utterly impossible . . . for them to listen to a thing I say? To take my words as having *some* value?'

The irony, of course, was that she wasn't interested in my answer. But I gave it nonetheless. 'Patience,' I would tell her. 'The man you are looking for is a rare sort. But you will find him. Meanwhile, you beguile these men with your fair looks and your interest in their stories, and . . .' A dismissive wave of the hand brought me to silence.

'I don't want to be a fawning audience. I don't mind listening to good stories, and some of their stories are moderately good. Or have the chance to become so. But that cannot be my only role. Can it, Melissa?'

And I'd lean over from my saddle and pat her arm and say, 'Patience.' Really, I was speaking to myself. Patience. And devise a plan. And get these two children (almost adults) through this season and the next and then . . . oh, I wanted to say, and then, I would rule the world and not have to deal with petty conversations and piddling concerns such as this one. But, but, but . . . I knew (though it pained me to admit it) that I wouldn't be able to turn my back on Bradamante once the age was done. Things would change and get better, under my rule, for certain. But it would take time. And I wanted to help her now.

In the evenings, when we had arrived at whatever regal lodging Rinaldo had secured for us, we would dine with our hosts and enjoy some sort of entertainment. Often, Ricardetto was the entertainment, sometimes with help from Bradamante. They would tell tales (she would recite a tale; he would tell a story) or he would play his lute and she would sing (and I would subtly add in some additional musicians to enhance the effect). They won praises from their hosts, making both twins blush, and even Rinaldo seemed pleased.

The first snows fell as we were crossing a jagged line of hills – their slopes held balsams and fir trees and ragged outcroppings of black rock. The knights who rode back to talk with Bradamante told tales of real mountains that dwarfed these hills and snowfalls halfway up a horse's legs. Bradamante gasped and shook her head in awe and bit her lip so she would offer no reply of her own except appreciation. I couldn't bear it.

But at last we reached the chateau of Duke Le Sur. Made of the same grey-black stone that jutted out from the hills, the chateau dwarfed Duke Aymon's manor, could have swallowed it whole and still had room for more. As we rode closer, I could see that we would not be the only guests. Indeed, half a dozen banners flew above the chateau's outer wall, and Rinaldo immediately ordered Duke Aymon's stag to be unfurled; Ricardetto had the honour of holding the banner aloft. Bradamante squinted ahead at all the flags. 'Whose is the wolf?' she asked the knight who was riding nearest.

'That'll be Baron Vanderley.' And on he went to name the other lords whose banners flew.

'And what are they all doing here?'

'Ah,' he said and gave a little laugh. 'I forget you haven't heard any of our talk for this whole ride. We've spoken of little else. The duke has promised one last contest before the winter sets in. Next spring, there will be no time for jousting if we ride to war.'

'So all these nobles have come to compete.'

'Indeed, my lady. Each of these nobles will have brought his best knight or two. And, besides all of them, there will be the hedge knights, those not attached to a lord, who will want to try their chances, see if they can earn a spot in some lord's keep.'

'And what are the rules for this contest? Do they fight according to Bedwin's terms?'

The knight gave a little start. 'I didn't realize my lady was well-versed in jousting.' He looked as surprised as if a rock had spoken to him. 'Yes, indeed. Those are the terms: three passes, with points given for striking, unseating, or rendering one's opponent unable to fight, and, of course, causing his death.'

Riding behind, I could safely roll my eyes. Leave it to a man to explain the terms that a woman had already suggested she knew quite well.

The chateau, I admit, was rather marvellous. For a pile of stone, it had some charming features. The stained glass in the chapel, where we went with Rinaldo to pray; the tapestries in the main hall, where the duke greeted us and kissed both of Bradamante's hands, twice. (He offered me a stiff bow.) And, my favourite, the parapet atop the highest tower, which overlooked a sheer cliff above a river. And this was not the muddy flat river near Duke Aymon's, this one foamed and raged; even from the top of the tower, I could hear the roar of the waters.

The servants who had brought me and Bradamante to our chamber (Ricardetto would be sleeping with the other squires, probably in a hay pile somewhere, much to his chagrin) were surprised when I asked them to show us the stairs to the tower, but they complied (I have mastered the sneer, the cold command, the voice of utter entitlement). Arm-in-arm, we walked around the tower. I leaned over to stare down the drop-off towards the river, then, on the other side, Bradamante peered into the yards and fields that extended out from the chateau's walls, half a dozen or more patches of bare packed earth that gave way to pastures and then fields where sheaves still stood, waiting to be gathered. I was enchanted by the whole scene: the pounding might of the river behind me, constrained by the cliff walls, the sweep of the cropland and rich, heady scent of ripe grain. Bradamante, on the other hand, stared only at the practice yard, where squires practised with sword and shield (ah, yes, there was Ricardetto . . . doing quite well and looking fine in the armour I had fashioned him). I put my arm around her shoulder and pulled her tight; the wind had brought the colour up to her pale cheeks, brought tears to her blue eyes as well. One streaked down her face and she licked it away as she turned to face me. 'Melissa,' she said, voice full of misery.

'You miss it,' I replied, matter-of-fact.

'Terribly.' And she returned her gaze to the fighting men. 'I am good at it. And it feels . . . right. But they will refuse to fight me. Or, if they agree, then the contest is rendered unfair or worthless because I am a woman. At best, it becomes a spectacle rather than a competition. They won't believe I am actually, on my own merit and skill, good. Better than them.' And she leaned over the parapet and spat, a big gob, over the edge. That's my girl. 'I shouldn't mind listening to their endless stories if at least they knew I could knock them down. It would make things . . . even.'

I gave her a smile. 'I have a plan.'

Pre-dawn, the day of the tournament, when five more noblemen's flags waved above the chateau's gate and every chamber, stable, hall and shrub was full of slumbering forms, I slipped through the door of the largest stable and found Ricardetto asleep atop a pile of straw. He had been up late the night before, playing his lute and dancing jigs, and now slept on his back, mouth open, snoring profoundly. I nudged his shoulder and he jerked awake.

'Melissa?'

I put a finger to my lips and helped him up from the straw. Then he followed me across the yard and into the chateau, up to the chamber I shared with Bradamante. She was already awake and the two of us plucked and brushed the straw from Ricardetto's clothes. (There was nothing to be done with the smell; more horsey than most horses). 'What is it?' Ricardetto asked, then yawned tremendously, sitting down on the edge of the chamber's bed. 'Why can't I have a chamber with a bed?' he asked.

'It is yours for the day, if you wish,' I replied.

He yawned once more. 'Oh, no. I have to get ready for the jousting. And soon. The lists are so long, they start ear-ear-ear . . .' Another yawn interrupted his speech. 'Ly.' And he lay back on the bed. 'So soft.'

'Yes, rather. You should enjoy it. What would you say to your sister taking your spot?' I asked.

This made him sit up. His blue eyes sparkled as he pushed his auburn hair back from his forehead. 'Would you?

Bradamante?' Then the pleasure fell from his voice. 'Rinaldo wouldn't be happy.'

'If all goes well, he won't know until later, when his unhappiness will matter for little.'

Ricardetto frowned slightly but said, 'I trust you, Melissa.' And, turning to his sister, he took her hand and kissed it. 'Fight well.' And then he lay back on the bed and fell promptly and soundly asleep.

A few moments of adjustment and he was swaddled in bedclothes and Bradamante wore his tunic and cap. If someone came too close, they would notice her longer hair and her whiskerless chin (truly, he had only a dozen or so, whiskers, that is, not chins) but we hurried along the passageways and across the yard, encountering only kitchen servants hurrying to the well, and they gave us a wide berth. I ordered a groom to saddle Storm for jousting and ready Wolf-Fang as a replacement, should anything go wrong. Then I helped Bradamante into her brother's suit of armour; it fitted her perfectly, with the help of a few magical adjustments. By the time I was situating her gorget, the first of the other squires had come in, yawning and scratching and calling out. 'Eager, are you, Ricardetto?' He jumped a bit when he saw me and gave a little bow. 'Good lady?' And then a curious look. 'You're the fighting abbess that Ricardetto told us about? My lady?'

I allowed a small glow to surround my head, a minor nimbus. 'Yes, I am. And now, Ricardetto and I must go and pray before the fighting.' And I held out a hand for Bradamante to take; a cold gauntlet pressed against my equally chilly fingers and we went, clanking step after clanking step, to ready sword, shield, and lances. The practice yards were a swirling chaos of pages and squires, of horses and grooms, of knights laughing or barking orders.

We pushed through the yards close to the keep; Bradamante led Storm and I, Wolf-Fang. A few men called greetings to Ricardetto or offered a friendly taunt or two. Bradamante raised a hand in reply. I helped her mount and put Storm through his paces, practising some sword forms to warm up, and then I handed her the lance and shield.

By then, other knights and squires had arrived in our yard, and one of the stewards from the duke's chateau, resplendent in a yellow-and-green coat and a green wool cap with a yellow plume at the peak, hallo-ed and called for order. A tedious reading of the duke's many titles, a flowery proclamation, and then the names and order. Those of lowest rank fought first. And if they won, they fought again, against a higher-ranked knight. I supposed there was some good reason for this, and that reason might be hierarchy and the fact that those on top liked to stay on top. As it was, Ricardetto, who had never jousted before, was at the bottom of the heap, jousting against another squire. Rinaldo, a paladin of the king, top of the lists, would not be fighting for several rounds.

Bradamante and I made our way to the assigned pitch. There, I checked her armour one more time. I admit that I longed to weave in some protections, some magical enchantment – not to her person, that would break the rules I had settled on with my brother – to her lance or shield. But more than protecting her, I wanted her to win with her own might, her own skill. This was difficult, but this, too, was Nurture. Knowing when to let go.

And so I removed her helm, kissed both her cheeks, reminded her to keep the tip of her lance up, and when she rolled her eyes and said, 'I know, Melissa,' I clamped the helm back down firmly, and sent her off.

Storm pawed and stamped at the ground once Bradamante had mounted and Wolf-Fang, whose lead I held in one hand, whickered in sympathy. The steward assigned to this pitch raised one hand and pointed towards Bradamante. 'Ricardetto! Brother of Rinaldo! Son of Duke Aymon and Beatrice!' He raised his other hand. 'Antonio! Squire to the knight Giorgio.' The two faced each other at opposite ends of the pitch and then, at the steward's signal, cantered forward. The first pass was a complete miss, the horses shying away from each other. The crowd groaned and booed. Bradamante wheeled Storm around and they set up for another pass. This time, her lance struck Antonio hard in the chest, while his blow glanced off her shield. 'Point to Ricardetto!' the steward cried. The third pass yielded the same result, and the steward bellowed, 'A win for Ricardetto. Up in the lists he goes!' The crowd gave a few shouts and cries, but already the next pair of squires was lining up for their turn.

Bradamante came over, and I helped her dismount. Together, we walked Storm around to cool him down – cool Bradamante down as well. Once we were away from the crowd, she lifted the visor of her helm. 'I won,' she said.

'How did that feel?' I asked, though the question was entirely superfluous. Her eyes glimmered and her skin glowed – almost as if she had some magic of her own suffusing her.

'Wonderful,' she said. 'I felt . . . invisible. But powerful. I was myself and not myself. More than myself.' She laughed. 'That doesn't make any sense, does it?'

'Oh, yes, it does. It's called potential. And I believe you are finally realizing yours.'

Twice more that morning, Bradamante jousted against squires. One she unhorsed on the second pass, another she won against with points. Neither landed a blow on her body, though one did strike her shield, hard. A bell sounded the time for respite: wine and bread and rest. Others began to unbuckle the heavy plates of armour, but Bradamante, of course, could not. She removed a gauntlet and lifted her visor to drink from a goblet of watered wine, managing a few swallows before giving a little yelp and clamping her visor back down. Rinaldo, looking fine in a fresh silk coat of royal blue, approached. 'Brother!' he called, landing a thump on Bradamante's shoulder. 'What jousting! The contest is bringing out the best in you; I have never seen you ride so well. You've made it through the lists of squires and now, on to the knights . . .' He seemed to notice me for the first time and nodded to me. 'Good Melissa. I've been looking for Bradamante. This would be an opportune moment for her to bestow a favour.' He thumped Bradamante's shoulder again. 'And not on her brother, for goodness' sake. Do you know who you're fighting next?' Bradamante shook her head, helm waggling back and forth. 'Sir Trito! That's the luck of the lists.' Again, he turned to me. 'Where should I find Bradamante?' he asked me.

'Alas, I fear she has a touch of the flux, and she remained in our chamber this morning.'

'You should attend to her, then,' Rinaldo said. 'I hope she will be better for this evening's celebration.'

'I know she feels the same,' I replied and gave a slight curtsy. Rinaldo turned and hailed another knight. When he had gone a safe distance, Bradamante lifted the visor. 'Trito! I hope I crush him to . . .'

'Focus, dearest. Don't let vengeance cloud your vision.'

She slammed her visor shut.

But she must have focused, and quite well. The first pass saw both of them land solid blows on each other's shields. Now that the field had been thinned, the rawest of the new squires nursing bruises and broken arms, the crowd had thickened and they roared to see 'Ricardetto' hold his own against this experienced knight. Bradamante wheeled Storm about and charged again. This time, her blow caught him square in the chest, sending him tumbling over the rear of his horse. In the tumult, his lance caught in the strap of her shield, breaking it, and setting her off balance. But she was uninjured and kept her seat. This made the crowd roar even louder. Trito lay on his back on the pitch; a squire chased down his horse. Another picked up his fallen lance. The steward knelt over the knight and lifted his helm. A moment. 'He yields!' the steward called. I didn't need to lift Bradamante's visor to feel the gloating radiance of her smile as the steward called again. 'Ricardetto wins the match.'

Now we shifted the saddle to Wolf-Fang, giving Bradamante a fresh mount as she took on another knight and unseated him as well. There were bells and trumpets and fanfares that meant that the top of the lists had been reached. Now the paladins – Rinaldo and Ganelon and Oliver – had joined the jousting. The last of the fighting; Bradamante was the only squire who had made it through the lists, together with a hedge knight who wore armour painted a fiery red (though it was now much chipped) and a noble from the north countries. She drew Ganelon for her match; I fiddled with the new strap on her shield and she settled Wolf-Fang beneath her, whispering to the horse, words I could not hear. The duke himself had come forth from the chateau to oversee these final contests and now Bradamante, shield firmly affixed to her arm, rode towards the duke's pavilion and bowed to him before returning to her end of the pitch. Ganelon rode a white horse and bore a shield that had plates of metal on it shined to mirror brilliance. They caught the light and sent it dazzling around.

Before I could say anything, Bradamante snapped at me. 'I know, I know. Don't look at his shield, it's a distraction.'

I reached up and patted her armoured thigh and said

nothing. I could hear the tension in her voice. The worry. And, beneath that, the hope – maybe even the knowledge – that she could win.

At the steward's signal, they charged. Lances levelled, the thunder of hooves. The crowd yelling and then the crash of metal and wood. Ganelon's mirrored shield went flying, and Bradamante slumped to the side of the saddle, but kept her seat. As she turned Wolf-Fang, I could see how she hunched over in pain. 'Point to Ganelon!' the steward cried. The other knight paused only to have his shield strapped back on. Bradamante straightened in her saddle and then they charged again. Discs of light danced off Ganelon's mirror, but this time Bradamante aimed her lance better, and caught the knight in the join of his armour, where chest plate met shoulder. A soft spot. And though she did not unhorse him, and though the lances were blunted, nonetheless, she lodged the wood in his flesh, so hard did she strike him, and the other knight shrieked in pain as the lance hung there.

Squires hurried to help Ganelon, steadying the horse and pulling the lance free. Another terrible shriek and a gush of blood over his shiny armour. Bradamante, riding back towards me, looked over her shoulder. 'Sir Ganelon yields!' the steward cried. I helped Bradamante down from Wolf-Fang and as the crowd yelled and hollered, she collapsed on the ground. 'Oh, my ribs,' she groaned, as she lifted the visor of her helm. 'I heard something break.'

'Enough,' I said. 'Take this victory and count it a success. You can yield before the next match.'

She pushed herself up halfway, wincing. 'Never! The next match is the final one. I have to enter.' Then she groaned again and lay back down. I let her wallow in her pain and rubbed Wolf-Fang's nose instead.

The horse's mouth was flecked with foam, but his breathing

came steady. He ignored my stroking and looked towards Bradamante. 'I know,' I told him. 'She's hurt. But she's being stubborn. Can you talk some sense into her?' The horse shook his head, bit and bridle clanking.

This made Bradamante laugh, which made her yelp with pain. 'Good horse,' she managed. 'Melissa. Help me to my feet.'

Just then the bell sounded and the steward strode to the middle of the pitch. 'The final match! Ricardetto against Rinaldo! Brother pitted against brother! Paladin and squire!' The rest of his words (and there were many) were lost in the roar of the crowd.

There was nothing fair in the match. Rinaldo had fought one bout – against the hedge knight – and faced Bradamante fresh and unscathed. She, on the other hand, had been encased in armour since dawn, had borne a dozen or more strikes to her shield and person, and now was nursing a few cracked ribs. Nonetheless, this was the match.

'Just do your best, dear,' I said, handing her a lance. The knights and squires gathered around us gave me strange looks. Word of the fighting abbess had spread, and I feared I was becoming a curiosity. Well, if they wanted to stare at me and not Bradamante, that was fine. And soon enough, when I ruled this age, they would know me for who and what I really was . . . 'And, really, what you've accomplished today is marvellous. Already a success. You don't need to prove yourself any further . . . it wouldn't do for you to injure yourself more . . .' Bradamante snatched the lance from my hand and spurred Wolf-Fang forward.

I was left, surrounded by smelly men, wringing my hands. I had set this up, after all. It was my plan. And it would be my fault if she broke a bone . . . or worse. For I knew that Rinaldo, though he thought he was fighting his own brother, wouldn't lessen his blows in the least. He would be goaded by the fear that a younger, less experienced, mere squire could best him, and so he would fight fiercely.

Indeed, the first pass saw him land a solid blow, striking Bradamante on the hip. Thankfully, Rinaldo's lance landed on the opposite side from her cracked ribs. 'Point to the Paladin Rinaldo!' the steward bellowed. Bradamante didn't pause at all, just turned Wolf-Fang about and charged again. This time, she angled Rinaldo's blow off her shield, landing her lance square against his chest and even, as she cantered past him, managing to strike him with her shield, making him rock back in the saddle. He slumped to one side, then the other, like a ship foundering in a heavy sea, but held his seat. 'Point to Ricardetto!' Now the crowd's roar was almost unbearable, and I wove just a bit of air around each of my ears, reducing the noise to a gnat's buzz. The third charge. Both lances struck, both lances shattered, an explosion of wood, and Bradamante went tumbling over Wolf-Fang's flanks. Rinaldo lost a stirrup, but grabbed the edge of the saddle and managed to stay ahorse, though bent over from the blow she landed. I pushed through the crowd, letting someone else chase down Wolf-Fang, and ran to Bradamante's side. 'Rinaldo wins!' the steward called. I lifted her torso, propping her up, and whispered into her helm, 'Are you all right?' A groan was the reply.

And then Rinaldo, leaning on a squire's arm, was beside us. He reached down and pulled Bradamante upright. 'Well done, brother,' he said. Someone had removed his helm, and his face, with its neat little black beard, was flushed with effort and success. 'You bruised me well. How do you fare, Ricardetto? Remove your helm, that I might see that you are well.'

I lifted the helmet from her head. Sweat-soaked though she was, her long hair tumbled down around her shoulders.

The crowd gasped. Rinaldo's eyes went wide. 'Bradamante?' he said, his voice husky. 'I just fought you?' I could see a war of emotion occur – he was embarrassed but also proud, fearful but also delighted. He could not deny that she had fought well . . . but didn't know what such an admission would mean.

Bradamante though, managed a smile. 'I am well, brother. You fought hard, and if I bruised you, then you bruised me more. But I will still dance tonight. Never fear.'

Around Rinaldo, squires and grooms buzzed like a swarm of bees. This one unbuckled his sword belt. Another knelt to remove his greaves. Servants approached, one with a goblet of wine, the other with a rag soaked with vinegar, to begin cleaning his wounds. Each of them, I thought, listened to the conversation between the siblings keenly, one ear pricked to what Rinaldo would say. As for Rinaldo, he quirked his eyebrows and licked his lips and seemed a dozen times on the cusp of saying many things. At last the servants got him out of his chest plate and, though he had done his best to ignore the ministrations, now he stood in a sweat-soaked tunic before his fully armoured sister as a servant washed blood from a gash in his side. A gash she had put there. He winced, caught himself in this display of weakness and bared his teeth in what might have been intended to be a smile. 'Sister,' he said, winced again. 'Fair Bradamante.' The servants, who had been clanking and clanging as they moved the armour, grew quiet. 'I would not have chosen this . . . pursuit for you. Arms and fighting are men's domain.' He drew himself up straight. 'But you have chosen it for yourself. And, that being the case, sister, I tell you that I want nothing more than for you to be the best. The best at jousting. The best at sparring. Nothing less.' He looked down at the cut in his side and gave her a smile that was pained, but genuine. 'I would say, based on today's showing, that you are well on your way.'

Bradamante's cheeks had flushed even deeper red as her brother spoke and now she sank into a gracious bow (armour does not allow for curtsying) and said, 'Thank you, brother. Your blessing is more than I could have wished for. And I hope in the coming months to learn from you and improve further.'

I heard a few cheers and huzzahs from the squires and servants, an underlying buzz as news of this exchange quickly spread. The duke himself leaned down from the pavilion where he'd viewed the jousting and called, 'We'll fete you both tonight!'

Rinaldo bowed and then gestured to his squires. 'Help my sister out of her armour.' And they swarmed around her, bowing and ducking and offering, 'm'lady', as they pulled at her straps and buckles. I found myself pushed aside and stepped back, only to end up next to Rinaldo. 'Ah, Abbess Melissa,' he said. 'Your tutelage has paid off.'

I drew myself up to my full height, shook my hair a little, to let the lustre shine in the late afternoon light. 'Your words to your sister were most gracious, sir. Many men would not grant that a woman could ever be good.'

Rinaldo's smile grew brittle. 'When I was a little boy, my mother used to say to me that once the milk has spilled from the pitcher, there's no way to put it back. One must manage the mess. That's what I am doing.' And he turned and, with one more bow to the duke, began the walk to the chateau.

When Bradamante and I reached our chamber (a slow journey; I had to almost carry her up the stairs), we found Ricardetto already arrayed in finery for the feast. Or just about. He wore an umber jacket, velvet, the colour of autumn leaves, its sleeves worked with a pattern of vines. But as we entered, he tore it off. 'No, no. Too sombre.' And he seized another jacket, this one silk – a vibrant green – with his father's leaping stag on the chest. 'Perhaps?' Only then did he seem to notice us and thrust the jacket back on the bed. 'Bradamante!' he cried and his voice warmed me. His was the pure sound of happiness, of pride, of joy for another – not a note of the doubt or falsehood I heard from so many men. He wrapped her in a hug and swung her about the chamber.

'Ow, ow, ow!' Bradamante cried and broke the embrace.

'You can't be hurt,' Ricardetto scoffed, looking her over from top to toe. 'For the past hour, servants have been carrying me news of my great victory on the jousting pitch. It seems I am now one of the best jousters in the land. Who managed to injure you?'

'Our brother,' she said and put her hand to her ribs. 'Or the knight before. I can't recall. Melissa?'

'Lie down,' I instructed. 'Drink that wine. It's fortified. And eat that cheese. You need rest.'

'I can't rest, Melissa, knowing that my brother might wear that hideous jacket to my feast,' and she seized the umber coat, sticking her tongue out at it. 'Yech. Who told you this colour suited you?'

'It is terrible, isn't it?' Ricardetto sulked. 'But then what to wear?' And they began sorting through the silks and the woollens, ignoring me entirely. I practically force-fed Bradamante the bread and the cheese. ('It's going to be a *feast*, Melissa, I don't need to eat before a feast,' she tried to insist.) And she did let me wrap her broken ribs (three of them, by my estimation). Ricardetto picked out her dress, skirts of grey silk the colour of a dove's wing, with a bodice of silk, blue of summer sky. I combed their hair, tying hers up with blue and grey ribbons, and pinning a cap (black, with a single

late-season rose affixed to the side) to Ricardetto's head, and
sent them off.

For myself, I took Ricardetto's lute and followed behind. I
carefully turned my lustre down low, reduced myself. I did
not wish to compete with my twins for brilliance. (I told
myself that this was Nurture, to think of the needs of others
and not my own. I told myself that my time for brilliance
would come, when I ruled the age. And also, it is true, I
enjoyed how brilliant the twins were.) Every squire, every
lady, every second cousin to the duke (and he had many)
wanted to offer congratulations on the jousting, share a laugh
with Ricardetto, compliment Bradamante's dress, gossip about
some knight or other. A slow descent, a slow walk across the
hall. A dozen knights kissed Bradamante's hand – a hand that
had, but lately, held a lance that charged down at them. She
smiled and spoke to each one in turn.

All eyes on them, I settled on a stool near a hearth and
slowly conjured (so that none in the hall would notice the
magic I worked) a few other musicians to join me. They were
no more than confections of air and water and, given my
proximity to the hearth, I borrowed a few sparks and some
smoke (since I could not summon those on my own . . . thanks
to my wretched brother, may he be dying of thirst). Salvers
of meat, platters of roasted vegetables, baskets of bread. The
noise of the feast – the stamping of feet, the yips of dogs as
they fought for scraps, the shouting for wine – overwhelmed
the hall. I played the lute. (Or, rather, I thought of a melody
and moved the air such that it seemed as though the lute
produced the noise. I have no idea how to actually play this
instrument. So many strings!) I knew no one could hear this
melody but me, as the air of the hall was raucous with feasting,
but I played it nonetheless, a song for the space between the
stars. A song that cast about for the moment yet to come, for

my twins' chance at greatness, my chance at domination. It was a song of doubt but also hope. It was as close as I would come to prayer.

When I opened my eyes at the end (I hadn't realized I had closed them) I found that one little spaniel had drawn near and sat on its haunches, staring up at me. 'Did you like the song, then?' I asked it. A passing serving woman paused, looked at me, at the dog. 'That one's stone deaf, my lady,' she said, and moved on. Nonetheless. The dog curled at my feet and I and my ethereal musicians began to play in earnest as the feast wound down and the drinking continued. Tables and benches were moved. They called for the sword dance and the paladins obliged, capering about with their blades (I would not call it a dance, but then, I am picky). The duke and his lady wife took a turn at the circlet and then called for all the visiting dukes and counts to join them in a round. I plucked the stiff and stately notes. Then raucous cheers, a shouted toast for today's victor. Rinaldo stood on a table and downed a goblet of wine. A shout for his sister to join him. She stood on the table, but only smiled, forgoing the wine. More shouts, 'Dance! Dance!'

Bradamante stepped down and Rinaldo followed. He offered her his hand and she took it. I gladly ceased the stately pomp of the round and began a lively melody, just a touch of two-step in it. Rinaldo wore a black silk jacket, black leggings, silver buckles on his shoes and a silver stag on his chest. His beard was neatly trimmed and combed. To my surprise, his steps did not falter. Bradamante led him nimbly and the two swayed and stepped and the crowd roared. Then Ricardetto stepped forward and bowed to his brother, who replied in kind, and took his twin's hand. I breathed in the woodsmoke from the hearth, the sweat from the men around me; I let it all feed into the music. Let the air and the water vibrate with the mood of this moment. Let it swirl around my twins, around every person in this hall, so that they would each hear a melody tuned to them. There were cries of joy, a whoop of delight. My twins held each other, turned each other round, dipped low, spun tight, shaped a song of their own.

It was late, very late and yet, when I climbed the stairs to my chamber (alone, the twins were still revelling down in the hall) and looked out of the window, Mars and Venus still burned bright in the sky. Lingering there, as if in warning to me. I know, I know, I wanted to tell them. The harvest's almost ready; the sheaves are gathered in; my twins are growing ripe – have grown ripe. They are ready, are they not? I felt they were – not perfect, of course. But where one had flaws, the other had ability, and that was enough, I hoped. But doubt crept in as I stared at those glowing planets. Doubt and fear and a little bit of plain old curiosity. My presence would scarcely be missed for a few moments . . .

A trip by chillest moonlight, an arc of blue-white luminosity, like a suspension bridge across the night sky. At the height of that span, I paused, pulling my disincorporated self tightly together, and *felt*. First, I felt for my brother – after all, I have a strong sense of self-preservation, and it is wise to know where he is rather than just blunder into him. But he seemed . . . somnolent, inactive. Like a volcano that's gone quiescent between eruptions. Hopefully he had fallen into a deep sleep, a long nap (we are both prone to this; one of the few traits we share in common), and it would be a long while before he woke. At any rate, he felt distant and so I went on and felt for his twins, the girl, Marfisa, first. I found her easily and then ran my fingers along the thread of her time, as it were, trying to find some moment of significance – I didn't want to linger or pop in only to find myself in the midst of a boring day (most days in the human world, I'd found, were boring). I sensed a spark, a sparkle, on a day just adjacent to this one – maybe even, by the time I got around to her part of the world, it would be the same day (time bends in funny ways on earth). A coincidence? I thought not. The convergence, the moment my brother and I had appointed, was nearing. This was no chance symmetry.

And so, down the arc of moonlight I flew, dropping into her life. She was at the edge of the desert, near the edge of a continent; as I lowered my descent, I swooped over a mountain range that separated desert from sea, and found her in the foothills, on the desert side. Sandy, dusty, sunny, and hot. I sheltered in the deepest shadow I could find, taking stock. And once I had shaken off the abrupt change in climate, I was surprised to note a certain similarity to the situation I had just left. For here, with the mountains as a distant and dramatic background, stood an impressive palace, its towers and gatehouse festooned with a dozen or more banners bearing the signs of various nobles: a golden sunburst on one, a palm tree on another, a lion, a plough-share, and on they ranged. Though the palace was built from the yellow stone native to this region, it otherwise resembled the duke's chateau in its formidable yet elegant structure. And like that chateau, beyond the palace's walls, level plain stretched. Here, it did not extend into acres of pasture and field but rather into desert sands.

Along the plains nearest the wall (and the shadow I was in lay very near the wall), tents stood, scattered about. Some were plain grey, as of sailcloth. Others were colourful and striped. Some were small enough that one would need to crouch down to enter and others were large enough for a family to live in. Horses were tethered here and there;

boys – most in well-worn tunics – darted and dodged through the pathways between the tents, some yelling and chasing, others intent on an errand. Young men swaggered about; most wore tunics marked with a noble's device; a few went around in long robes – some were tattered and patched and others were fancifully embroidered.

Just beyond these tents were viewing pavilions overlooking jousting pitches and wrestling rings. But for the temperature, I could still have been at the duke's chateau. Now oriented, I flitted from shadow to shadow, looking for the girl. I found her outside a tent – a large one, silken, dyed the rich yellow of saffron with two red stripes, one near the top and one near the bottom. There, Marfisa sat, long hair tied back with a leather cord, scarf loose about her neck, idly sharpening the edge of a knife. Though she wore a long beige robe with a sash about her waist and leather boots – the same sort of clothing as many of the men around her – she was unmistakably a woman. Gone were the hunched shoulders and shrouded face that had marked her years in the city guard. She had grown a little, or maybe that was just the difference of having her shoulders back, her head up. Her cheekbones seemed sharper, her dark eyes keener, as if the intervening span of time had honed her. I noted thick calluses on her palms, from gripping swords and lances, wind-chapped skin on her forehead and cheeks. And yet, there was a feminine beauty about her – the perfect bow of her lips, and how deeply red they were; and when she stood, briefly, to resettle her robe and search her belt (for a different knife to sharpen) I could see the curves of her torso beneath the billowing fabric. Then she settled again, obscuring her hips and chest, and once again, she was just another body. Her hands moved the edge against the whetstone in a practised rhythm and her gaze moved among the men around her, men who oiled bridles or worked kinks out of chain mail. Nearest to her sat Rami, consulting a list, pulling at his bottom lip.

'They all want to challenge you, Marfisa,' Rami said, his voice light and teasing; his robe was an impossible white, with three saffron stripes that matched the tent's colour, made of a soft, silky material (quite the contrast to Marfisa's beige, burlap-seeming attire). 'Look here. The clerk has put down six names for you, and only one for me. Where is there justice in the world?' The other men chuckled.

'You would wish to have six men out for your blood?' Marfisa replied.

Rami shook his head, sighed and rubbed his hand over his scalp; there was the merest layer of dense, curly dark hair that rasped against his palm. 'I would wish to have six men believe I was the best, and vie to prove that, in truth, they were. There was time when I was considered . . .'

'That's not why they challenged me,' Marfisa interrupted. 'They do not think I am the best. Far from it. They think I do not belong. They wish not to knock me down a peg, but knock me out entirely.' Her words sparked with anger and startled me into keener listening – they were nearly an echo of what Bradamante had said to me. Not quite a mirror image, but like looking into a pond. Imperfect, but somehow truer.

Rami spread his hands out; each finger bore a ring, silver and gold and some set with stones, that dazzled in the sunlight. 'Peace, sister. I do not think you are wrong. But this is the way of knights. We fight fiercely against each other, to injure, to settle scores, and sometimes to kill. But we are brothers outside of the pitch. No?'

'Yes,' Marfisa said acidly. 'Brothers.' She cast a glance at the nearby men, all of whom immediately bent over their tasks with renewed intensity. 'I am not included in those ranks.

I know,' she continued, holding up a hand, bare of any ornament save calluses and scabbed-over nicks, to forestall Rami's comment, 'that you will say I am welcome with you, a sister as good as a brother. And it is true. But with who else? These men who challenge me . . . I will say it plain . . . they would as soon take me against my will as they would unseat me from my horse. To them, the two are the same. Conquest of a woman.

'Am I wrong?' She looked about at the men, who remained silent. 'Is that how you would treat a sister? Is that what you think of when you go to joust your fellow knights, who are men? I do not think so.'

A few of the men gave quiet chuckles, a nudge with an elbow.

'Peace,' Rami said. 'You are right. I would not argue with you any more than I would joust with you. In both endeavours, I would end up skewered.' He laughed, a deep, booming sound that brought a scant smile to Marfisa's lips.

'So, what do I do, brother?'

'Fight them and win,' Rami replied.

Marfisa rolled her eyes. 'That was my plan already.'

Within an hour, at the sound of a distant drumming and clash of cymbals, Rami helped her into dark and battered armour – the very armour she had won from Khalid, just refitted to her size. I watched her take a moment, after the groom had led out her chestnut charger, to lean her forehead against the horse's brow. Nose-to-nose they stood, in a moment that looked oddly like prayer. Then she clapped on her helm and set her hand on the groom's shoulder to mount. They passed up her shield first – Khalid's old shield, now so much pocked and splintered that no device was evident – and then her lance.

And out she rode, onto the tourney field. I could not help but compare her to Bradamante – the two events were parallel.

Were, perhaps, occurring at the exact same moment – and there, in my shadow, I felt a sense of vertigo. Time – like onion skin, one impossibly thin layer atop another. Were these the same times, only separated by space? Did one determine the other? I shook myself, huddled tighter in the shadow. This was no moment for foolish philosophy. This was time to hope the girl had overestimated her abilities . . . though I doubted this . . . still, it was time to watch her and learn what her weaknesses might be so that, when the stars aligned, it would be Bradamante who emerged victorious.

Rami sat on a raised platform with other nobles. They, like him, wore spotless white linen robes, with chains of office around their necks, or jewelled daggers in their colourful sashes, and they laughed and chatted like a pack of magpies. Rami was every bit as resplendent as they were, every bit as royal as they were, but he still sat apart. Because he was foreign, yes, because he was darker, true. And because, in his heart, he was rooting for the girl, for Marfisa, and they were not.

Lists were read, challenges were issued. Two knights fought with sword and shield to settle a score between them (one accused the other of spreading a false rumour) and the victor, a knight with a peacock on his shield, dragged the other off the field, taking him as his hostage, to ransom. Horses were paraded before the nobles, and they bickered and dithered about how much they would pay for each. A musician played an oud and sang a (truly terrible) song in praise of some local ruler.

And then the jousting began. Some knights rode out and shouted words of praise to the nobles. Some rode out and hurled insults at their opponents. And one rode out in complete silence. Marfisa.

If I had not watched her get ready, I would not know she

was a woman. The armour encased her completely, hid her self away. Just as it did with Bradamante. But the other knights knew her, and the crowd did too. And as she took the field, the volume increased. Shrieks rose up, hate-filled cries. *Bitch! Cheat!* Again and again. But the word that resounded loudest was *Woman!* Oh, this was what Bradamante had feared. This was what Bradamante couldn't face: being hated. Being reviled. Instead, she had ridden onto the pitch to cries of appreciation and encouragement. I shrank a bit, resenting the crowd's raucous rudeness, impressed by the girl's undaunted strength to face it. Fearful of what this strength meant for *my* chances to win.

I watched as she unhorsed her opponents. One, two, three. More than any other knight on the field. Down they went, as if her lance were magical and knocked them off at the lightest touch. I watched her turn her chestnut horse and ready herself for another charge, another opponent. The crowd only grew louder, increasing their demands. *Knock that bitch down! Kill her!* And it was clear that the knights that fought her fought for more than honour, more than the prize purse. They fought to prove themselves men, as if she was the rock that they must strike their blade against, to shatter or be shattered.

And it occurred to me that there was no way she could win. She was trapped. If she lost, well, she lost. Everything. If one man could drag another away and hold him hostage for losing a bout, then what would a man who defeated Marfisa do to her? And if she won? There was no winning – only more fighting. Indeed, even as she unseated her last opponent, her sixth victory of the day, the crowd's jeers and hoots only grew louder.

Squires and servants helped her fallen opponent to his feet. Marfisa steered her charger to the centre of the pitch, waiting in front of the pavilion of noblemen. She lifted the visor of her helm and gave a small bow of her head to her opponent. I saw her mouth form the words, *Well fought*, though they did not carry over the noise of the crowd. The knight she had unhorsed, now on his feet, though supported by two squires, answered by spitting in her direction. She turned back to face the watching noblemen. Again, she spoke, trying to lift her voice above the jeers. 'I have won. I have defeated all your knights. I ask of you no prize of money. Only of rank.' Her lips twisted. 'Of the semblance of honour.'

The noble who sat foremost on the pavilion – who wore a circlet of gold around his dark hair – held a hand up. The crowd quieted somewhat. 'It is not possible for a woman such as you to have honour,' he replied. And though his words were calm, a flush suffused his tan cheeks, and his dark eyes glinted with malice. 'And I would never raise you in rank. You belong among the lowest.'

Marfisa snapped the visor of her helm down and spurred her horse, trotting away from the pitch. As she rode off, the crowd surged and cried, and soon began to pelt her with trash. Bits of bread, chicken bones, and, then, rocks. She nudged her mount to a gallop and did not stop until she reached Rami's tent. There, it seemed a protected space. Quiet. Calm. She dismounted and handed the horse over to a groom. One of the men who had watched her sharpen her knife earlier helped her now with the buckles and ties. She stacked the plates of Khalid's armour neatly by the entrance to the tent, set her shield on top of it, and retreated inside. Out came the whetstone, the knife. When Rami entered, he tossed the fat purse with her winnings on the ground beside her. 'I argued for your prize in silver if they wouldn't give you the prize you truly deserved. Marfisa. It stings, but they will . . .'

She held up a hand to forestall his comments. 'They won't,' she said, her voice tight and pinched with anger.

Rami sighed, his broad shoulders rising up almost to his ears and then dropping low, giving up the argument. 'What's this?' He held the flap of the tent open and pointed to the shield.

'Would you summon the armourer for me, friend?' she asked, and I heard the effort it took for her to keep her words light and relaxed.

'Of course. What is wrong with your plate?' He picked up the armour and examined it.

'Everything,' she replied.

Servants brought figs and wine and cheese and olives and fresh-baked bread. Rami duly brought the armourer to the girl, a pox-scarred fellow who bowed low before he settled himself on a cushion. 'What can I do for you, my lady . . . Sir Knight . . . ?'

'Marfisa,' she said. 'That only is my title. For now and always. A single name is enough, is it not? I have no father. I had a brother once, but he is lost.' She waved a hand in front of her face, as if clearing away a cobweb. 'That is a story I cannot tell. I am only Marfisa. Alone. I wish for you to make me a suit of armour that will protect me, yes, but will also be honest. No more of this plate from another man. No more a boxy approximation. I wish the armour to be fitted to my body, as my body is. Do you understand?' And she stood and cast aside the coarse beige robe. Beneath, she wore the sort of tight-fitting leather jerkin and leggings that any fighter would use to lessen the chafing of the armour and its straps. The armourer gasped; even Rami jerked in surprise. In this place – much as in Bradamante's land – women kept their bodies covered, or revealed them only in sanctioned ways. Marfisa's leathers showed nothing of her flesh, but everything of her shape. And for all that men insisted that this body determined everything about a person's capability, they seemed little able to face her form: her hips, her waist, her breasts. They would insist it made her who she was and they would also insist not to see it. 'This is the body that you say limits me?' Marfisa said, her voice low and harsh. 'This is the body that will defeat you.'

'Fitted to your shape?' the armourer said hesitantly.

'*My* shape,' she said. 'These men. Some wear helms shaped like grotesque creatures, or with horns, to scare their foes. Others don plates that make it seem their chest and stomachs are sculpted of bronze, when we all know their stomachs are distended with wine. I do not want to deceive. I want everyone who approaches me to know that I am a woman. First and foremost. I do not want to be a man.'

The armourer swallowed. Bowed. Took his leave.

'Marfisa,' Rami began. She cut him off with a wave of her hand.

'Who is the man who paints the best shields?' she demanded. Rami heaved himself to his feet. 'I'll fetch him.'

Tense days passed there, on the margin of the Great Desert. Other knights jousted or sparred. Marfisa kept to her tent. Messengers came and went from the palace and word spread through the camp: *war*. A call to arms from a king who gathered forces at a port on the sea, just on the other side of the mountains. Some knights rode off in haste. Some nobles returned home to gather more men. Others remained in camp and gnawed on rumours and gossip. Marfisa stayed in her tent. Until the day her armour and shield were ready.

First, she took receipt of the shield. A verdant green field. A sparkling silver phoenix. Her wings spread, her taloned feet just rising out of a red-gold fire. She was beautiful. With a hooked beak and a glaring eye, she was deadly, too. And then, the armour. It, too, was silver, resplendent as a mirror. And when Marfisa put it on, as Rami fastened the back plate to the front plate, it seemed as though it had been poured over her. Gone was the squareness, the flatness of her previous plate. This armour had curves and roundness; it bore the shape of her, boldly female.

'Aren't you concerned,' Rami said, 'that this will make you a target?'

'I am ready to be seen,' Marfisa replied; her words danced with grim happiness as she gazed at herself in a looking glass.

He moved to take her plate off, but she shook her head. 'I will travel like this. I am never long between fights. I am a target, as you say.' She pursed her lips, then began to stalk about the tent, moving as if the armour weighed nothing, gathering up her few belongings and tossing them into her saddlebags and muttering to herself. 'Perhaps I ought never to take this armour off. I don't want to hear them say that there is a woman hiding within that plate.' Her voice grew louder. 'There is a woman within this armour. This is a woman's armour. This armour is a woman. I am not pretending to be a man. Let it be clear.' The last words rattled with rage.

Rami bent over to examine the painting on the shield, fingering the fine feathers of the phoenix. 'What is this all about, little sister? And did you say you are travelling? Now?'

'They think they can hurt me by naming me a woman. They think I wish to hide what I am. But I do not. I do not wish to be like them. I want to be better than them.'

'You already are, Marfisa.'

'But they do not see it.' She paused in gathering her belongings and stood in front of the mirror, staring at herself.

Rami shrugged. 'Perhaps they will.'

She shook her head. 'I cannot win on their terms. That is,

I do win. Every day, again and again. I follow their rules but their rules do not follow me.' She sighed. 'Rami. I am separate. Why do I try to belong?'

He gave her a rueful smile. 'I know, little sister, a taste of what you mean. To be thought barely adequate, you must be twice as good as any of them. I know what this feels like. Do not let it make you bitter,' he said.

'Too late.' She turned from the mirror and faced him. 'I will leave this place. I will go to fight in this war that is on everyone's lips.'

Rami's eyebrows shot up. 'You will fight for King—'

'I will fight for the man who will recognize my worth, or I will fight for myself.'

'You may well be an army of one, I fear.' Rami chuckled. 'But you still might win.' He clapped his hands together. 'Shall I have my horse saddled then? Fold up the tent?'

'What? Why?'

'I'm coming with you, of course.'

'I don't need your protection.'

'I would never suggest such a thing.' He spread his hands wide. 'But perhaps you'd enjoy my company?'

I was most concerned. As the two of them loaded up donkeys and mounted their horses, I settled in a shadow beside the road leading from the camp to the mountains. They would surely pass this way. Little hope that they'd succumb to a storm or starve to death as they crossed those peaks. No. She was on her way, this girl, this Marfisa. And she seemed to aim with deadly accuracy right towards Bradamante's heart. Thinking of the two of them – it was like comparing a fox to a terrier.

And now, here she came. In her armour, atop her sturdy horse. Rami rode in a robe – an unusually sedate one for him; tan, with trim of darker brown. To keep the dust of the road

231

from his face, Rami had wrapped a burnoose about his head and neck and now only his eyes were visible. Behind them trailed two laden donkeys led by Rami's two servants. For a king's son, he travelled light. Marfisa had the visor of her helm lifted and she peered ahead, to where the mountains loomed. 'It will be a long way over those peaks,' she murmured. 'And longer still after, to reach the sea. And whatever lies beyond the sea.'

'Have you seen the ocean before, little one?' Rami asked.

Marfisa gave a little snort. 'I grew up on an island.'

'Truly?' Rami replied.

She still stared at the mountains. 'An island in the middle of the ocean.' She grimaced. 'It isn't a story I can tell.'

'Try,' he said gently, nudging his horse nearer to hers, waving his servants to ride farther back. (Which forced me to abandon the rather comfortable shadow I had found among their baggage ... swapping it instead for a bumpier one next to Rami's saddlebags.)

'You promise that you won't laugh at me?'

'If I do laugh, I will apologize profusely. But laughter is hard to prevent and hard to forbid.'

This brought a smile to her lips. 'Very well. When I was little, I lived on an island in the middle of the ocean. With a twin brother. And a demon. He was tall and thin and had the shape of a human. He had long, black nails, that looked like bird claws, on each finger. His eyes glinted red. I hated the demon. I loved my brother. And when I was still just a little girl, sailors came to the shore of the island and stole me away.'

A long pause, interrupted only by the call of one crow to another.

'That's all?' Rami prompted.

Marfisa shook her head. 'There's so much more. Rami ... there is ... this story fills me. Sometimes it fills my heart, making it pound until I think it will burst. And other times it fills my lungs, so thick that I can barely draw air. But I cannot tell it.' Her voice wavered and I thought for a moment that she might be close to tears. 'I cannot tell it,' she echoed.

Rami reached out, placed his hand on her armoured shoulder. 'A story is like a baby. It comes forth when the time is right. Let me tell you, Marfisa, of another island . . .' And his voice fell into the pleasant cadence that bards use, when they intend to while away half the night with a tale of strange lands, foreign customs, and fantastic beasts. I longed to linger there in the shadows, to hear what he might tell. But I had to go. Time was short and I wanted to check on her brother.

I sorted through shadows until I sensed him (I did so look forward to finally ruling this world, entirely. Not being relegated to half of my powers. Not being so constrained by ridiculous rules. Not having to squeeze through shadows . . . soon, soon), felt the threads of his life. No surprise, the tension grew, thrumming taut, right at this moment. He, too, like Marfisa, like Bradamante, was at a moment of change. Oh, the time was so close. And (this was surprising) so was the place. Just the other side of the mountains. I took a good deal of pleasure in passing over the peaks in the blink of an eye, knowing that Marfisa would spend weeks struggling over them, perhaps losing a toe or two to frostbite (one can hope, can't one?). And slipping through shadows on the other side, feeling the temperature around me rise, tasting the salt in the air, trading the calls of crows for the squawks of seagulls. Feeling my way through throngs of men – a few knights on horses, but mostly an unwashed mass of barely armed soldiers. Some king's army, waiting to be slaughtered.

I was relieved to find my brother's boy, Ruggiero, at some distance from the bulk of the men. I followed the shoreline, over a marshy patch that buzzed with flies, then veered slightly inland. A tricky navigation of a span of sere desert – only sand, barely a shadow for me to hide in – and then I found him. There, in between two grey and yellow hills, an oasis sat. Palms sprouted, like the last patch of hair on a balding man's head, and cast thick shade around a pool of water. Just beyond the palms, a few tents were pitched. These were not the showy confections of Rami's liking, but rather designed to blend into the sand, to offer a bit of protection from sun and wind. Camels, donkeys, and two horses were tethered not far from the tents, beneath the palm trees. I could hear some humans near the tents, and some others, closer in to the centre of the oasis. That's where the boy was.

Except he was a man now. Finished with his growth, Ruggiero had filled out. Broad shoulders, muscled arms and legs. He had even grown a straggly beard, his whiskers as dark as the hair on his head. But in his eyes – the wide spacing of them, and his lips – the arched bow of them, he looked like his sister. No resplendent armour for him. At the moment I found him, he wore a grubby tunic and leggings and wielded no weapon beyond a shepherd's staff, as he helped two men bring water to a flock of sheep and goats. One of the men herded the sheep, slowly corralling them into a tighter space, a bit distant from the tents but still in the palms' shade. Ruggiero filled leather buckets with water and passed them to the other man, who spilled them into makeshift troughs. The sheep butted and bleated to get a drink. A few tried to break away from the flock and reach the pool of water, but the shepherds caught them quickly. The water of an oasis is a precious thing, one might say sacred. Anyone could draw its water, but no one should let animals befoul the pool.

234

I watched this simple task, drinking in a sense of this boy, this man, this twin, this Ruggiero. He worked steadily, silently. The other men cursed the sheep, cursed the flies, cursed the heat. He said nothing, only hummed a bit to himself. Only once did his composure break, when a young woman approached, her footsteps rustling on the dried and fallen palm fronds. The sound made him jump, spill water, as he pivoted and faced her, knees bent, ready to spring. 'What is it?' he barked and she shied away.

'The meal is ready,' she said and dashed off.

One man stayed with the flock, while Ruggiero and the other returned to the tents. There, an older woman stirred a pot while a middle-aged woman nursed a child. The young woman, the one who had summoned Ruggiero, said, 'Your knight was calling for you.' Ruggiero nodded and ducked low to enter a tent. (I followed; shadows were easy to come by here.) Inside, the odour of illness assaulted me. Sweet rot. I expected to see a gangrenous limb, but the knight – who lay atop a nest of blankets – had no visible injury. Sir Badr was a fraction of the man he had been, wasted away to a twist of skin and bones. The smell of decay came from his mouth, from his breath, from somewhere inside him. Ruggiero propped up the knight's head, dribbled liquid from a wineskin into his mouth. The man looked like the nursing infant outside, eyes closed, lips fumbling. Around swallows, he murmured and muttered. 'Look, you have to look.' Most of his words were nonsense. But now and then he managed an intelligible phrase. Ruggiero tried to cover him in blankets, but Badr threw them off, seized Ruggiero's wrist. 'Mars!' he said, beseechingly. 'Look! It's not where it ought to be.' And then he sank back into raving mutters.

Ruggiero wetted a cloth, rubbed Badr's forehead and cheeks. Waited till the man had quieted, fallen into sleep or stupor, and then crawled out of the tent. I was glad to leave and could tell by the deep breath that he took that Ruggiero was as well. The fug of sickness was heavy.

The young woman handed him a bowl, full of lentils cooked with greens and some root vegetables. He settled near the fire, though the evening was warm; the smoke did something to keep the flies at bay. He ate. The others talked. The sun set. Ruggiero rose and went to the horses, checking their eyes and hooves before the last of the light faded. Stars appeared and, with visible reluctance, he looked up. (So did I.) Mars flamed in the sky, as red as the coals the lentils had cooked on. He ran his fingers through his dark hair, digging his nails into his scalp, as if he could scratch loose understanding. He stared for a very long time, until the screech of a night-bird startled him from his reverie.

At some odd hour, Ruggiero went over to the flocks and took his turn at watch. The sheep were quiet. The oasis a dark mass. The shepherd whose watch he relieved nodded in thanks and disappeared into the night. Ruggiero walked around the pen, satisfied himself that nothing lurked in wait, and then settled, staff across his knees. For a time, he gazed out into the emptiness of the desert, but then, as if answering a call he could not resist, he looked up, where Mars still blazed.

'Your knight is going to die.' The voice came out of the darkness and in a moment, Ruggiero was on his feet, a knife in his hands, the staff left on the ground. 'Peace,' the voice said. It was the old woman who'd cooked the meal. She stepped closer, bent down and picked up the staff he'd let drop. 'I don't mean to be cruel. But he will die soon.'

'I know,' Ruggiero said. 'And it will be a mercy. He is in pain.'

'What will you do, when he dies?' The old woman still held the staff, turning it over in her hands.

Ruggiero tipped his head back. 'Is Mars . . . where it ought to be?'

The woman laughed. 'Nothing is where it ought to be.' She shoved the staff at him. 'Put that knife away. Be a shepherd.'

He sheathed the knife and took the staff but said, 'I am not meant to be a shepherd. I am meant . . . to guard. To fight.'

The old woman pursed her lips as she stared at him. 'I saw you, when the bandits tried to take our flocks. You fought and you killed.' Ruggiero looked away from her. 'You have courage. But you don't like to kill. You don't like to hurt. So you oughtn't fight, if it causes you such anguish.'

He sighed but made no answer. Together, they stood in silence and gazed at the sky. 'What power can move Mars from its natural course?' he asked at last.

The woman shook her head. 'Powers far beyond ours. And if we are lucky, they will ignore us.' (Oh, I thought, you are not so lucky.) She sucked at her teeth. 'Mars is the sign of war. It may be out of tune because the king gathers his army. Have we not seen knights and men at arms straggling everywhere about the desert?'

'It's more than that,' Ruggiero said.

'What will you do when he dies?' the woman asked again.

'I'd like to help with your flocks,' Ruggiero mumbled. 'Sir Badr, before he fell ill, spoke of quests and glory. I have learned much from him. The sword and the lance, how to ride a horse and care for one, too. But I don't . . . without him . . .' He cursed softly under his breath. 'I don't want to be alone. Again.'

The woman patted his shoulder. 'Don't stay with us. The path you wish to avoid is often the path you must take. But I don't think you will be alone for long.' She pointed again to the night sky and now the red flare of Mars was joined by the green glow of Venus. 'Look how they move

– the two of them, as if they whispered secrets to each other. Yes, they move. Towards . . .' Her finger traced an arc, reaching, pointing at the double stars of Gemini. 'Towards the twins.'

At this word, Ruggiero startled. 'I am a twin,' he whispered.

'I know,' the woman said. 'I can feel that you are missing half of yourself. That is why you cling to the knight who will die soon. That is why you want to cling to the flocks, my family, when he dies. Why you must not.' She gestured once again at the stars. 'I think they are shining for you.'

Ruggiero shook his head. 'I don't want . . .'

'They don't care what you want.'

The night wind rattled the palm fronds. 'Tell me a story,' Ruggiero said, petulant as a little boy. 'Tell me a story about twins. A boy and a girl.'

The old woman smiled, though the darkness swallowed it. 'Once upon a time,' she began.

In the morning, Ruggiero crawled into the tent and found Sir Badr dead. The men helped him bury the corpse under a palm tree on the edge of the oasis. Helped him heap up stones so that no beast would disturb the grave. As the other men went to ready the flocks, Ruggiero saddled one horse. The old woman came near, gave him dates and almonds and dried mutton. 'Good fortune to you,' she said as he mounted and rode away towards the sea, towards the gathering tide of men and war. By the time he turned and looked back, the tents had already disappeared.

Winter. The duke had invited Bradamante and Ricardetto, and of course Rinaldo, to stay as his honoured guests at the chateau and travel to join the king in the spring. And so, when I returned from my observations of Ruggiero and Marfisa, I found my own twins settled into comfortable chambers and learning all the nuances of the life of the noble and idle. Traits that assuredly would *not* assist them in the coming contest. Bradamante delighted in spending hours with the ladies. They talked endlessly of potential marriage partners or complained of current husbands and sewed volumes of embroidery – handkerchiefs, jackets, scarves, shirts, robes; I felt lucky to leave that room without my flesh embroidered. I would linger there out of desire to be near Bradamante, working a drop spindle or helping to turn one of the larger spinning wheels, occasionally feeling compelled to try my hand at some embroidery (I was terrible at it), listening to their stories (or gossip, if that's all there was to listen to), lasting an hour, maybe two, before I grew restless. Then I might wander, pacing the chill hallways, circling the parapets, or even trudging across the snowy yards. Sometimes the twins would accompany me and we would pass an afternoon at the stable, currying Wolf-Fang and Storm. Once in a great while, the duke would declare that it was time to hunt, and off the whole chateau would go. Servants first, to clear trails in the snow and make sure the quarry was ready to be hunted. Men second, to pursue said quarry. And women third, to pursue the men.

I sound gloomy. I was gloomy. I had reached, I admit, a slough of despond. I would like to blame it on the cloudy weather, on the cold and confinement. But the truth is, I was full of doubt and self-recrimination. I could not stop thinking about those other twins. My brother's twins. My brother . . . my Other . . . It seemed so long since I had been properly myself. Properly *home* (though that was not quite the word for it . . . the place where we belonged . . . the place we came from . . . the place we went back to . . .). As I strode along the icy parapets, I would replay scenes from Marfisa's life, or go over again the stories that Ruggiero had been told. I would try to imagine how my twins would meet them, where, under what circumstances. Everything I imagined filled me with doubt, filled me with a bubbling sense of anxiety that made me tremble until I would dash down off the parapets and charge into Bradamante's chamber and demand that she put on armour and practise her fighting and she would laugh and seize my hands – her own fingers so warm and mine so cold – and say, *Melissa. Don't be ridiculous.* As if she were the adult, the angel, the heaven-sent, and I was the foolish child. And I would force a laugh and we might sit and watch the snow fall for an hour or more. And when I pressed – when I dragged her and Ricardetto from their comfortable chambers out into the snow, or when I leapt from shadowed corners, pouncing on them and forcing them to defend themselves, or when I hauled Ricardetto into the ladies' sewing room to tell stories, they would shove me rudely away, scold me, even. Grow angry. And soon enough they began to avoid me entirely. Evenings had been my one sanctuary – a time when both twins would spin tales for children (and adults), a time when Ricardetto might play his lute and, sometimes, a few people might take to the floor and dance. But if I appeared in the hall, the twins would withdraw, as if fearing what I might call on them to do. And so I began to keep to my chambers more and more.

It is my fault. That is the conclusion I have come to. Or not fault, but a necessary, though unfortunate, by-product of my Nurture. That my twins are comfortable. Loved. Settled. I would have them a bit rougher, a bit sharper . . . no, no I would not. What they are, they are because I shaped them with care and tenderness and hope. I would have them keen with *want*, sharpened by *desire*, instead of being full and content. No, no. This is why they were avoiding me; I had raised them to be what they are. I just wish I didn't feel so full of doubt.

Winter continued. I grew languid. Felt enervated. Could barely rouse myself from bed. When the angle of the sun shifted and the days stretched longer, and the icicles that dangled from the rain spouts of the chateau began to drip ceaselessly, I called for a servant to bring a large silver bowl and a ewer of fresh-drawn water. I hauled myself from my bed when the requested items arrived and forced myself to concentrate. I felt too weak, too defeated to venture forth by shadow or moonbeam. So scrying it would have to be. As soon as the servant had withdrawn, I poured the water into the bowl.

It took all my concentration and effort (I was growing so weak down here, in this body) to draw air over the surface of the water, to let it ruffle and ripple. I summoned in my mind a picture of Ruggiero; I recalled the breadth of his shoulders, the hue of his skin – tan and gold and reddened by sun. How his eyes turned down at the corners, just a bit, and were wide-spaced on either side of his sharp and jutting nose. I formed a judgement, too, not that it mattered: handsome, in a striking way. Not neat and trim and perfect angles, but compelling. The air swirled the water again, took my image into it. A tiny whirlpool formed in the middle of the bowl, spun furiously for a moment. Stilled. And, like a fish rising up through the depths of a pond, Ruggiero's face surfaced. I leaned forward and watched.

He led his horse through crowds of men. I noticed he wore his saddlebags slung over his shoulder, as if he had learned that a thief might take them from his horse if he left them there. One hand on the horse's bridle, the other on the pommel of his sword. He used his broad shoulders to manoeuvre himself. The men were mostly like him, armed and young. Some wore mail. Some had horses. Others carried a spear.

241

Some wore bare rags and others had fresh tabards in a lord's colours. Ahead, I could see the spindly masts of ships rising up, like bare tree trunks; that was where he headed. Eventually, he broke through the crowds and reached the piers, where ships – large and small – bobbed on the water. He exchanged words I could not hear with a guard, a broad-chested man with a cudgel, broken-nosed and intimidating enough to stare down men with swords. The guard pointed him further down the pier, and Ruggiero trudged on, the horse plodding beside him, until he reached a man – perhaps a noble, but a minor one – who wore clean brown leggings and a loose-fitting shirt the colour of flour. Barefoot. He was dressed for the sea, and when he turned at Ruggiero's steps, he pursed his lips, as if judging the weight of the horse, the armour, the man. 'What is it? I haven't much time.'

'My name is Ruggiero, and I . . .'

'I haven't time for your lineage. I'm sure your story is sorrowful. There's a crowd of men waiting to board these ships.' He pointed down the pier the way Ruggiero had come. 'I don't know who let you pass, but I'll have his ears. Off with you, wait with the others.'

'I was squire to Sir Badr,' Ruggiero said, even as he retreated a step.

'Badr,' the man breathed.

'And I've served as a sailor before I was a knight. I can be useful. On sea and land.' The other man barely seemed to listen, entranced by the name Ruggiero had spoken. 'This is his armour, his shield, given to me.'

'He is dead?' the man asked, inspecting the shield that Ruggiero untied from the horse's back and held up.

'He is. I travelled with him through the Levant, to Jerusalem . . .'

'I haven't time for tales. You say you know ships? And you

242

can use that sword?' He waited for Ruggiero to nod. 'Then get yourself loaded. I'll hear your tales when we are under sail.'

The man began to walk away, but Ruggiero, steeling himself, called. 'Wait! What's the payment?'

A smile crossed the man's face. 'You are Badr's squire. Smart fellow. A silver a kill. All the food you're served. Load up.'

And I left Ruggiero, getting his baulky horse up the gangplank to the ship's deck. I knew enough: he would be crossing the sea. He would be coming to this land. A mercenary, a soldier for hire, to fight in the army opposite my twins. I let go of his time, held in place just the hints of his face, those features he shared with his sister: the shape of the jaw, the set of the eyes. I pictured her as I had last seen her, that fierce focus on the horizon. The water of the bowl stilled. The circles rippled out, concentric, from the middle to the edges, as if I'd dropped a pebble in.

And there she was. Riding side-by-side with Rami, the servants still lagging a bit behind with the donkeys. The mountains were behind them now, and they rode through just-tilled fields. Ahead, there was a huddled mass of buildings, still indistinct at this distance, indicating a town. And if I squinted (and used a little magic) I could discern, past the buildings, the bare spires of ship masts. Marfisa still wore the armour (did she take it off to sleep?) as she rode and I noticed that everyone she passed looked at her. Peasants working the fields paused in their digging to stare. Merchants driving carts full of wares let their jaws hang open as they took her in. She gleamed. She shone. She was unmissable, unmistakable.

They slowed their pace as they drew near the town, eventually reining up beside an inn where they paused to water the horses and the donkeys. Marfisa dismounted, stretched, and lifted her visor to survey the inn, the road, the town that now lay just ahead. She nodded, and turned back to Rami, who gently stroked the nose of his horse.

'I will take my leave of you now, Rami,' Marfisa said, her words quick and blunt.

Rami gazed at her, a soft fondness in his eyes. 'I feared you would say that. And I know you better than to argue.' He shook his head and looked off into the distance, towards the town, past it, towards the masts that were now clearly visible. 'I cannot fight in this war. It is not my war. Not my father's war. I would travel with you, if you wished it.'

Marfisa shook her head. 'I was meant to be alone.' Her words were smooth and cold as polished stone.

A large smile split Rami's face. 'Ah, no, little sister. You were not. You were born a twin. You yourself told me this. So you were born to be with another. Only at this moment, you are searching for that other. This is so.'

A bit of colour rose in her cheeks. 'I have enjoyed riding with you, these past months. I have enjoyed your friendship.' That last word caught in her throat.

'And I yours. And when you have found what or who you are searching for, come to Axum, and I will show you my father's kingdom.'

'Would I be a curiosity there?'

'You would be a welcome guest. Are you certain you will not take some coin from me?' He held out a leather purse. 'A gift, friend to friend.' She shook her head. 'I beg you to be careful.'

She smiled. 'I will be fierce. I will sell myself to no man, serve no man who does not value me truly, for all that I am, not despite what I am.'

Rami looked as if he might open his mouth and say something more, but he merely nodded. They clasped hands, thumped each other on the shoulder, and parted ways.

* * *

And there. I let the moment fade, sat in my chill chamber, the bowl of water on the floor, the bottom of the silver bowl gone black, as if charred by smoke and soot. There. They were on their ways. They were coming towards me. No, not towards me. Towards my twins. The season had turned, the stars were aligned. The moment drew near. I tried to shake myself from my stupor, to regain some vigour, summon the urge to rally my twins and lead them out to meet this challenge. But I was . . . weary. And before I could shake this terrible ennui, footsteps clattered up the stairs. My heart gave a little leap – it was my twins, coming to find me, oh, they cared and we would . . . but it was a servant, knocking on the door, edging it open, and telling me in breathless words that the king's messengers had summoned all his knights and soldiers to come to his aid.

The chateau boiled over with plans for departure. Carts and wagons were loaded with supplies and provisions. Horses were saddled. Troops were mustered. Before, I might have shoved my way to the front, or at least claimed a position at my twins' side. But now, I felt like a stick, carried along by the spring floods, going where I was pushed. Now in an eddy, now surging along the current. I, who had set these events in motion, now felt myself subsumed by them.

It was not a pleasant sensation.

From my chamber window, I could see all the arrangements and preparations. The masses of men moving out. Rinaldo conferring with the duke. I waited for my twins to come to my door, to ask me for help. To need me. I, who had raised them and nurtured them and taught them everything they knew.

But they did not come.

*　*　*

And in that lonely room, I felt again that this was the hardest part of Nurture. Letting go. Being done. Well, not *done*. But not the same active, hands-on, Nurture. Let them go. Could I do it? Did I have a choice?

I didn't trust myself not to meddle. If I went down to that muddy yard, I would be fussing with Ricardetto's bridle, arguing with Bradamante over her clothes. They would resent me further and I would help no one. I watched from my window, long enough to see them emerge. Bradamante had found some point of compromise; she wore a split skirt, leathers beneath, so she could ride astride Wolf-Fang. But her dress was a gown, and a luxurious one at that. And someone – not me, not me, alas – had combed her hair until it gleamed, lustrous and red-brown, and caught it in a silver net dotted with pearls, so that she glinted and glittered in the morning sun. She smiled at the men around her, though I suspected the smile did little to allay her nerves (I could comfort her . . . I could make those men cringe in fear . . .). And Ricardetto, not to be outdone by his sister, wore a dark green coat, its front worked with pearls and thread to display a hunting scene – pearl eyes for the hart, pearl eyes for the hunter. And a jaunty cap – useless against the cold spring air, I would have urged him to something warmer – with a matching dark green plume.

They mounted and waited in the yard. They did not look up at me. They rode out. They did not glance back. Perhaps they assumed I was right there with them; I always had been. Perhaps they didn't care at all.

When the yard was quiet but for a few servants who began sweeping and shovelling the debris the men and horses had left, I climbed from my chamber to the chateau's highest tower. To the still-icy parapet. The stars had been moved. The challenge had been set. There was nothing I could do but wait for the time to come. Well, one thing I could do. I could make certain that my brother didn't meddle with anything in these final moments. Yes, that would give me some clear purpose and keep me from pining over my twins. There, on the parapet, alone – even the guard of this spot had answered the call to war – I stepped to the edge, climbed atop the wall. The wind wrapped around me. I called it, a gust, a howl, a cyclone. I leaned into it, let it support me, let it release me to fall. I fell . . . what freedom in falling. No choice, only one direction to go in. As I hurtled down, governed only by the laws of this planet, I wondered what it would be like to die. This, death, something I would never know, never understand. And I feared, in that moment of falling, that because I could not understand death, I could not understand life either.

The ground came closer and before I could reach it, I let the air lift me up. Changed my arms to wings. My fingers to feathers. My golden hair to a tufted crest. My nose to a beak. I caught a thermal, let it lurch me higher, around, and higher again. Until I was almost back where I belonged. High above. Looking down. On what would be my land. My world. My age. To rule.

Why had I never been a bird before? Flying was wonderful. The air was my element. True, birds did have very small brains, but I need not be limited by that. I revelled in the sensation of wings, of near-weightlessness, and it almost made me forget the moment of despair that I had felt when my twins left me. At length, I came to myself – my real self, not my Melissa self – and oriented towards my brother, my Other. Where was he? Where were they? I widened the sweep of my arc, a huge circle, swinging as far north as to see the icy castle where Fiordispina had been raised, and as far south as the kingdom that Rami's father ruled. I felt my brother nowhere. I swooped down on the tropical island where he had spent years with the twins (I will not say raised them) and stomped my taloned feet amid the ashes of his fire. Long since dead and cold. No sign of him here. I tried (believe me, I tried) to talk with the parrots of that island, to get some form of information about when he had last been there, but the only thing they had to say about my brother was *good riddance*. Well, in that we would agree.

I say that. And I mean it. But I also . . . missed him. Hmmm. Perhaps I was curious what he was up to. Or I would not have minded a bit of conversation with the only other being in the universe who had a chance of understanding me. And so I took to the sky again and tried another arc. I was not *spying*. I was looking for my brother, Atlante, as he was now known. So, of course, I had to look at my twins and make sure he wasn't planning a covert attack.

They had crossed the muddy roads out of the mountains, gathering more forces to the duke's men, as other knights and nobles and lords joined, until they already seemed a mighty army. I settled in the boughs of an oak tree and watched them all tromp past. What a mess. They camped for a night in a mucky field some peasant had spent the day tilling and planting – an entire season's crop ruined by this herd of men, who got up the next morning, pissed where they had slept and carried on, as if they neither knew nor cared where their food came from. There was Rinaldo, near the front. Ricardetto not far behind. By his wild gesticulations, I knew he was telling a story and the raucous laughter of his appreciative audience reached even my ears, high above. And Bradamante, riding a bit apart, beside her twin. Letting him, for once, do the talking. Now and then she would acknowledge some knight or lord who rode up to greet her and engage in conversation. Oh, I wished to overhear her every word. I regretted that I had turned up my nose at her gossip with the ladies, I so missed the sound of her voice, even her complaining. Maybe she wouldn't mind if a friendly bird alighted nearby . . .

I shook myself out of my revelry. *Don't be a fool. You're looking for your brother.* And he was not here. So, off, off. Down to where the boats had landed on this side of the sea. Another army, another muddy track. Here, though, signs of more violent destruction – they were invaders, after all. A burned village. A ransacked town. Ruggiero rode in a small cluster of knights on a ridge above and beside the main force – a sort of scouting party, I surmised. They wore mail coats and carried sword and shield, travelling light in other words, for speed. Already, he bore a bruise on one cheek – dark purple-blue. And a wideness to his eyes that spoke of a certain haunting. I knew he had killed before, but the rawness of battle, the wanton destruction of taking over and invading the homes of simple merchants and peasants must have bothered him deeply, even as he earned his silvers. I watched the group ride ahead, watched them divide and explore the various roads. Watched him lay an ambush for a lone rider, a messenger, gut the man's horse, drive the pommel of his sword against the man's head. Then kneel and check that he still breathed. Stay kneeling for a moment, a minute, his own chest and shoulders heaving. Before rising, his face a mask, and returning to meet his fellows.

I left him there, left him to his gory tasks. Where was my brother? My last stop, Marfisa. She had somehow managed to inveigle her way onto a river barge (I suspected, knowing her, that it had involved rudeness against her person, a challenge to a duel, her summary defeat of her opponent, and her commandeering the ferry as a result). At any rate, as I settled on the stones of a church tower, I watched her disembark from the barge, the ferrymen bowing as she passed. Her armour gleamed, sending the sunlight clattering off its shiny surface. She led her horse up the river bank and held her head high as she walked across the square of a modest town, towards the inn. And there, with firm resolve and only one minor fight (resulting in an unconscious, but not bloodied, groom) she had acquired a room and very soon the wife of the innkeeper was serving her wine and bread and cheese and asking her a multitude of questions about how, exactly, did a woman become a knight and was it very difficult to learn the sword?

Quite entertaining. Hopeful, I might even say. But no sign of my brother. I took a last sweeping circle of the sky and picked a spot in what seemed likely to be, very soon, the middle of the world – or the middle of the world that I cared about. The point of convergence of these armies, these persons. As a spot, it wasn't much. A boggy bit of ground, a few hummocked ridges. A deep glade of forest. And a bunch of fields, currently occupied by peasants with their pitchforks and hoes. Soon, it would be a bloody, churned mess. I flapped down to a tree near the forest's edge, picked a bough twined round with mistletoe – a fine balance of coverage and visibility – and settled myself in the greenery. I yawned (not so easy to do with a beak). Snuffled. Rustled my feathers. It was oddly comfortable to tuck my head under my wing. And before I knew it, I had fallen asleep.

Some inner sense of balance innate to birds must have kept me from falling off the bough. For I slept deeply, losing all sense of time and place and self. Slept through dreams of soaring, dreams of walking (it makes sense: if humans dream of flying, birds would dream of running), and into that deeper space beyond dreams. When I awoke, it was to the skittering night sounds of the forest – insect buzz and owl call – and the sky above, visible through the thin spring leaves. Venus glowing. Touching, almost touching, no, touching one of those twin stars, and as I watched, Mars appearing – against all planetary odds, against every astronomical calculation – and edging up to the other twin. There . . . the moment had arrived.

I watched the sky until dawn drained the darkness and the stars and planets faded away. Still there, of course, just invisible. And then I took stock of myself – I must have slept for a long while. My plumage was dull and ruffled. So, as the sun rose, I preened myself and, somewhere in the midst of tidying my pinions, thought to wonder what sort of bird I was. Hmmm, a mélange. I had a tufted crest of yellow-gold, the cruel beak of a raptor, the long legs of a heron. This would not do. I sighed (also hard to do with a beak) and considered the likely day ahead – what was currently a pasture was going to be a battlefield and then a graveyard. Very well. I closed my bird eyes and concentrated, feeling the flesh take the proper form of a vulture. I cleared my throat, heard my bird voice, *Auwghkh*. Rather unpleasant. From my vantage, I could see now the tents of one of the armies, see men stirring. Banners fluttered in the morning breeze, enough so that I could discern this was the army of Rinaldo's king, the army where I'd find my twins. Even my vulture eyes couldn't spot the other army, but I could hear them, on the other side of the forest glade – hear their drums, hear the stamp of their horses' hooves. And it seemed that now human ears could detect these sounds as well, for the camp burst into activity. A horn blasted, three times, and men ran about.

Where was Bradamante? Already the number of knights in armour on horses was disorienting. I'm sure, closer to the ground, they could be differentiated. But from my perch, it was just a mass of metal. I pondered going down. I pondered taking a different form – I could be a squire or a groom. I could be invisible. I could be anything I wanted . . . I hunched my vulture shoulders. What I wanted . . . what I wanted . . . why did that feel like such an empty, gaping hole? I wanted to win of course. (But deep in my bird brain, a small voice chirped: what would it mean to win? The death of Ruggiero and Marfisa? But I liked them, too. Wanted them in my future world . . . wanted . . .)

My thoughts were interrupted by the churn of air, the flap of mighty wings, and I let out an involuntary vulture squawk (*Auauwgh!*) as another bird alighted on my bough, a mere foot away.

It was, without question, the oddest bird I had ever seen. It had a bill like a toucan, a draping tail like a peacock (though not as brilliantly coloured), and was all over striped and shaded like a tabby cat. 'Sister,' it croaked (its voice sounded more frog than bird).

'What are you supposed to be?' I sneered. (I didn't mean to, but this is part and parcel of being half of a bonded polarity – I can't help but sneer whenever he is close.)

'A simurgh,' he croaked haughtily.

I squawked a cruel laugh. 'Definitely not. No legend I've ever read supposes it to have stripes like a cat.'

'It is lion-like!'

'Lions are not tabby kittens.'

'There is a variety of striped lion that is found in the steppes.'

I rolled my eyes. 'Moreover, simurghs are always, always, always female. And I do believe that female is my half of the polarity. So back off.'

There was a ruffling sound, rather like a feather duster being shaken, a lengthy croak, and then I was side-by-side with another vulture (though he was balder and uglier than I was). 'Sister,' he said.

There was something comforting in having him back by my side. I hate to admit it, but it is only with him that I feel like myself. As if I need that opposite against which to define myself. What would it feel like to be whole and not half?

'What are you doing here?' I asked.

'The same as you, I imagine. Observing the end of our bet. Preparing to rule the age to come. Imagining you in the Farthest Deeps, exiled. You know.'

'Have you been watching your twins? I am not so certain they will emerge victorious.'

'I haven't needed to watch. I knew from the moment I selected them that they would win,' he snarked.

I tried to purse my lips, to answer him with a sneer, but this is impossible to do with a beak, and I ended up just sneezing (also hard to do with a beak) and muttered, 'We shall see.'

He ruffled his feathers and replied smugly, 'Yes, we shall.'

Indeed, below us the ranks of the army had formed up. As servants and pages broke down the tents and carters tried to haul supplies away from what would soon be a battlefield, knights rode back and forth on their mounts, organizing lines of halberdiers and pikemen, the foot soldiers who would lead the charge and absorb most of the casualties. With a great deal of shouting and horn-blowing and milling about, the lines at last surged away from the camp and onto the cleared field below us. I craned my neck and searched the other side, seeing in the distance the opposing army, marching to take up their own end of the field. If my brother had possessed lips to lick, he would have licked them. This was going to be bloody. As it was, I swear, he curved that vulture beak into a grin and leered at me. 'Which ones are yours?' he asked.

I scanned the lines again and found Duke Aymon's leaping stag on a banner, held aloft by some poor squire (I hoped he had another weapon at his disposal). 'There,' I said, 'beneath the stag.' Rinaldo was easy to pick out; he had painted his armour blue, his father's colour, and also had a stag painted onto the front plate. He sat atop his warhorse, which pawed the ground, his lance vertical in its holder, his visor raised as he peered out over the lines of men towards the enemy. Behind him, on Storm, I spotted Ricardetto. He wore the armour I'd fashioned, and still held his helm in a gauntleted hand, his auburn hair shorn shorter than the last time I'd seen him – maybe that was the new style, and maybe Rinaldo had talked him into the practicality of shorter hair beneath a helmet. He looked pensive, scared, but determined (or maybe I was being hopeful). But as to Bradamante, I saw no sign. A dozen other armoured knights gathered behind the stag banner. Some with painted plate, some with armour dented from recent use. Forgetting, for a moment, my brother's presence, being totally absorbed now with locating Bradamante, I pushed off from the bough and circled low over the troops. Low enough to catch her scent. (A few troops spotted me circling; I hoped they didn't think me an ill omen.) There she was, two down the line from Rinaldo. Her armour painted blue like his, though her shield was painted plain white, and riding a horse that was not Wolf-Fang. I circled back up to my bough, thinking . . . perhaps she had altered her appearance so that none would be able to locate her as Bradamante, as the woman fighting on their side. No need to increase her presence as a target.

'Worried?' my brother croaked as I settled on the bough again.

'Curious,' I replied. 'It's part of being nurturing.' A blast from the horns interrupted our conversation and we both peered down. The armies were marching towards each other. Slowly now. Somewhere, drums rolled. The armies churned and roiled, like two waves approaching the same beach. The closer they drew to each other, the faster they moved. The men were screaming before they made contact and then they collided. The foot soldiers bunched together thickly, hacking at each other in an utter devastation of a melee. Even my brother looked a little sickened by the sight (or he was enjoying himself. It's hard to tell with a vulture).

In the style of this time (or so I gathered), some knights called out and claimed the right of challenge, pointing to an opponent, and, through an elaborate system of dipping and waving their banners, agreed to duel. So, as the lines of foot soldiers decimated each other, the knights pranced away for their tidy little combats. Well, the better (or richer or more noble) of the knights did. The others, the hedge knights, the hired hands, stayed on and supported the foot soldiers, hacking with the swords and maces. Rinaldo claimed a duel with a knight whose red banner bore a black eagle. Ricardetto challenged someone who flew a white banner with a golden sun. Bradamante rode back and forth behind the foot, finally issuing a challenge to a black-armoured knight. Oh. He looked quite fierce, with horns coming out of his helmet and his shield all black as well, and were those barbs on his lance? That was quite excessive, in my opinion. But off she trotted. I swallowed, my vulture's throat dry.

'Which ones are mine?' my brother asked.

'Oh, curious?' I said.

'No. Bored.'

I found Ruggiero – he used Sir Badr's old shield, which bore the unusual device of a man holding a lion on a lead. It was the symbol of a saint that the old knight had revered. Lions and lambs and taming wild beasts. Or something. No doubt Ruggiero had absorbed the mystical lesson. 'There.' I pointed. 'The one on the white-and-grey horse.'

'Why isn't he off . . . jousting . . . with the others?' my brother asked.

'He's a mercenary. Here for the pay. I think the jousting is just for the nobles.'

'Ah. So they won't get hurt?'

'No. They'll kill each other, I'm fairly sure. Or at least the loser is likely to die. But it is a noble death. Not like being kicked in the head in this morass.' As I said this, Ruggiero's horse reared back and stove in the head of a foot soldier, who crumpled to the ground. No sooner had the horse landed, then Ruggiero was again cutting about with his sword. He might as well have been a woodsman hewing at trees with an axe.

'And the other one?'

I scanned the field once more, eager to fly off and observe my twins. But eager not to seem eager in front of my brother (he'd use any emotion to his advantage). 'I don't see her . . . Oh, wait.' Something gleamed in the sun on one of the ridges that hemmed in the field. 'Is that her?' Another glitter. Yes. That was the sun catching on her mirror-like armour. She stood on that ridge, looking down at the battle below her, at the knights jousting, and, removing her helm so that her long, lustrous hair flowed visibly over her gorget and shoulders, sounded a horn – one like the hunters use to call the hounds. Winding, sharp. She yelled something, and I stirred the air to bring her words towards us: *I challenge you. All of you. Any of you. Who dares belittle the name of woman? I will fight any who thinks he can best me.*

My brother's vulture face showed some alarm. If vultures had eyebrows, his would have shot up. But all he said was, 'my, my'.

For myself, I wavered between concern for her safety (not a helpful emotion, Melissa!), admiration of her courage (also not helpful), and a general feeling that things were going to get gory, quickly. The sounds of the battle grew louder – more shrieks, from horses as well as humans. More awful clatter and clash of weapons. 'Why,' I asked, raising my voice above the fray, 'does the battle have to come first? Why couldn't we begin with dancing? Or story-telling? I could do with a good story right about now. Why this?' I gestured awkwardly with one wing towards the melee.

'Because,' my brother replied, voice laden with insufferable forbearance, 'if the order was different, there would be a chance that you would win. By having the battle first, most signs – almost every sign I've been able to read and discern and decipher in the last seventeen miserable years on this ball of dirt – point to the sweeping victory of my twins shortly after the onset of the battle.'

My outrage grew so suddenly that all I could manage was a strangled *Auwqk!*

He smiled. The bastard actually managed to get that vulture beak bent in a smile. 'There were, mind you, some lines – not *that* many of them – that showed very different, very unfavourable outcomes if our twins should meet under any conditions other than the battlefield.'

My voice came back, grating and low. 'You dirty, cheating, unbelievable . . . you've manipulated this. You've pulled some strings . . .'

'Prove it.' He fluffed himself up and gazed down at the field. 'This is destiny. This is fate. This was meant to be.'

All those times I had visited the island and seen him toiling at arcane magic. I thought he had been curious. Or bored. Or acquiring a new hobby. What a trusting fool I was! I was the one who had been bored and learned to embroider and now, what would that rule-abiding goody-two-shoes behaviour get me? Exile in the Farthest Deeps. 'You stinking, rotten . . .' I rose up from the branch and began to beat my brother with my wings, tearing at his eyes with my beak, seizing clumps of his plumage with my talons. He let out a shriek and tried to fight back and soon we were tumbling to the ground together, feathers flying.

We landed with a thump and each dissipated to our ethereal forms. Briefly, I was tempted to rush to my twins and give them all the magical aid I could manage. But my brother would only do the same – it would be a quick, savage ending, a fight we had fought many times before: the two of us pitted against each other, neither one of us able to win. The two of us locked together for all time, dependent and despising one another. I had thought this would be the end to it . . . or this would be an end at least for an age.

I reincorporated. Forcing my essence into flesh. Becoming, once more, Melissa. Only this time, styled for the battlefield. Greaves and gauntlets. A visorless helm. In one hand, a sturdy sword and in the other a shield, adorned with a black-and-yellow honeybee. To anyone familiar with statues from the ancient world, I looked rather like some depictions of Athena. Fortunately, no one on this battlefield had such familiarity (it wasn't the time or the place to be truly inventive. A little creative copying was fine). My brother had popped back into his demon appearance. Red eyes, black fingernails, long black hair. I upped my glow a bit. He glanced at the sky, pale blue and nearly cloudless. 'The moment is nearly come. Shall we?' He gave a mocking little bow and extended a hand, as if I would take it.

'No interfering,' I hissed and began to pick my way across the ground.

'*I* don't need to.'

I looked him up and down. 'You're too visible.'

'So are you.'

'Very well. Gnats. On the count of three.' He nodded. 'One, two, three.'

And we both squished ourselves (most uncomfortably, at least for me) in the merest little form of winged insects and buzzed off.

Corpses littered the field. The melee had split into clumps of men. Some still fighting near the centre of the field. Others fleeing and being pursued. One group, more enterprising, had strategically retreated to the top of a ridge and was managing to fire arrows into anyone who approached. All this mayhem. Had my brother brought this battle about, this whole war, in order to get his twins to win? How many deaths? Or would humans have done this themselves, without his intervention? And was I complicit? Was I any better than my brother, since I had signed on to the same bet, intent on using this world for my own purposes? Well, my purposes were . . .

'Isn't that yours?' my brother said, his voice a whining buzz.

I looked up. Indeed, it was Ricardetto. His lance was gone, but he still rode Storm, brandishing his sword and half of his shield (the other half appeared to have been sheared away, by sword or axe). He was riding seemingly at random, tracing an undiscernible pattern across the battlefield. Had he taken too many blows to the head? Then I saw him pause by a fallen horse and examine the bodies around it, say, 'Bradamante?' but it was not. Poor boy. Across the field another knight hallo-ed, bellowing out a challenge. Ricardetto stiffened, but turned his horse and raised his sword in answer. I couldn't watch.

'Pity,' my brother said, flicking his wings. 'I imagine he's a fine dancer.'

'He's a better story-teller,' I murmured. 'But, yes, a good dancer.'

My brother buzzed, a pleased sound. 'Onwards?'

We flew towards the ridge where Marfisa had issued her challenge. Around us, more bodies, some groans, some feeble attempts at motion. The noise came from the edges, where knights still clashed and charged, intent on their private warfare. We reached the height of land Marfisa commanded and found her, ahorse and gleaming, her visor once again lifted, shouting to the wind, 'Who is next? Who dares to challenge me? Who says that women are weak and do not deserve to wield a sword?' Around her, bodies decorated the ground. Horses, their riderless saddles askew, their reins trailing the ground, stood nervously on the margin of field and forest, wondering when their knights might arise and find them.

'No one?' Marfisa bellowed. She swung her sword, its edges coated carmine, over her head. 'Must I seek out someone of high rank? Or is the king ready to grant me a title of my own?' She was raving, near lunacy, I feared.

And then a horse charged up the slope, rider in battered armour that might have once been painted blue but now was chipped and flecked.

'At last! A challenger,' Marfisa crowed. 'Who are you, *brave* knight. You must have some degree of skill to have lasted this long in battle, or have you been hiding while others fight?'

'I come not to challenge, but to enquire . . .' the other knight said.

'I'm here to fight, not talk. I'll take marriage proposals after we duel. Draw your sword, since your lance is shattered.' She sneered this last with all the bravado she could muster, and I stood, gobsmacked, worried for her – this much rage, this much hate, this much bitterness . . . it would undo her, and she was such a fine human, with so much potential, just in need of nurturing. And as I was focused on her, worried about her, my brother nudged me with one of his sticky little gnat feet and said, 'Isn't that your other one?'

With a wing, he pointed at the challenging knight, with the battered blue armour. Blue. It was Bradamante! I opened my mouth to call to her, but she was already lifting her helm – not just her visor, but her whole helmet, and loosing the spill of her auburn hair. 'Good lady knight,' she called.

'I am not a knight and many would say I'm not a . . .' Marfisa paused in her reply. 'What the devil?'

Bradamante nudged her horse closer. Her shield was still strapped to her left arm, and in her right hand she held her helmet. Her pale cheeks were flushed from the exertion of fighting, and the hair of her forehead was dark and dampened with sweat. 'My name is Bradamante,' she said. 'And I would know yours – never before have I met another woman . . .'

Marfisa's gaze travelled all over Bradamante – the armour, the horse, the sword, the shield. Taking the measure of her. Her lips rose into a snarl, fell in doubt, and I wished I could be in her shadow once more, feel her thoughts – now I could only wonder and worry. It was a cold sneer that settled on her lips. 'You pretend to be a man. Look at you. Your armour, like a turtle's shell. You think that if you look like one, if no one knows you are a woman, you will be safe? They will respect you?' She turned her head and spat. 'You are twice a fool. They'll hate you more.'

Bradamante bowed her head. 'I know,' she said with a meekness I had never heard from her before. 'You are right.' I nearly gave a squawk though I was no longer a vulture. She had never conceded such to me! 'I don't want to fight you. I want to learn from you,' she said.

Marfisa's sneer faltered but didn't fall. 'You are probably weak and feeble. You probably don't know how to fight . . .'

She was goading my girl, and I could see Bradamante tremble, bite her lip, her jaw clenched. Oh, she wanted to answer, she wanted to prove herself. 'I can fight,' she said at last, words in a loud, frustrated burst. 'I don't need to learn *that*. I need to learn . . .'

But her outcry (which I desperately longed to hear the end of) was cut short by the pounding of hooves, the onrush of a warrior in dull grey armour. He wore a rounded helm that came to a point on top – the style favoured by the opposing army (I knew this much of the two sides) and bore a shield with a fish jumping above water, and somehow – a miracle this late in the battle – an intact lance.

An intact lance that he now levelled at Bradamante, charging up the slope. And she, caught by surprise, dropped her helm and made to draw her sword, angling up her shield, her only protection. She managed to turn the lance's blow a mere degree, stave off the brunt of its force, but still, it crashed against her – sideways, at least; she dodged the killing point – but took the impact to her shoulder and head. She slumped, swayed in the saddle, her blue eyes rolling back into her skull. The man – the rogue, the coward – who had charged her wheeled about to make a second charge, to skewer her (I heard my brother cackle; how could he manage that in gnat form?) when another set of hooves came drumming up the slope and a voice called the very words I'd been thinking. 'Rogue! Coward! To charge an unready knight!'

And there was Ruggiero – there was no mistaking his peculiar shield, his grey-and-white horse, the sound of his voice proclaiming righteousness. He had no lance, only his sword. And his boots and greaves were crimson with gore – he had waded through the lines again and again. 'Fight me! If you are truly a knight, if you have any honour.'

The rogue faced Ruggiero, and I released a breath I hadn't realized I'd been holding in, relieved to see the lance trained on someone other than Bradamante (who still swayed in her saddle, her head now bleeding copiously). 'That's no knight,' the rogue brayed. 'That's a whore, a woman dressed in some armour she stole, parading about.'

'You have no honour,' Ruggiero called back. 'I know you by your shield. You are Rodomonte. Fight me.'

'And by your shield, I know that you are nobody. A hired sword? It is beneath my dignity to fight you.'

Ruggiero roared and his horse surged forward. The rogue, Rodomonte, couched his lance and made to charge. I heard my brother's gleeful gnat buzz – he did love the sight of blood, it little mattered whose it was (so long as it wasn't his own). A blur of motion, a crash of sword and shield; I winced at the impact. Marfisa had charged at the same moment as her brother had; both had laid into Rodomonte. Ruggiero had got inside the man's charge and levelled his blade against Rodomonte's neck, striking perfectly the tiny gap between gorget and helm, severing head from body. And Marfisa had struck, side sinister, finding the seam of Rodomonte's plate, and plunging the tip of her lance in between his ribs, a foot or more.

And now, brother and sister – though unknown to each other – rode past their strikes, and turned to watch the knight crumple, the horse whinny and rear, shed itself of rider (whose head had already rolled free) and whicker off towards the trees. Ruggiero reined up his horse, lifted his visor, and disgorged a bit of vomit. Marfisa lifted her visor and sneered. 'Sick? It can't be your first kill?'

'That doesn't make it any better,' Ruggiero replied. The two of them locked gazes, and I wondered if they could see the similarities – so blatant to me. Even in the small parts of their faces visible, the eyes, the nose, the mouth, they were so clearly twins. Behind them, Bradamante still swayed in her saddle, muttering and murmuring. Ruggiero nudged his horse away from Marfisa and went to Bradamante's side.

'That's it,' Marfisa jeered. 'Go to help the damsel in distress.'

'A fellow knight needs aid.'

'Oh yes, honour among thieves.'

'Are you going to help? Or insult me?'

'I was considering running you both through.'

My brother buzzed more loudly, sounding delighted, jostling me with a wing, but I ignored him and focused on the fools in front of me. Bradamante pushed herself upright. 'I don't need your help,' she slurred, ill-advisedly. The effort of those words made her lurch to the side, perilously close to falling from her saddle. Ruggiero reached out and grabbed her arm, steadying her, holding her as she continued to sway, though he looked back over his shoulder, as if to make sure that Marfisa wasn't actually going to charge.

And a good thing he was looking because yet another horse came pounding up the slope towards them, another knight, wielding a sword somewhat haphazardly, shouting, 'Unhand my sister!'

Oh, Ricardetto.

'Run him through!' my brother squealed, beating his wings furiously. Marfisa was, indeed, readying her sword. I winced, preparing to turn away – I didn't have Ruggiero's weak stomach, but I couldn't bear to see my boy slaughtered – but she just thumped him (hard) on the shield with the flat of her sword.

It was enough to make Ricardetto pause, look at her, give a little start. 'Beg pardon, my lady,' he said, and bowed in his saddle. 'But that's my sister he's manhandling.'

'He's helping her, you idiot,' she replied. 'And what are you doing, letting your sister come onto the battlefield?'

'Letting?' Ricardetto laughed, a startling sound that echoed in his helm. He lifted his visor. 'Letting? As if I could stop her. She's much the better fighter. And I could never tell her what to do, in fighting or anything else. Now, pardon me,' he said and trotted to Bradamante's side, glaring at Ruggiero. 'I will handle things from here. Bradamante?' He rummaged behind his saddle and came up with a wineskin. With quick, efficient motions, he shed his gauntlets, pulled off his helm, and put an arm around Bradamante's shoulder. Her head flopped over and she slumped against him. 'Oh, dear sister,' he whispered and put the wineskin to her lips, gently squeezing the sides. The wine gushed out, some going into her mouth and some pouring over her lips, running down her neck, cutting through the lines of half-dried blood that stained her pale skin.

Ruggiero watched. 'You're twins,' he said at last. 'Look how similar you are. If not for your whiskers, and her long hair . . . one of you could be the other.'

'Indeed,' Ricardetto said, distractedly, as he wiped Bradamante's lips with his kerchief (perfumed no doubt; only he would ride into battle and still keep a square of linen so pristine). He glanced up at Ruggiero, took in the young man's wide-eyed stare. 'What? Have you never seen twins before? Is it so uncommon in the corner of the world where you come from?'

Ruggiero shook his head, as if clearing a dream from it. 'No, no. I mean, yes, twins are uncommon. But no, I have seen twins before. Yes. Yes, I am a twin. I have a sister. Or had one, but she was taken from me. No doubt she is long since dead. I lost her long ago.'

Ricardetto paused in his ministrations to Bradamante. Ever curious for a story, he asked, 'How was she lost?'

'Stolen, by sailors, from the island on which we were raised.'

'What?' This from Marfisa. She had been lingering on the margins, sword still unsheathed, prowling about, waiting for one of them to fight. But now she stopped and stared at Ruggiero, her eyes boring into his. 'An island? Was there a lioness?'

'Yes,' said Ruggiero, meeting her gaze and then letting his eyes range over her. 'My sister and I would wrestle her cubs . . .'

Marfisa let her sword drop slowly, as if the air were water. 'And my brother and I would curl up with them at night, to sleep on the beach . . .'

They stepped towards each other and it was like watching someone reach for their reflection in a mirror or lake. The looks of awe on their faces, of recognition.

'I've been searching for you,' Ruggiero said. 'Or I did, for a time. But I gave up hope . . .'

'I did too,' Marfisa said, and her voice was wrenched from her, thick with emotion that I had never heard from her before. 'I have been all alone.'

'Alone,' Ruggiero echoed. And they stepped towards each other and would have embraced, but at that moment, my wretched brother, with a pop like a cork emerging from a bottle, traded his gnat body for his demon form, appearing right there with his black fingernails and red eyes. And the dramatic bastard even puffed a little smoke around himself. Ricardetto screamed, 'God save us!'

And Marfisa yelled, 'You!', her shriek enough to curdle blood.

I had no choice but to appear as well (that's how opposites are. We must balance each other), squeezing myself into my angelic appearance. I hate to rush incorporation, but there I was, blinking and squinting, and trying to remember how many vertebrae were in a spine – oh, forget it – and getting ready to fend off whatever magic my brother was about to unleash.

'Melissa!' Ricardetto said, his shout thick with relief. 'Thank God. Save Bradamante. Save all of us.' And he threw his arms about me. Flattering, yes. I had waited quite a while for some gratitude. But also a touch embarrassing. Here was my brother, all fearsome – with his twins, blades still drawn, strong and keen. And my twins, one bloody and semi-conscious, the other scared out of his wits.

'Get Bradamante down from her horse,' I said, keeping an eye on my brother. He stood, hands held in front of him, palms facing out, still smoking slightly, a lilac-silver sheen all around him. It was imposing, I admit. I turned my glow up.

'This is your destiny,' he said to his twins, his voice a low purr. 'This is the moment I prepared you for.'

'You prepared us for nothing,' Ruggiero said, manoeuvring to put himself between his sister and my brother.

'Pardon me,' my brother said, voice dripping with sarcasm. 'I misspoke. This is the moment I have prepared for you. So obey me.'

Marfisa elbowed her brother aside and put herself between him and my brother. 'I obey no man. Particularly you.'

'You'll want to obey me,' he said. 'And I am much more than a man.'

I edged towards Bradamante, thinking my brother sufficiently distracted, and worked a bit of healing on her (I know, the rules of our agreement forbade this, but it seemed that he had bent those rules long ago). A touch of bone, a lot of air, a little water. She groaned. Her eyes fluttered. 'Get the wine,' I whispered to Ricardetto. He reached for the skin and squeezed hard, sending a surge of liquid into his mouth. 'For her, you idiot,' I said, but with affection.

'I know, I know.' And he tenderly dribbled wine between her lips and blotted at her forehead with his silly kerchief (embroidered – perhaps by me! – with a leaping stag).

Meanwhile, my brother continued on, in that low voice that was part entrancing, part intimidating (or so he intended. Marfisa did not look intimidated at all). 'Fight these two.' He waved a hand towards my twins. 'Kill them. And I will make you rulers of this world.'

'That is not the deal we had,' I said. 'It was to be an orderly competition, consisting of three contests.'

He glared at me, red eyes gleaming. 'It was never going to be such a thing. Only one skill matters. You have insisted for years that humans are more than this. But I will prove that they are not.' He looked back at his twins. 'Kill them.'

It showed the depth to which my brother did not understand human beings that he thought his twins would leap to obey. That they were either puppets whose strings he could pull with the merest tug of his fingers or that they would trust him to make good on his promises. Humans have wills of their own (Bradamante taught me this lesson, daily). Trust cannot be casually assumed – and with Marfisa and Ruggiero, I knew, trust was slow to be acquired. And that was owing almost entirely to the neglect he had shown them; my brother was the one who had betrayed them.

'Melissa,' Ricardetto said from behind me. 'Do you know this . . . demon?'

'He is my . . . Other. My twin, in a sense.'

Bradamante had regained her feet, though she leaned against her horse, steadying herself with one hand. Ricardetto assayed that she was upright and then stepped closer to me. I felt his warm presence, remembered the way he used to tuck himself into my skirts, or nestle against my side to hear a story read. He looked my Other up and down. Studied Ruggiero and

Marfisa as well, both of them still with swords in hand, the one with battered armour, the other clad in what seemed to be liquid silver. 'It is funny, is it not,' Ricardetto said, and offered his most winning smile to everyone, including my Other, 'to have so many twins in one spot?'

'We are not *twins*, strictly speaking,' I said. 'We are . . . never mind.'

Ricardetto wasn't listening to me anyway; he was fixated on Ruggiero and Marfisa. 'The two of you,' he said. 'I can only see your faces, that bit allowed by the aperture of your helm. And yet, those features visible could easily be exchanged, the one for the other.' The two twins stared at him, then stared at each other. 'And everyone says the same is true for me and my sister, Bradamante.' He stroked his chin. 'Especially when I shave my whiskers.' Ricardetto rounded on me. 'And yet you, good Melissa, look nothing like your twin. Where you are blond, he is dark; your eyes blue and his . . . red. Only in your heights are you similar.'

I kept my eyes on my brother, though I spoke to Ricardetto. 'This is the way with twins. Perhaps with other pairs of people as well, I do not know. Either they are like to like, or they are as repellent as oil to water. You and your sister are doubles. My brother and I form a single whole – if you could get us to combine.'

'Which we will not,' my Other hissed.

'Indeed.' I smiled around at all the twins. 'This is, in truth, an unnatural convergence, one that my brother and I manufactured. Hence the overabundance of twins. I chose you two,' I gestured to Bradamante and Ricardetto, 'to raise and shape. To nurture and train. To bring you to compete, *fairly*, against these two.' I gestured to Marfisa and Rougierro. 'Whom my brother raised.'

'He didn't raise us,' Marfisa snarled. 'He ignored us. He

let us raise ourselves. He let us be taken and tossed about the world.'

'You've turned out well enough,' my brother sneered. 'For my purposes. A nearly perfect weapon. Now kill them.'

'Never knowing our parents. Losing each other when we were mere children. Wandering alone,' Ruggiero said.

'And it's honed both of you, made you sharp little blades, hasn't it?' my brother said, his voice a disturbing croon.

'What if we were meant to be something other than weapons? Something more?' Marfisa demanded.

'You are what you were meant to be. Enough of this nonsense.' He raised his hands one more time, spreading his fingers out, and spoke to his twins. 'If you do not kill these two, I will have to. And you will regret disobeying me.'

I tensed at his words. 'Our agreement. We said we wouldn't harm . . .'

'I say many things I do not mean.'

With one fluid motion, without pause to lower her visor, Marfisa swung her sword round and levelled a mighty blow at my brother. Were he a mortal man, he would have been cleaved in half. But he simply disincorporated, disappearing in a dramatic puff of smoke. Marfisa let out a strangled cry. 'I hate him!' she said. And her brother stepped close, put an arm around her shoulder, hugged her near. I saw her tense, for just a moment, this sort of contact at once unfamiliar, at once summoning up a long-ago memory, when someone cared, when she belonged, in part, with someone else. She buried her head against his armoured chest.

'He's not gone, is he?' Ricardetto asked.

I shook my head. 'He'll return. It'll be unpleasant.' I sighed. 'It always is. Let me set some charms and wards, so we at least have warning.' I wove them with light and air, a fine golden net, close-knit to be almost a mesh, and cast it upwards, as if I might be fishing in the sky. It formed a dome, a small space, but enough for us to be protected for a moment, maybe more. You never knew with my brother.

Bradamante stepped towards us, a little wobbly on her legs, and took her brother's hand. 'Melissa. You said you had designed a competition?'

Leave it to Bradamante to want that. 'Yes, my dear. Three events. Contest by arms. A contest in story-telling. And a competition in dance.'

Bradamante shook her head gently. 'I am much too weary to dance. But I would love to hear a story.'

'As would I,' said Ricardetto. 'But I don't think it should be a competition. The best stories are told together – one person listens, the other shares, then the listener retells it, makes it better, makes it truer. You can't tell stories on your own.'

Marfisa sighed. She looked up into her twin's face. 'I think we have many stories to tell each other.' She glanced over to Bradamante. 'And I, too, am weary.'

'Let us take off our armour and rest a while,' Ruggiero said. 'The battle has abated.'

I nodded. 'You are safe here. I will see to that.'

Marfisa scowled at the others. 'I swore not to take this armour off. Until I had my vengeance against all men. Until they valued me for what I am.'

'That,' Ricardetto said, as he helped Bradamante with the straps that held her plate tight, 'sounds like the beginning of a fantastic story.'

I listened to the clatter of their armour, the heavy clank of swords being unbelted. The jingle of saddles and bridles, as horses were freed of their burdens. Earth and air and water and a quick bit of hunting (in a manner of speaking) and I had summoned a minor feast for them. Roast pheasant, parsnips, bread. Ricardetto was holding Marfisa's chest plate, his own image swimming in its shining surface. 'How did you acquire such plate?' he asked.

Marfisa ignored him and stared at her brother. 'What happened after I was taken from the island?'

'I was going to ask the same of you,' he laughed. Then he spotted the feast I'd prepared. 'Food!' he cried.

I let my body go, floated up to the fine mesh I'd created. Wove together some more strands, set them spinning in the wind. They twirled and floated and began to chime in tune. A simple melody, a peaceful song, some music to sustain these four as they ate and talked. As they shared food and stories and came to understand each other and themselves. Music to last through dinner, through the night, that would carry them off to sleep if they desired, that would let them dance if they so wished.

And then I stepped outside the charmed web and waited for my brother. Above, the sky darkened and deepened towards night. The stars, I noticed, had gone back to where they belonged. No more Mars glowing oddly. No more Venus out of its orbit.

Only one abnormal light, the orange of flames, streaking towards me like a meteor. My brother, of course. I put up a shield and he splashed against its surface, all showy flare. He looked at the golden mesh I had woven and gnashed his teeth. (Metaphorically. We had both disincorporated.) 'Let them be,' I said, placatingly.

'They disobeyed,' my brother replied.

'They're human. That's what they do.'

'I want vengeance. I want what's due to me,' he insisted, his voice snarled and ugly.

'Be careful what you wish for,' I said, 'particularly in the way of justice. You broke rules you had sworn to.'

He made a dismissive noise. 'Psssh. Words.'

I looked down through the mesh. Ricardetto had his lute out (had he really carried that into battle?) and sat near to Marfisa, plucking a few notes but mostly listening to her as she spoke, her hands tracing patterns in the air. What was she describing? The spice merchant? The sailors who stole her? Rami? Bradamante, meanwhile, was trying to show Ruggiero the mincing steps of a roundel, but he was turning the stately dance into a hornpipe.

'Let them have their world,' I insisted to my brother. 'We have other places to go.'

'They are cold and dark and boring,' he grumped.

I reached a gentle tendril towards him and was surprised when he did not draw away. 'They are what we make them. And perhaps, together, we could make them better.'

And, arm-in-metaphorical-arm, we turned our backs on our twins, on the earth, and turned instead towards each other. Walking up and over and through, turning sideways and slipping between the stars, back to where we belonged.

ACKNOWLEDGEMENTS

So many people and places and possibilities go into writing (and rewriting) a novel. I am very grateful for the support of my colleagues and administrators at Phillips Exeter Academy. I am surrounded by good people who care about writing and who understand what it means to labor away at a manuscript. I am grateful, too, for the students at the Academy; their toil and engagement with the practice of writing is inspirational in many ways.

As ever, I am thankful to my spouse, Ilona, who never grudges me time and space to write and listens to me whine (occasionally) and gush (less occasionally) about what I am working on and lets me remain in sullen silence when appropriate.

There is no doubt that this book would not have existed without the expertise and involvement of my wonderful agent, Alison Fargis. She is a cheerleader, a coach, and a huge booster of my work. And right next to Alison, a big thanks to editor Vicky Leech. She steered me through multiple drafts and insisted that I take the time to rethink when I needed to; her comments were always precise and helpful.

And thank you, reader, for picking up this volume and giving a strange story a chance. None of this would be possible without you.